BORN
ANDROMEDA

K. M. WATTS

interlude **press**

CHICAGO

Copyright © 2023 by Kaylie Tucker
All rights reserved
Published by Duet of Interlude Press
An imprint of Chicago Review Press Incorporated
814 North Franklin Street
Chicago, Illinois 60610
ISBN 978-1-951954-21-5

Library of Congress Control Number: 2022943462

Cover and interior design: CB Messer

Printed in the United States of America

*To Edgar, without whose love and support I
never would have accomplished this.*

*And to Papa, who began my love of books so many
years ago, and whose belief in me never wavered.*

My love for you both is undying.

CHAPTER ONE

IT IS SAID, IN THE Princess Handbook, that a princess should be courteous and well-mannered. She should exude grace and dignity, be the face of the monarchy for which she stands. A princess should never steal the spotlight from those above her station, nor should she strive to be in any spotlight at all, for that matter. It is for the best, really, that she maintains a background role to those who know better than herself. But above all else, a princess should behave in her private life as she does in public. A standard must be upheld, for a princess is the example which all others will strive to emulate.

Or rather, that's what a princess handbook would say if there were such a thing. As it is, any books on royal etiquette have long since been tossed aside in preference for oral repetition, passed down from mother to daughter. Perhaps if there had been a book, with clearly detailed instructions and easily recognizable points, it would have been some help to Andromeda. If she had been able to tear out a page and stick it to her bathroom mirror, she could point to it and say, *"This. This is what I should be."* But as it stands, there is nothing so easily identifiable. Because why would anyone make anything easy?

So really, it's her family's fault that she was now tucked beneath the engine of an SG8 Moon Cruiser. It took up half her bedroom, the expensive armoire her uncle gave her for her tenth birthday shoved back beside the bed to accommodate it.

"Damn it, just turn!"

Andromeda used both her hands to force the wrench to move, and little by little it did, until with a final grunt the bolt came loose. A sigh racked her body as she allowed her arms to fall to either side of her. A bead of sweat slid down her temple and found its way into her ear.

"Ah, gross!" She rubbed her ear against her shoulder, and when that didn't work, used her knuckle to wipe out the moisture.

She finished unscrewing the bolt and set it beside her head as the sound of her door being opened alerted her that someone was coming. Two pairs of feet approached, then stopped beside her. A moment later, a face appeared in the gap between the floor and the engine.

Andromeda smiled at the dark eyes of her handmaiden, Korra. "Hey, perfect timing. Could you hand me that screwdriver?"

Korra raised her eyebrows as she got onto her knees, her black braids swishing against the floor. "I thought your father told you not to bring any more machinery into your room?"

Andromeda shrugged and rubbed her forehead with the back of her hand. "What he doesn't know won't hurt him."

Another face appeared beside Korra's, this one featuring green eyes and golden locks. Emmi, her second handmaiden, scrunched up her face. "How could he not notice you having a giant motor brought to your room?"

Andromeda slid from beneath the engine, her shirt hiking up and exposing the smooth skin of her stomach. "As it turns out, kings have more important matters to worry about than disobedient daughters."

They helped her to her feet, and Emmi tugged at Andromeda's grease-covered shirt with a wrinkled nose. "What about your mother?"

"Oh, you know my mom. As long as I'm falling in line with their plans, she doesn't care what I do with my free time."

Emmi and Korra glanced at each other, then Korra nodded and turned to the princess. "So, it's still happening?"

Andromeda pulled off her shirt and threw it to the floor, not turning to look at her friends. She knew what they were talking about and would rather not discuss it. The less she needed to think about the fast-approaching horror, the better. But Emmi and Korra were ladies of the court at heart, daughters of lords, and there was nothing they liked better than a bit of gossip. Given that said gossip was about herself, Andromeda found it exhausting.

"You mean my impending wedding to an unknown man? Yes, it's still happening. Mother and Father are insistent about it."

Korra rolled her eyes. "He's not unknown, Andy. Eden is the crown prince of Someron."

Andromeda pulled the clips from her hair and allowed her black curls to fall. That was easy for her friend to say—she wasn't the one being auctioned off to the highest bidder. "Yeah, well, that's pretty much all I know about him. He could have two heads and a drug addiction for all I know."

Emmi laughed as Andromeda pulled off her brown work pants. "I'm pretty sure that information would have leaked."

With a kick of her foot, Andromeda shoved her dirty clothes under the bed. "You don't know that. Most people know little about my... affliction."

Korra bent down to retrieve the dirty clothes and flashed her an annoyed look. "You don't have an affliction. You're just... modified. As it doesn't affect your appearance much, I don't think the media would be particularly bothered."

Andromeda flexed her metal fingers. She very much doubted what Korra said. People on the outside had been trying to catch a glimpse of her for years, ever since her accident. Not that she cared if they saw her or not. They would undoubtedly tear her to shreds regardless of her appearance, as the media were known to do. Already, the headlines filtered through her head.

Princess Andromeda, Still Beautiful Despite Horrific Accident! It's a Miracle!

Heir to the Celestine Empire Not as Horrifying as We All Imagined! Prince Eden Has Lucked Out!

Vain Princess Uses People's Tax Money to Get Cosmetic Surgery! More on the Spoiled Child of Luxury at Six!

"Yes, well, I suppose they'll finally get to see what they've always wanted once I marry Eden. The restrictions on royal children in the media will lift, and I will assume my place as a public figurehead." Andromeda snatched a comb from the nearby table and ran it through her tangled curls. Her friends watched for a few moments before Emmi picked up a second comb from the bedside table and helped. Andromeda pressed her lips together. She wanted to say that she was perfectly capable of doing this on her own but held her tongue. Reprimanding her friends wouldn't do her any good.

Korra seemed to sense Andromeda's frustration. "Why don't we go for a walk in the gardens?"

Oh, great. Another walk through the same gardens she'd been through a thousand times. "Fine. Just help me back into my dress. Mother and Father would die of embarrassment if I were anything less than a proper lady."

As a child, she'd been allowed to wear jeans and shirts in public, but now that she was older, her parents thought it best for her to dress formally at all times.

Emmi pulled Andromeda's dress over her head and tightened the laced-up strings on the back. "Didn't your aunt just get caught swimming in a fountain, wearing nothing but her underclothes? I thought I saw that on TV, or was it just a dream?"

Andromeda smirked and straightened the sleeves of her dress. "No, that really happened. Father likes to pretend he doesn't know her, his own sister." She cleared her throat and spoke in a deep voice.

"My sister does not represent the royal family in actions or beliefs. She is acting of her own ill-advised accord."

Both of her friends laughed and adjusted the finishing touches on her dress.

"You do a pretty good impression of him," Korra said with a smile.

"I've had a lot of practice."

"OK, you look top notch. Now, let's go." Emmi tugged at Andromeda's dress, leading her toward the door.

All three girls made their way out of the room and down the hall. As they walked, Andromeda glanced out one of the grand windows. Earth sat in the sky, green and blue and lovely as ever. God, how she wished she'd been born there instead of on this cold rock. She wanted to see the majestic mountains and vast canyons, to walk through the tall redwoods and swim in the ocean. It had always been her dream, but her father had never allowed her to go. She loved her home on the moon, but her soul yearned for Earth and all it could offer.

Celestine was just so industrial. Beautiful and shiny and stream-lined, but completely and utterly fake. As her eyes moved down to look at the city that lay beyond the palace walls, all she could see were sleek, straight-edged buildings and numerous ships flying in between. Nowhere out there would you find a naturally grown flower or a blade of grass that hadn't been artificially curated. There were no grand forests or powerful oceans. Every nook and corner had been planned and placed just so, with no need to set out and discover something new. Not at all like on Earth.

Earth did as it liked. She had watched the films about horrible storms that had thrashed the land and left terrible destruction in their wake. As a child, she'd read countless books about how water and wind worked for thousands of years to build massive canyons. Oh, what she would give to feel wind.

By the time they had made their way onto the royal grounds, she'd worked herself into a mood. Annoyance at the artificial life around her wasn't uncommon, but she'd learned to keep her mouth shut on the matter. They had made it clear when she was young that everything would go more smoothly for her if she accepted the status quo.

The front lawn stretched out for nearly a mile, broken up by fountains and hedges every thirty feet. Andromeda was sure that whoever had put them there had measured it down to the millimeter. Beyond the front lawn, Andromeda could make out the soaring iron gates that separated the palace from the rest of the city. Above and around them sat the massive dome that protected Celestine from the harsh emptiness of space, its presence no longer noticeable after so many years. The appearance of clouds and a light blue sky gave a feeling of comfort, even if they were just images projected above them. There was, of course, no true atmosphere on the moon. Just the one her ancestors had created. Everything here on Celestine was created by man, forged to look like a copy of Earth, from the green grass that stretched as far as the eye could see, to the oak trees that gave them shade, to the sky above them that made them feel safe. All fake.

The gardeners and groundskeepers scattered throughout the gardens barely looked up as the trio passed, only nodding and mumbling a, "Hello, Your Highness" or "Good afternoon, Princess." Andromeda nodded but paid them little mind. They were as much of the norm as the statues they polished.

Andromeda glanced back at the castle as they moved through the garden, her eyes tracking upward to the soaring towers of glass, artfully designed to hide the steel that held it all in place. At least, one would assume it was glass, given its transparent nature. In reality, it was clear polycarbonate, constructed to appear delicate while actually able to withstand massive impact. They had built the main bulk of the castle with white stone and steel to allow privacy to those who lived within while still maintaining a classic look of regality. Andromeda had always thought it looked too dramatic, as though it couldn't decide whether it wanted to be a relic of the past or a beacon of the present.

As the three made their way into the grove of trees, Emmi grabbed Andromeda's hand. "Look, there's Carson!"

Andromeda looked ahead, and sure enough she saw the gardener. Though he was in his mid-thirties, he was handsome. Blond hair and a strong jaw set him apart from the rest, and Emmi had developed a bit of a crush on him.

Korra frowned at Emmi. "Don't act like a fool."

He smiled when he saw them approaching. "Good afternoon, Your Highness. I hope you're having a lovely day?"

Andromeda nodded and smiled back. "I am, thank you for asking. And you?"

He tilted his head and ran a hand through his hair. "I can't complain. Getting to see your lovely faces certainly helps."

A slight blush rose to Andromeda's cheeks. She'd known Carson since she was a child, and he had always had a familiar attitude toward her. But now that she was older, she thought his words perhaps held a different meaning. If her father ever heard him speaking to her in that manner, he would likely have him thrown out of Celestine.

"You are too kind. But if you'll excuse us, we were just on our way for a walk through the gardens."

Carson bowed and held out his arm. "Of course, Your Highness. I wouldn't want to keep you."

"Oh, he's so handsome!" Emmi squealed once they were out of earshot, her eyes bright with adoration. "I think I might be in love with him."

Korra huffed and rolled her eyes. "You are not in love with him. Besides, he only has eyes for Andromeda." She gave Andromeda a playful poke to her ribs. "Have you two been sneaking out for rolls in the garden?"

Andromeda's jaw dropped. "Of course not!"

Emmi raised a skeptical brow. "No? Well, what about that girl from court? The daughter of that one lord. She seemed to take a keen interest in you."

"No," Andromeda said firmly. "There's nothing going on between me and anyone."

Just the thought of it made her chest burn. It was distinctly forbidden for anyone of royal birth to sleep with anyone outside of marriage, and it infuriated her. She'd grown up watching television shows about girls and women being who they wanted to be, discovering themselves and the world around them. They were heroines and adventurers and free. And that was something she would never be.

It was easy to recall the first time she'd realized her entire life was already planned out for her. She'd been ten years old, dancing around her room while her mother hummed and wrote in her journal. She'd had a lesson that day about the expeditions into deep space, about the founders of their current civilization and those who still ventured out to map the stars. It had been with the joy and naïveté of a child that she had told her mother that when she grew up, she wanted to be an explorer on one of those ships. Her mother had looked at her so sharply, the crease in her brow deep.

"No, Andromeda," her mother had said. "When you are grown, you will be queen. That will be your job."

She remembered the sinking feeling in her stomach as her mother went back to writing. As she realized she'd have no part in the choice of what her life would be or who she'd become. It was clear that was not up to her.

Andromeda shook herself from the memory. "Come on, I want to put my feet in the water."

She ran to the nearest of the massive marble fountains and lifted her dress, swinging her left leg over first, then her right. She sat down on the edge of the fountain, and despite her best efforts, the front of her dress dipped into the crystal-clear water. Andromeda wiggled her toes and watched as the water moved around them.

Korra watched her with a quizzical frown. "I've always wondered, why do you still like doing this? When you were younger, sure, but ever since your accident… I mean, can you even feel the water?"

Andromeda considered the question. "It's not that I can't feel it, I just can't feel it the same." She leaned forward and placed both hands into the water. "On this hand," she said, wiggling her right elbow, "the water feels sharp and almost burns. I can feel how the water moves the tiny hairs on my arm and goes into my pores." She turned her head to her left and looked down, wiggling her left shoulder. "But this one, it feels cold, but it's dull. It's like it knows it should be cold, but it doesn't care, so it's not trying too hard." She removed her hands from the water, staring at her left hand. She opened and closed it, turning it from wrist to palm up. It always amazed her how the synthetic skin over robotic fingers looked so much like her own.

Korra nodded. "Hmm, that's interesting. Then tell me, how does this feel?" She dipped her hand into the water, and with an upward motion, threw a handful of water into Andromeda's face. Andromeda shrieked and leapt up.

"Oh, that's it!" She scooped up as much water as she could and flung it at Korra. To avoid being soaked, Korra fell backward off the fountain and onto the grass. Unfortunately for her, she wasn't quick enough, and most of the water still found its way onto her. The three of them jumped into the fountain and spent the next several minutes chasing each other through the knee-deep water, kicking and splashing, their laughter carrying through the garden.

By the time they made it back into the castle, all three were soaking wet and starving. Andromeda attempted to contain her wet mass of curls, but it was really no use. What she really needed was a dry dress and perhaps a warm pastry. Chef always saved her some from the morning spread, and today wouldn't be any different. But before they made it halfway to the kitchen, a voice called to them.

"Your Highness!" Johan huffed, taking hurried strides as he approached. He was her father's assistant, and it wasn't uncommon to see him rushing about the property.

"Johan," Andromeda said with a smile, "is everything all right?"

"Yes, everything is fine, Princess. Your father has requested to see you immediately."

Andromeda raised her eyebrows. "Did he say what for?"

"Not to me, Princess."

"Very well. I'll see you two back in my room in an hour?"

"Sure," Korra and Emmi said in unison.

Andromeda followed Johan and tried to calm the nerves that fluttered in her stomach. There were only a few things she could think of that would make her father call to her urgently, and at present, she didn't want to deal with any of them. As they reached the large oak doors to her father's office, Andromeda took a deep breath. Johan opened the doors and stood back, allowing Andromeda to enter. Her parents, King Alder and Queen Adella of Celestine, also known as the Moon Kingdom, sat behind a massive desk. As she walked in, Johan shut the door behind her. Her father looked up from his papers.

"Please have a seat, Andromeda."

She did, sitting in the high-backed chair across from her parents. It felt as if she were about to be scolded, and she picked at her nails, anxious for someone to speak.

Her mother looked her over. "Andromeda, why are you all wet?"

She shrugged. "I fell."

Her mother raised an eyebrow. "Fell?"

"Yes. Into a fountain."

Her father frowned, but her mother let slip the smallest of smiles.

"So, why did you call for me?"

Her mother leaned forward onto the desk. "You're eighteen now, Andromeda. We need to discuss important life decisions you will be making."

"What, like my career path?" she prodded, being purposefully difficult.

Her father pursed his lips. "Andromeda, the only career path you will take is royal. You will be queen of Celestine someday, and you need to act like it."

Andromeda blew a stray black curl out of her face. "And how am I supposed to do that?"

Her mother smiled. "As you know, you are promised to Prince Eden of Someron. Your father and his have been in constant talks over these past months, and they have come to an agreement."

Andromeda stared at her parents in silence. She'd known this was coming. She had known it her whole life. Yet, that didn't stop the wave of nausea from coming over her. She wasn't ready. She needed time to grow up and experience life, to travel and see the great seas of Earth. To fall in love on her own terms. But none of this mattered, and it would do no good to argue with her parents. Every royal of Celestine was required to marry at eighteen to ensure many heirs and a strong marriage bond. She had known since she first learned to talk that she'd marry once she came of age. It just wasn't until recently that she'd begun to fully understand what marriage would entail. She took a deep breath before speaking.

"I understand. When will he come?"

"He will arrive tomorrow afternoon."

"Wha-What? Tomorrow? That's too soon!" she protested. "I thought I would surely have at least a few more months, if not a year!"

"There's no point in postponing it, Andromeda," her father said firmly. "King Beckett and I are in agreement on the terms. Prince Eden will be here for five days, and then you will go to Earth for two weeks to meet his people and see his kingdom. After that, you will return home and wed here in Celestine."

Andromeda bit her lip. In only two and a-half weeks, she'd be wed. She'd be a *wife*. Eugh, just the thought made her want to shudder.

"What if I don't like him?"

"You will learn to," her father insisted.

Andromeda flopped back in her chair. "How romantic."

"You'd be surprised," her mother said.

"He will leave Earth tomorrow morning and making the six-hour trip here. I expect you to look the part of a princess and greet him and his family with us."

Andromeda sighed. "Yes, Father."

"Excellent. That was all. You may go now."

Andromeda stood slowly. Part of her wanted to scream at her parents, to shout that there must be some mistake. She hadn't been born to be a wife or a queen or any of the other silly titles they attempted to assign her. In the end, she just gave them a simple curtsy before leaving.

The palace moved by her in a blur as she made her way to her room. Andromeda tried to slow her racing mind, but it was to no avail. Marriage wouldn't suit her. She didn't want to smile at a man she didn't know and laugh at jokes she didn't find funny. She didn't want to be touched or looked at or told how *lovely* she was. But even as those thoughts swirled in her mind, she knew there was nothing she could do. Sure, she could pout and stomp her foot and threaten to not eat, but what good would that do? She'd still have to marry, only without a hint of dignity or grace. And if she had anything, it was that. She'd been raised to be a queen well enough that her fake smile almost looked real.

By the time she made it to her room, a persistent ache had formed behind her right eye, forewarning of a coming migraine.

"Andy!"

Andromeda spun to find both of her friends sitting on her bed. In her haze, she'd forgotten they would be in here.

"Well?" Emmi asked. "What did they want?"

She flopped down in a chair in front of her mirror with a sigh. "Prince Eden is coming tomorrow."

Both of her friends gasped.

"Tomorrow?" Korra repeated. "Will you be marrying right away?"

Andromeda tilted her chair onto its back legs. "Within three weeks."

Her friends glanced at each other. After a moment Emmi asked, "What do you think about that?"

Andromeda shrugged and chewed her lip. "Does it matter?"

"Of course it matters!" Korra said as she leaned forward on her elbows.

A single curl twisted around Andromeda's finger. "Not to my parents."

"But… " Emmi bit her lip. "Don't you want to be happy?"

Andromeda felt like her friend had hit her in the gut. She leapt up from the chair, allowing it to crash backward. "Of course I want to be happy! What sort of stupid question is that? Who doesn't want to be happy? Who doesn't want to have the freedom to be who they want to be? But as my mother says, I'll learn to be happy. That's the price I pay to be royalty. I've always known it, so there's no point in fighting it."

Even as she said the words, they felt false. Like reading the script of a stage play you had read a hundred times and acted out just as often. They burned in her throat. She needed to calm down, so she grabbed the wrench off her dresser and turned to where her engine was. She froze. The engine, which had taken up a large corner of her room, was gone.

"What the hell?" She turned on her friends. "Where is my engine?"

Emmi gulped and looked at Korra, who was frowning. "There were some workers here a while ago, while you were with your parents. They removed it. They said it was on the orders of your father."

Andromeda closed her eyes and turned away. She could feel the tendrils of a breakdown creeping around her consciousness. Her hands began to flutter and shake at her sides, a coping mechanism her body often took on when her mind became anxious or overwhelmed. She didn't need them seeing this. A princess must always be put together.

"Could you guys go? I really need some rest for tomorrow."

There was silence for a moment before Korra asked, "Do you need us to prepare you for bed?"

"No!" Andromeda snapped. She bit her lip, forcing herself to hold it together. "No, but thank you. I can do it myself. Please, just... please go."

Andromeda turned away as they made their way to the door.

Emmi's voice was gentle when she spoke. "If you need us, just call on the com."

Andromeda nodded and heard the door open and close. She sank to the floor with a gasp that shook her entire body. The dizziness that filled her head was familiar. Not familiar like a family member or friend, but familiar like that face you see often in a crowded space. A flash of eyes and a crude smile that makes your heart beat faster as you wonder if you have a stalker. She crawled backward until her back hit the bed. Her arms wrapped around each other as she silently cursed her traitorous mechanical heart that was pounding like it wanted to escape from her chest. Like it knew it didn't belong there, it was only an imposter in place of something real.

Everything was happening too fast. She was getting married. She was going to devote the rest of her life to a person she didn't know. Possibly someone unkind, someone who would also not approve of her working on engines or putting her toes in a fountain. She'd hand a piece of control over her life to a stranger. Perhaps not as large a piece as her parents currently had, but at least they had good intentions. This person could be evil for all she knew.

Her fingernails dug into her scalp, and the sharp pain of it grounded her. She opened her eyes and looked around in the dim light of her room. In a matter of weeks, she'd no longer have her own room, but a shared one. The thought made her feel nauseated.

Then there was another part of her mind, a part she hated to even acknowledge. What if he didn't want her? While she didn't want him, being denied by someone she was being forced to marry would sting terribly. Andromeda knew she was considered conventionally attractive, so that wasn't her worry. But her multiple disabilities would be enough to make anyone hesitant. Not only was nearly half her body made of metal and wiring, but her golden eyes that looked back at her in the mirror were a constant reminder that she was different.

She'd been born with moon sickness, an uncommon deformity that caused her to have bright golden eyes. However, what made Andromeda unique was that every other child born with it died within weeks of their birth. Somehow, she had survived. She'd asked her mother and father how they thought it was possible, but they had simply shrugged and told her she was special.

Andromeda wasn't sure how long she laid on the floor, her arms wrapped tightly around her chest, but when her breathing finally slowed and her mind calmed, it was dark outside. She unwrapped herself and stretched, her stiff muscles protesting the movement.

Gripping the edge of the bedframe, she pulled herself up and looked in the mirror. She was a mess. Her hair was a wild bush of haphazard curls, and her face was blotchy and streaked with tears. Allowing herself one last shuddering breath, she made her way to the washroom.

She washed her face, dressed in her sleeping gown, and closed the curtains before climbing into bed. After such an intense breakdown, she was left drained and empty. The only way to cure it was with sleep. Yet try as she might, it took her several hours for sleep to come, and once it did, she was plagued with nightmares of a handsome prince laughing and poking her with a stick.

CHAPTER TWO

ANDROMEDA STOOD OUTSIDE THE DOORS to the throne room and tried to get her breathing under control. Her heart pounded erratically, and for a moment she worried her artificial valves were malfunctioning. She assured herself it was only her nerves. In a matter of minutes she would meet a man whom she might spend the rest of her life with. A man whom she might have children with, if possible. She had never felt so much pressure to be better than she was.

Her mother's hand came down to rest on her wrist, which was currently twitching. She hadn't even realized her hands had been fluttering.

"None of that, dear."

Andromeda bit back a sigh. Right. Don't twitch, don't flutter, don't tap. *Don't be you.*

The doors opened, and she saw her father was already seated in his massive high-backed throne on the raised dais at the end of the room. She and her mother ascended the stairs, and her mother took her seat beside him. Andromeda sat on the cushioned bench on the other side of her father and fiddled nervously with her hands.

He glanced over at her and gave her a gentle smile. "How are you feeling?"

"Like I'm going to throw up all this expensive hardware you put in me."

He nodded. "I understand how you feel. I've been where you are, twice. You'll do great."

Right. Everyone could keep telling her how great she would do until they were blue in the face. It didn't change the fact that her stomach felt like someone had stuffed it full of live mealworms.

A messenger entered the room through the two large double doors before them, and Andy's heart jumped. She had thought it was the royal family.

The messenger bowed. "The Someron ship has landed. The royals are descending from the flight deck now. They will enter momentarily."

"Thank you." Her father looked at Andromeda again. "Remember, be polite."

She fought the urge to roll her eyes. "Yes, Father, I know."

He didn't need to remind her how to be a princess.

"I am glad you agreed to do this so gracefully. It's my dream to see you happily married."

Andromeda forced a smile. "I know, Father."

The doors to the room opened, and this time it was no messenger. Trumpets announced the royal party. The flag bearers entered first, then four golden-clad royal guardsmen. Behind them entered the royal family. The king and queen walked side by side. The king was a robust man with a thick beard and gleaming blue eyes, while the queen's long red hair fluttered behind her elegantly. They made a lovely pair, but it was who walked behind them that caught Andromeda's attention. He was tall and slim with sleek black hair, and striking cheekbones she could see from where she sat. To say he was handsome would be an understatement, and his eyes were glued to her. Andromeda's heart fluttered, anxiety taking hold. As they approached the bottom of the stairs, her parents stood. They descended, and Andromeda followed behind. She kept her head high and her eyes straight ahead, trying to seem as regal as possible.

When both royal families were standing before each other, her father extended his hand in welcome. Rather than taking it, King Beckett threw his arms around King Alder in a hearty embrace. Her father stood still, seemingly unsure of what to do. Andromeda couldn't help the small laugh that escaped her. She glanced up to see Prince Eden still staring at her, his blue eyes piercing. She quickly composed herself and looked back at her father.

"This is no time for handshakes, old friend!" King Beckett chuckled. "How many years have we known each other, Alder? Thirty?"

"Somewhere around that long, yes." Her father smiled and pulled himself from King Beckett's embrace.

"And now look at us! Our children about to wed! Joining our two kingdoms as one and uniting everyone between the moon and Someron!"

Andromeda raised her eyebrows. He certainly liked the way his voice sounded. His eyes turned to her.

"And here she is! I haven't seen you since you were a tiny little thing. You couldn't have been more than six! Now you look… " he trailed off, his eyes roaming over her figure.

Andromeda waited in silence for him to finish his sentence.

"Stunning! You're positively radiant! Isn't she, darling?" he asked, turning to his queen.

Queen Elowyn's eyes grazed over her, and Andromeda felt like she might as well be naked. The queen's lips turned up at the corners. "Yes, I agree. Exquisite."

"You sound surprised," her mother said in a tone most would consider lighthearted, but Andromeda knew her mother well.

She could practically feel the ice seeping from her mother's voice. Andromeda stared in surprise, unsure of what would cause her mother to react that way.

"Not at all," Elowyn responded with a smile. "With parents such as you, how could you have anything but a perfect child?"

"How indeed," her mother said, ice still clinging to her words.

"Well, it doesn't matter what we think. Let the kids meet!" Beckett said, standing aside to allow his son through. Eden sauntered forward, his long legs bringing him in front of her. He was even more handsome up close. Andromeda wasn't sure what to do and was about to stick out her hand for a handshake when he took her gloved hand in his and bowed, pressing a kiss to her knuckles.

"It's an absolute pleasure to meet you, Andromeda. The stories of your beauty don't do you justice."

Andromeda glanced at her mother, who gave her a smile of encouragement.

"Um, thank you, Prince Eden. You are... very handsome as well."

God, why did she have to be so awkward? If there were ever a time for her to not sound like an idiot, it was now.

Eden smiled anyway and straightened, still holding her hand. "Thank you for saying so. It means a great deal coming from you."

"Let's allow these two to get more acquainted. Alder, show me to that wine cellar of yours!" King Beckett turned and pulled her father away by the arm, while the queens followed behind.

Eden watched their parents leave and then looked to her. "Is there somewhere we can talk?"

Andromeda fidgeted with the hem of her sleeve. "Um, we should have some privacy in the gardens."

"The gardens sound lovely."

She led him out the double doors and down the hall to the entrance of the gardens. Once outside, they walked in silence for a while. Overhead, the great dome that protected most of the moon's surface glistened, only visible when the sun hit it in the right way. Eden tilted his head up.

"The history of your kingdom is really quite fascinating. I learned all about it before coming here. That dome is eight thousand feet high and was built nearly one thousand years ago, after the Great War ended. Eight armies fought in the Great War; and six of them came to a truce. They came together to defeat the others, and when it was all over, Earth was divided into five kingdoms. Someron, Castellonia, Ameriadia, Afretious, and Austrota. The sixth king, your ancestor, used earthen technology to build this world on the moon. Now it's one of the most powerful and prosperous of all the kingdoms."

Andromeda raised an eyebrow. "I didn't realize I'd be receiving a history lesson on my own kingdom."

Eden smirked. "Apologies. Should I have waited for you to tell me?"

"Oh, I wouldn't dare think to bore you with such mundane conversation."

That surprised a laugh out of him. "Are you calling me boring?"

Andromeda clasped her hands behind her back and tried to hide a self-satisfied smile. "That would be terribly rude of me."

"And are you? Rude, I mean."

She glanced at him out of the corner of her eye and found him watching her. "If I were? Would that make this whole situation unbearable for you?"

"Oh, I wouldn't say that. I'll allow you your faults if you allow me mine."

Andromeda finally looked at him fully. "Well, Prince Eden, that would depend entirely upon what yours are."

A moment passed where neither said anything. Eden was still smiling when he turned away and changed the subject.

"I've never seen some of these plants. What are they?"

"Well, that," Andromeda said, pointing to a long-stemmed flower that curled upward, "is a Cavitous Bellatona. They were bred here on Celestine, and they can only grow in moon soil."

He reached out to touch a red bulbous flower. "And this?"

"Don't touch that!" She snatched his hand out of the air.

He stared at her in alarm. "Why not?"

"That's a Draculous flower. If its oils get onto your skin, it can seep into your bloodstream and cause your blood to thicken, which can lead to a heart attack or stroke."

Eden made a face of horror. "Then why is it in your garden?"

She shrugged. "Oh, you know. Beauty before practicality."

Eden seemed to keep his hands much closer to his sides after that. He walked over to a set of potted flowers. Purple petals twisted around a bright golden center.

"Oh, these are lovely."

A smile lit up her face. "Those are Andromedas."

He raised his eyebrows. "Were you named after them?"

"No, they were created after I was born. They were a gift from my father for my fifth birthday. The entire castle was filled with them. Every room smelled like them for at least a year afterward." She leaned down and inhaled deeply, a smile still on her lips.

"That was a very kind thing of your father to do."

She nodded. "He is a very kind man."

"I don't remember my father ever doing anything like that for me."

Andromeda examined his face, surprised by his bitter tone. "Really?"

"No. I wasn't always the eldest."

Oh, right. Andromeda remembered something about that. "I forgot. Your older brother died, didn't he?"

"Yes. There was a mechanical failure on his ship. Everyone on board died."

"How did it happen?"

Eden turned his face away from her, the corners of his lips pulling down. "I don't know. I'm not a ship expert." His tone made it clear he didn't want to talk about it anymore.

Andromeda flushed and looked away. Right. It wasn't appropriate to talk about someone's dead brother the first time you meet them.

"I'm so sorry. I-I should have known that wasn't something you wanted to talk about."

When he looked at her, it was with a smile that didn't reach his eyes. "It's fine. I've had three years to grieve, but it's still terribly hard for me sometimes."

He sat down on the edge of a fountain, and Andromeda followed. "I can understand that. I would be heartbroken if I lost either of my little sisters."

He pressed his hands against the cool stone and leaned back, tilting his face up and taking a deep breath. "So, do you mind if I ask you a personal question as well?"

Andromeda's stomach twisted, but she knew she couldn't refuse. "Sure."

"How did you end up like... this?" He waved his hand over the left side of her body.

Though nobody could see the metal beneath the synthetic skin, everybody knew it was there. She'd known she'd have to explain it, eventually; she had just hoped it wouldn't be on the first day she met him.

"You don't have to tell me if you don't want. It's just that we were given no details on the particulars."

"No, it's fine. It happened five years ago while I was on a trip to meet with my aunt. I remember the ship was flying low to the surface, only about three hundred feet above the ground. I remembered my father telling me the minimum altitude for a dome ship was six hundred feet, so I unbuckled my seat belt to talk to the captain." Andromeda took a deep breath.

"There was a jolt, then everything exploded. All I can remember next is fire, pain, and falling. When they found me, I was nearly dead."

"My God," Eden whispered. "How did you survive?"

"I shouldn't have. But the doctors worked for ten days straight to save my life. When I woke up, they had replaced nearly half of my body. Top-of-the-line robotics, they said." She turned her face away. The pain and conflict she felt at these memories weren't for him. Perhaps someday it could be something she'd share, but for now her pain was hers and hers alone.

"Do they know how the accident happened?"

Andromeda ran her hand over the coarse gray stone of the fountain. "Yes. Apparently, the captain of the ship had been drinking. We collided with another ship. One side of the craft was ripped off, and it pulled me out with it."

Andromeda stared into space, the memory of those agonizing months after the accident vivid in her mind.

"They found the captain guilty, and my father executed him himself."

Eden shook his head, watching her. "That entire ordeal must have been so hard for you."

"It was. When I woke up with so much of me changed, I couldn't come to terms with it. I hated myself. I've really had to accept my new reality, but I still struggle with it, even today."

Andromeda looked down and ran her hands over her legs. Both her legs, the left side of her ribs, some of her left-side organs, half her heart, her left arm and shoulder, and part of her skull had been replaced. Her brain was still mostly hers, at least. A metal chip had been embedded in her right lobe, which helped operate all the parts, to keep her in sync.

"Well, if it makes you feel any better, I like the way you look."

She forced a tight smile. "Thanks."

It didn't. It wasn't about her looks. It was about the loss. Losing so much of her, half the body she had been born with, ripped away in a moment. She was incredibly grateful for the technology that had saved her life, and she had grown to appreciate the robotics that were now her body. But she still sometimes dreamed about the way she had felt before the accident. The sharp pain of hitting her shin on a table. The way her feet would ache after running for long distances. The smooth silk of sheets rubbing against bare legs. All of that was gone now.

Eden nudged her shoulder. "Let's talk about happier things. What do you enjoy doing?"

"I-I enjoy spending time with my friends. And reading. Oh, and I love working on machines!"

He raised an eyebrow. "Machines?"

"Yes. Engines, motors, smaller tech. I enjoy taking things apart and putting them back together."

"Why?"

She blinked. "What do you mean, why? I just do. Why does anyone enjoy doing anything?"

He raised his hands in mock surrender. "Hey, sorry. I didn't mean to offend you. I've just never heard of a princess who doubles as a mechanic."

She pressed her lips together and looked away. "Well, now you have. Not that weird, I think."

He chuckled. "No, not that weird. Just surprising. But anyway, yeah, I enjoy spending time with friends and reading as well. Though I have had little time for that over these past three years. I've had to catch up on learning how to be a king someday."

"Oh, yes, of course! I do that as well. I spend a lot of my time with my mother and father, learning to be an effective ruler."

"Yeah, it can be a lot. The weight of millions of souls on my shoulders can be a tough burden to carry. It was never something I thought I would have to deal with when I was younger."

"You're lucky," she sighed. "At least you had years of freedom. I've known I would be queen since the day I was born."

"It doesn't have to be so bad, you know. If you have a good support system, and someone who cares for you by your side, you'll be OK. I hope that we will both have that."

Andromeda glanced at him out of the corner of her eye. He was smiling serenely, his eyes just hinting at mischief. "You're terribly charming, you know that?"

Eden smirked. "I've been told once or twice. Are you charmed?"

"Well enough, for now." She wouldn't give him too much satisfaction. He could work for that if he wanted it.

She rested her hand on the fountain, and he placed his over hers. She looked down at it, his hand wide enough to completely obscure her own, and swallowed. People didn't normally touch her. At least, not people she didn't know.

"You're also very familiar, Prince Eden."

Rather than remove his hand, as he should have, he shrugged. "And you really are stunning."

She had to bite back a harsh retort. "Yes, you've mentioned that."

He seemed to notice the irritation in her voice and pulled away. "I should be going to find my parents. I look forward to seeing you a great deal more over these next several days." He leaned in and pressed a kiss to her right cheek.

"Yes, I look forward to it as well." She tried to mean it.

Prince Eden turned and walked back through the rows of flowers to the castle. Andromeda ran a hand over the spot he had kissed her. She wasn't being fair to him. It wasn't his fault they were being forced to marry any more than it was hers. She got up to leave as well but, as she did, caught sight of a dress poking out the side of the wall of shrubberies. She frowned and moved to look behind it.

"What are you two doing?" she shouted.

Rosetta and Eleanora, her sisters, spun around. Both girls looked a great deal like their mother, unlike Andromeda, with black silky hair and dark eyes.

"We weren't spying!" Eleanora insisted, giving them away. At thirteen, she was the younger of the two.

Andromeda frowned.

"OK, so we were. So what?" Rosetta, who was fifteen, asked.

"Prince Eden and I were trying to be alone. Couldn't you have given us some privacy?"

Rosetta snickered. "Shouldn't you two have a chaperone?"

Andromeda placed her hands on her hips. "Oh, shut up, he's my fiancé."

"You're so lucky." Eleanora pouted. "He's gorgeous."

"And so tall!" Rosetta added.

"I guess." Andromeda shrugged, feigning indifference.

Rosetta rolled her eyes. "You know he is, don't lie. Your kids are going to be beautiful."

Andromeda looked away, not wanting to talk about that. "You two better get back to the castle and get ready for dinner."

"Fine. But first you have to admit how good looking he is," Rosetta insisted.

Andromeda sighed. "OK! He's hot. Are you happy?"

"Not in the slightest. You get all the luck with guys." Rosetta frowned before running to the castle, pulling Eleanora with her.

"*Sisters,*" Andromeda grumbled under her breath.

CHAPTER THREE

ANDROMEDA'S RED SATIN DRESS SWISHED across the tiles of the hall. Her black curls had been pulled back into a thick braid, made slick and straight with oils, and the ruby circlet around her head matched her dress.

The wide halls were empty, with most of the staff in the kitchen, perfecting dinner. She had walked these halls more times than she could count, but somehow they felt different now, as though preparing to throw her from them at any chance. As though she didn't belong anymore.

She took her time walking, trying to gather her thoughts. Tonight, both royal families would dine together, and Eden's parents would surely ask questions. She wasn't looking forward to it. Hopefully, her parents would soften the blow. As she reached the doors to the dining hall, she peeked in. The rest of her family and Eden's were already there, engaged in polite discussion. Eden was missing.

As though summoned by her thoughts, a soft voice spoke behind her. "Are you afraid to go in?"

Andromeda spun around, her hand flying to her chest. Eden stood behind her, his blue eyes taking her in, a smile on his lips.

"God, you scared me." She took a deep breath. "Why would I be afraid? I just wanted to see who was already here." She tried to slow her pounding heart for fear the mechanics would give out.

"Are you sure you weren't trying to see if I was there?"

Andromeda raised an eyebrow. Well, wasn't he cocky? "No more so than anyone else. What are you doing standing out here?"

He shrugged. "I just got here."

Not likely. Andromeda had excellent hearing, especially in her left ear, and would have heard his footsteps approaching. She glanced at the marble columns beside the door. Had he been hiding behind them? What a strange thing to do.

"Were you waiting for me?" she asked, trying her best to sound flirtatious. It felt false on her lips, a pale imitation of what someone who genuinely wanted to flirt would say.

Eden smirked. "You caught me."

They stood quite close now. Andromeda fidgeted with the turquoise ring on her finger. The urge to shake and flap her hands was strong, but she restrained it. It wouldn't do to make him uncomfortable. He looked her over slowly, and once his eyes settled back on her face, he lifted his hand toward her. She jerked back ungracefully, and he froze near her hair.

"I'm sorry, I didn't mean to startle you. There's a stray curl coming out of your braid."

She reached up and felt for the curl, pushing it back into place. "Oh, right. Sorry."

"Do I make you nervous?"

"Yes." It was the truth. "Do I make you?"

His smile softened. "I'm terrified."

"You don't look it."

He shrugged. "I'm a great actor."

"Have you considered becoming one?"

"What?"

"An actor."

He laughed. "No more than you've considered becoming a mechanic. Our paths have already been set for us."

Andromeda opened her mouth, but just then the doors to the dining hall opened.

"What are you two doing out here alone?" King Beckett asked. "Getting a little more comfortable together?" He quirked an eyebrow and gave them a devilish grin.

Eden shook his head. "We both just got here. I was about to escort the princess into the room."

"How about we sit and eat?" her father suggested, looking from one to the other.

"Of course." Eden nodded and held out his arm for Andromeda.

She took it and allowed him to escort her to her chair. Everyone else made their way to the table and took their seats, with Eden taking the spot directly across from Andromeda.

Once everyone settled, she studied Eden. Now over her initial nerves, she could notice other subtleties about him. The curve of his lips and the sly gleam in his eyes made her feel as though he knew something she didn't, like he had his own private jokes. He seemed to enjoy eye contact, something she tried to avoid, but she couldn't fault him for that. Most other people didn't have a problem with it either. Andromeda had accepted long ago that she was different, even before the accident, and that was OK. She liked herself.

Soon the food was brought out, and everyone ate.

"So, Eden, what do you do in your free time?" Rosetta asked.

He chewed his steak slowly before he answered. "I spend most of my free time with Father, learning how to govern my kingdom."

"Surely that's not what you do *all* the time?" Rosetta said, pouting her lips slightly. "What about when you're alone?"

He dabbed delicately at his mouth with his napkin. "Well, I like to write."

"What do you write?"

"I don't know, my thoughts I suppose." He fidgeted slightly in his seat.

"That's enough questions, Rosetta," her mother chided.

"And you, Andromeda? What do you like to do?" Queen Elowyn asked.

Andromeda paused mid-bite. "Um, mostly what Eden said. My training to become queen never ceases."

"Don't be modest, dear," her mother said. "Andromeda has a brilliant mind. She's always fixing something."

King Beckett slapped his hand on the table. "Ah, a true politician!"

Rosetta snickered, earning a glare from Andromeda. "If by politician you mean mechanic, sure."

"You do manual labor?" Queen Elowyn asked, her delicate brows furrowing much like Eden's had earlier.

Andromeda tilted her chin upward. "Yes, I do. I'm good at it. Just last month I repaired an engine that our main mechanic said was unsalvageable."

"A princess should not sully herself in the work of commoners." Queen Elowyn's eyes narrowed.

That familiar flame burned in her chest. "On the contrary, I think it's incredibly important for those in power to not forget the struggle of the average person."

Rather than respond, Elowyn turned to Adella. "You let her do this?"

Her mother didn't look up from cutting her meat as she spoke. "Frankly, Elowyn, I don't think it's your business what I let my daughter do. Especially after what I've heard you let your son get up to."

The table went silent and Andromeda stared at her mother in surprise. There was that animosity again. And what did she mean by that? She glanced at Queen Elowyn, who was fuming.

Her father cleared his throat. "That doesn't matter now. Once Andromeda and Eden are married, she will assume her royal duties full time. There will be no place for playing around with toy engines."

Andromeda's stomach dropped at his words. She knew her father disagreed with her hobbies, but she had hoped he would support her in front of the other royal family. Instead, he had offered her up on a platter. Yes, she'd be a good girl. She would be a perfect wife and future queen, even if that meant giving up a piece of who she was. She would do as they told her. Andromeda realized she had been staring frozen at her plate for several moments when her father spoke again.

"Prince Eden, I thought I would have a pod brought out for you and Andromeda to go for a picnic tomorrow."

Andromeda swallowed the lump in her throat and forced herself to look up at Eden. He was watching her with a gentle expression.

"That sounds wonderful, Your Majesty. I would love to spend more time with your daughter."

"I'm sure you would," Eleanora muttered under her breath, prompting a kick from Andromeda.

They finished the rest of their dinner mostly in silence. When they were done, Eden stood and placed his napkin on the table. "With your permission, Your Majesty, I would like to escort your daughter to her room."

"Of course." Her father nodded. "And I'll have guards waiting outside her door to take you to your room. We wouldn't want anyone to get lost."

Andromeda rolled her eyes, but Eden only inclined his head. "Of course."

She took Eden's offered arm and walked with him out of the room and down the hall.

"So that was… interesting," he said with a smirk.

"Yeah, that's one word for it," she muttered.

It would have been better if he hadn't offered to walk with her. She was in no mood to smile and curtsy for him. Being alone was the only thing she wanted right now, to recharge. But he was looking at her, so she pressed her lips into a thin smile. "It was a bit awkward."

"Mm, our mothers seem tense."

She shrugged. "Yeah, I don't know what that was about."

They continued to walk in silence. Andromeda fidgeted with her hands and tried to think of something to say.

"What's that?" he asked, pointing to a set of double doors.

"Those lead out to a balcony overlooking the front of the castle."

"Can we go out?"

Nerves returned to her stomach. "Why?"

He gave her a serene smile. "I could use a bit of fresh air."

She wanted to say that the air inside was the same as the air outside, all manufactured, but she didn't. She was sure she was already coming across as a brat as it was.

"Yeah, sure."

The temperature on the terrace was the same as inside, just like always. Eden walked to the marble balcony and placed his hands on the balustrade.

"Your kingdom is beautiful."

She stood beside him, looking out over the distant twinkling lights of the city. "Thank you. It seems boring to me, having been nowhere else. I can't wait to go to Earth."

"And I can't wait to show you everything I love. When we go, I want you to be comfortable."

She let her eyes dart to his face. He really was trying. "Thank you. I appreciate it. I-I'm sure I will be."

Eden's eyes lit up. "I'm so happy to hear you say that. To be honest, when I was told I would marry you, I was afraid. I worried we would have nothing in common. That there would be no chemistry between us."

She raised an eyebrow. As far as she could tell, that was exactly the case. But if the way he was looking at her was any indication, he felt differently.

"You think we have chemistry?"

"Of course. You're exquisite."

Ah, there it was again. She was exquisite. She was beautiful. She was attractive. He was basing his entire opinion of her off her looks. She gave him a thin smile.

"Yes, you mentioned that. But what else? What else do you like about me?"

A crease formed between his brows. "Well, I admit I don't know you very well yet. But you seem kind and intelligent."

She looked away. Kind and intelligent. Things that could be said about anyone. "So then, what exactly do we have in common?"

Eden tilted his head. "I'm sorry, have I offended you?"

Andromeda clenched her teeth and closed her eyes. God, what was wrong with her? Eden was only trying to be nice and make the best out of the situation, and yet she was snapping at him like he had personally planned to ruin her life. She forced herself to smile.

"No, no, you haven't. I'm sorry. I'm just tired."

The worry eased from his face. "Ah, yes, I understand."

Andromeda turned back to the door, but suddenly his hand was on her face, forcing her to stop. She blinked up at him, his face too close. Her breath stuck in her chest as he leaned forward and pressed his lips to hers. She was completely still beneath him for several seconds before her mind caught up with what was happening. She placed a hand on his chest and took a step back.

He frowned. "Is something wrong?"

Andromeda swallowed hard. Yes, something was wrong. All of this was wrong. Eden was kind and gentle, he was her fiancé, and yet even as he had kissed her, she felt nothing. No nerves. No joy. No butterflies. Just... nothing. He was handsome. There should be no reason for her to want to push him away now, to run to her room and lock the door. She seemed to have lucked out in who was chosen for her to marry.

And there it was. There was the crux of the problem. He had been chosen for her. Eden was a placeholder for where love was supposed to grow in her life. People fell in love and married all the time, but that gift was being denied to her. Just like the artificial heart that beat in her chest at that moment, he was an artificial love that she was expected to get used to. Someone she would learn to love. But she didn't want to learn to love someone, she wanted love to grow naturally, and by choice. She bit back tears.

"No, nothing is wrong. We're just moving a bit fast. And like I said, I'm tired."

She lifted her left hand to her face, but winced in pain. Oh, great.

Eden tilted his head. "Are you OK?"

Andromeda used her right arm to push the left back down. "Oh, it's nothing. This arm just gets stuck sometimes."

He looked from her arm, then back to her face. "Should I take you to a doctor? Or a... I don't know, mechanic?"

"No, it's all right. I can fix it myself once I get back to my room."

"OK, then I better get you there quickly before your father has your royal guard hunt me down."

She knew he was kidding, but honestly that wouldn't surprise her. He walked her the rest of the way to her room. They turned to each other, and Andromeda thought he was going to kiss her again. Instead, he took her hand and gave it a gentle peck.

"I look forward to seeing you tomorrow, my lovely Andromeda."

With that, he turned and left her standing outside her door. She watched him until he rounded the corner and was out of sight, then hurried into her room and closed it behind her. Once alone in her room, she walked to the box of tools on her nightstand. She found her scalpel in her toolbox and twisted her arm until she felt where it had gotten stuck, right above the bend in her elbow. She cut into the synthetic skin in a vertical line, all the way from mid-forearm to the crook in her elbow. The sight of cutting her skin open used to frighten her, but not anymore. She had done it so many times now it was like unzipping a coat. Her thumb and index finger pulled the skin away. The sight of her open arm never ceased to intrigue her. A mix of shining metal and clear tubes that served as veins intertwined with each other in a beautiful display of modern technology. She flexed her arm and watched as the parts moved at her every thought.

She set the scalpel on the nightstand and pulled out a small can of lubricant the doctors had made specially for her, then bent her arm back and forth until she located the problem. One of her elbow joints was stuck. She poked the thin nose of the nozzle into the tiny space where the joint was and squirted lubricant. Her elbow flexed several times until it felt loose and free. She smiled and placed the can back into the box. Once she had pinched the skin back together, she pulled out a tiny welder her doctor had made. It became only hot enough to reconnect the skin, but not melt or distort it. When she was finished, she rubbed her fingers over the finished product of her once again smooth skin.

With that problem solved, she flopped onto her bed. If only everything in her life could be fixed with tools and a bit of oil. She grabbed the remote that laid on her bedside table and turned on the screen that was attached to her wall. The face of a news host appeared, all blonde hair and bright smiles.

"We're once again on royal watch. As you all know, the Someron ship landed early this afternoon. We've heard from a source close to the royal family that Princess Andromeda and Prince Eden are getting along very well. They were spotted walking together in the gardens, and our source tells us they looked cozy together. Well, it looks like we won't have to wait long for another royal baby!"

Andromeda groaned and pressed the pillow to her face. She should have suspected that she and Eden were being watched. They always were. And soon her face was going to be plastered to every news screen and tabloid in the world. That's what happened when you married. When the Royal Children Protection Act ended, she'd step into the spotlight to take her role as a public figure, and the world would spend the rest of her life criticizing every little thing she did.

In a fit of fury, Andromeda flung the pillow across the room at the screen. It missed, hitting the wall instead. She felt it again, the building in her chest as her breath became shorter. It had only been a day since her last panic attack. She normally went months without one, yet she was about to have two in as many days. She dug her fingers into the mattress and squeezed her eyes shut.

It felt like her life was spinning out of control. She wanted to feel something for Eden, to feel a small glimmer of hope that this would all be OK. But how could it be, when none of it was up to her? Perhaps if she had met him in another life, if they had been given time and room to grow, then maybe she could have loved him. But not like this. Yet it was her only option. She'd marry him whether she wanted to or not, and it would be up to her to make it a pleasant situation. She'd smile and hold his hand and tell everyone about a love she did not feel. And they would eat it up. Because that's what she was to them. Entertainment. A fantasy.

Her life was not her own. This was the toll that was required for her to live the life that she had. She had a palace and money and luxury.

The cost was autonomy. She'd have her choices made for her until she was queen, and even then, she'd have her husband to answer to.

Andromeda sat up and turned off the screen. She desperately wanted to work on her engine, but that too had been taken from her. Unless... Her father would have had the engine sent down to the royal transport garage. At this time of night, nobody would be working in there. It took her only a minute to decide. She would not ask permission. Clumsily, she untied the laces on the back of her dress and then pulled it over her head. Once the ruby crown and other jewelry were all off and secured in her desk drawer, she pulled on her comfortable brown work pants and a loose-fitting black top. She kept her hair in the braid.

When all her tools were packed into her satchel, she cracked open her door and peered down the hallway. It was dark and empty, just as she liked it. She stepped out and locked her door behind her, ensuring nobody would try to enter. It wouldn't be ideal if half the castle thought she was off with Eden.

She moved silently down the hall, keeping in mind the spots that creaked. She didn't reach her first obstacle until she got to the stairs. Two maids were making their way up, but they didn't spot her, as they were too busy in conversation. She waited in the shadows of the curtains until they were gone. Her footsteps were silent as she slipped out from the curtains and ran down the stairs.

It took several more minutes and a few more hiding spots before she reached the back door of the garage. She peered in and was relieved to see that it appeared empty. Once the door was closed behind her, she made her way past several ships until she saw her engine. It didn't look like it had been touched. She let out a sigh of relief.

Her hand ran over the sleek metal. This felt like home. This was where she belonged. Dropping her satchel to the ground, she pulled out the tools and got to work. The feel of oil on her hands made her smile. Taking out her wrench, she focused on what she knew would be a problematic bolt.

"Come on, turn," she mumbled.

It didn't budge, so she added more pressure. "Come on. Turn, you stupid freaking mother—"

"Ahem."

Andromeda's hand slipped, and the wrench went sailing through the air before landing and sliding across the ground into a pair of boots. She leapt to her feet. A man stood a few feet away, his eyes moving from the wrench to Andromeda. Dark red hair flopped into green eyes.

She cleared her throat. "Oh, er, sorry. I thought I was alone in here."

He raised an eyebrow as he scooped up the wrench. "It's no problem, I thought the same."

Andromeda took him in. She had never seen him before; she was sure of that. He looked a few years older than her and was at least half a foot taller. Broad shoulders filled out his shirt, and she couldn't help but notice the top few buttons were undone. He held out the wrench, which she took with a quick thanks.

"So, do you work in here?" he asked.

She blinked. He didn't know who she was? He must be new. "Um, yes, sometimes. You?"

He shrugged one shoulder. "I'm new here."

"Ah, I see." They lapsed into an awkward silence. "Right, well, I'll just be going."

He held up his hands. "Oh, no, don't let me stop you. Do you need some help?"

She pressed her lips together. "No, I'm fine."

"Really?" He raised an eyebrow. "It looked like you were having some trouble with that bolt. If you need someone big and strong to do it—"

"No!" she snapped. "I am perfectly capable—" She stopped when she saw the wide grin spread across his face, a twinkle of mischief in his eyes. She narrowed her eyes. "You're joking, aren't you?"

He pouted his lip and held up his hands. "Maybe. Maybe not. That's up to you."

She crossed her arms. "What's your name?"

"Allen. Yours?"

She thought about it. "Andy."

"Well, Andy, it's a pleasure to meet you. As I said, continue as you were. Something about that bolt's mother, I think."

Andromeda couldn't help it. She laughed. It felt like a pressure being taken off her chest. Allen laughed as well, a wonderful, easy laugh, his eyes crinkling in the corners. She shook her head and leaned against the engine.

"Sorry you had to hear that. That wasn't very ladylike."

Allen scoffed. "Ladylike? What do I care for ladylike? Go ahead, cuss up a storm."

She grinned and looked down. "No, I couldn't."

He rolled his eyes. "Oh, come on. Just one? Here, I'll start. Shit."

Her eyes flashed up to his face. Nobody ever cussed in front of her. But he was looking at her with such openness and amusement. She bit her lip.

"Damn."

He nodded. "Good. Crap."

She straightened up. "Ass."

"Bitch."

"Fuck!" She slapped her hand over mouth, eyes going wide and a smile splitting across her face. She had only ever cussed in front of her friends, and even then, they had chastised her for it. But Allen was laughing.

"See! Doesn't that feel good? You don't have to sensor yourself all the time to please others."

Her smile slid off her face. Of course, he didn't know who she was. He didn't know what predicament she was in. He seemed to notice her change in mood and frowned.

"I'm sorry, was it something I said?"

She shook her head. "No, sorry, it's fine."

"It's clearly not. Please, tell me."

She looked back into his open, concerned eyes. "It's just, not everyone has that option. Some of us don't have a choice in what we do."

She sat down on the floor by the engine, and after a moment of silence, he came to sit beside her. He left a foot of space between them, but the sudden proximity made the hairs on her arm stand on end.

"Of course you have a choice in what you do. You aren't in prison."

"May as well be," she muttered. At his questioning look, she continued. "It's just, my parents. They have a course set out for me I have to follow."

"What sort of course?"

"You know, my job, where I'll live... who I'll marry."

"That's ridiculous. Nobody can make those decisions but you."

She laughed humorlessly. "As it turns out, everyone *but* me gets to make those decisions."

He was silent for several moments, and she could feel his eyes on her face. "So, leave."

"I can't."

"Sure you can," he insisted.

"No, I really can't! All of my family is here. I have responsibilities."

"Responsibilities that you don't want and didn't ask for."

"Yes, but mine all the same."

He let out a huff of air. "Trust me, someone else will take up those responsibilities if you leave. You only have this one life, don't waste it doing what everyone else wants you to do."

She looked back at him. What he was saying would be so nice. To run away. To leave the decisions and marriage and obligations behind. Maybe go to Earth and open her own shop.

"What about my family?"

"They would still be here if you wanted to come back."

She laughed. "How can you say that? You don't even know me."

He ran a hand through his hair and shrugged. "No, I don't. But I've been where you are before. Questioning my life. Doing everything for everyone else."

"So, what did you do?"

"Exactly what I said. I left. I found my own way in the world."

Andromeda bit her lip. "I admit, that would be nice. But my family would never allow it. They would hunt me down and bring me back. There would be consequences, and not just for me. Maybe someday, though, I'll get the chance to do what I like."

He looked saddened by her answer. "Andy, nobody is ever going to give you control. It's something you have to take."

For a man that she didn't know, he was getting awfully personal. She decided to lighten the mood.

With a smirk, she asked, "And how, theoretically, would I go about leaving?"

He tilted his head, considering it. "Just pack a bag, grab some money, and hop on the next ship to Earth."

She raised her eyebrows. "Are you asking me to run away with you, Allen?"

His mouth fell open, and his eyes widened. "What? I—no, that's not what... " He saw her smile and laughed. "OK, I suppose I deserved that." His smile faded slowly. "But, I mean, if you needed help getting out, of course I could—"

"No!" No, that was not an option. He would be charged with attempted kidnapping of a royal, regardless of how Andromeda would try to defend him. And she wouldn't get someone else in trouble for her selfishness. "No. It's a nice thought, but really, I'm fine. I'm happy."

The lie felt bitter on her lips, and Allen didn't seem to believe her. He opened his mouth to say something, but at that moment they heard the garage door open and voices coming in. They both scrambled to their feet.

"Crap," she whispered. "I'm not supposed to be in here."

Allen looked at her, then peeked over the engine at the two men who were walking toward them. "Quick. I'll distract them. Run to the door when I do."

She frowned. "Are you sure?"

"Yes, now go!"

She spared him one last look before darting around the side of the engine. Allen's voice came from behind her.

"Evening, gentleman. Here to pick up some late-night hours?"

She didn't hear the other men's response as she made a run for the door. Once outside, she pressed her back to the door and let out a slow breath. Allen had really saved her butt. She bit her lip, his cool green eyes clouding her vision for a moment more before she set out for her room.

CHAPTER FOUR

OVER THE NEXT FEW DAYS, Andromeda did her best to play her part. She attended all the planned dates for her and Eden and shook all the right hands. Eden was charming, as always. He said the right thing and smiled in the right way, always seeming to know how to make a situation right. And yet, more than one time, Andromeda found her mind wandering to red hair and green eyes.

She tried a few times to go back to the garage, but each instance had ended in either her friends or her sisters interrupting her. Yet, that hadn't stopped her from scanning the grounds for a flash of red hair each time she walked with Eden. She wasn't even sure why her mind lingered on him.

It had just been so nice to talk to someone who didn't know who she was. He hadn't looked at her as his princess or a celebrity. He'd seen her as a person. And he had been kind. Not because it was expected of him, but because he wanted to be. It was refreshing. It didn't hurt that he was handsome. Perhaps in another life, one where she wasn't a princess, there could have been something between them.

The morning of her departure came with little fanfare, as it was kept a secret from the public. She would be going to Earth separately from Eden, in a modified container ship so as to arrive stealthily and avoid any security risks that might come along with the two heirs traveling together. That was all fine with Andromeda. Any chance to escape the scrutiny of large crowds was preferable.

A package had been delivered that morning from Eden, and she'd opened it to find a beautiful emerald necklace. It had come with a note from him as well, telling her it contained a jewel from her future crown and that he wanted her to carry a piece of him with her until they were reunited. It was all a bit much, which was on brand for Eden.

Before boarding the ship, she hugged and kissed her parents and sisters good-bye. Her mother was emotional, but Andromeda assured her there was no need. She'd be back in a matter of weeks. It would be a lie to say she wasn't nervous about leaving, as this would be the first time she'd ever left her family, but the nerves were overshadowed by the excitement of seeing Earth. With one final tight hug, her mother released her.

Andromeda boarded the ship and glanced back once more at her family. The door slid shut, blocking her view of them, and she rushed to the window to peer out. They still stood there, smiling and waiting. She considered telling the pilots to open the doors so she could run back out to them. But she didn't. What would be the point in delaying this? Instead, she took her seat and fastened herself in.

"Are you ready, Princess?"

"I am."

The roar of the ship as it came to life reverberated through her, making her grip the armrest. She hadn't been on a ship this large since her accident, and flashbacks of it filled her mind. She closed her eyes and leaned back as they took off, shooting upward and heading for the sky port. The acceleration pressed Andromeda flat in her chair. They landed in the double-sealed port and waited for their turn to leave the atmosphere. Typically, a royal had first right of passage, but since she was undercover, they had to wait. It took about fifteen minutes for them to be cleared. As they left the dome, Andromeda couldn't take her eyes off the window. The bright sky of the dome faded into darkness. She looked back and saw that her palace was a distant dot, growing smaller by the second as the void of space consumed them. Well, that was it. She was on her own now. No family to protect her, no friends to reassure her. From this point on, she would rely on herself. She reclined her chair back. Might as well rest before stepping onto the firing range.

"Can you wake me up before we land?" she asked the pilot.

He bowed his head. "Of course, Princess."

It took only a few minutes for the ship to rock her into a restless slumber.

When she awoke, it was abrupt, as if someone had shaken her. A glance at the clock told her they had only been flying for three hours. However, when she turned to the pilots, she knew something was wrong. They moved quickly, flicking switches and muttering.

"Is everything OK?" she called.

One pilot turned to her, his brow creased and his eyes wide. "Oh, um, yes, Princess! Everything's fine."

He was lying. She unbuckled her seatbelt to see what was wrong. As she approached, they turned and saw her.

"Princess! Please, go sit—"

Before the pilot could finish his sentence, the ship lurched to the right, slamming Andromeda into the wall and then onto the floor. Oh, God, not again! They had crashed and she would be ripped out of the ship, and this time she wouldn't land on the ground. She would die.

The sound of the pilot's panicked voice reached her. "Princess! Are you all right?"

She pressed her hand to her head; the impact was making her dizzy. "I-I'm fine."

"You need to hide, Princess!" a pilot shouted, drawing his gun.

"Hide? Why?"

"We're about to be boarded."

Her head swam. What he was saying didn't make any sense. They were still in space. The only reason they would be boarded was for an emergency.

"Boarded? By whom?"

Before they could answer, she heard the outer door of the ship open.

"Princess, go!"

With steadily rising fear, she rolled under the seat beside her, tucking her legs against her chest. A second later, the inner doors opened.

Six pairs of boots entered.

"Reboard your own ship immediately!" one pilot shouted.

The newcomers chuckled.

"Why would we do that?" a gruff voice asked.

"What you are doing is illegal!" The pilot sounded terrified.

"What I want to know," said the gruff voice, "is why a cargo ship that can carry twelve tons of merchandise is empty. Why're you going to Earth?"

"That's none of your business, sir! Now, leave!"

"I don't think we will."

Two blasts went off, and the two pilots fell to the ground. Andromeda covered her mouth to stifle her scream. These men had to be pirates, and she had heard of the terrible things pirates did. But they never came so close to Celestine. What were they doing here?

"Search the ship," the gruff voice ordered.

The leader, Andromeda assumed. She searched for a way out, but knew there was none. If they had boarded her ship, that meant they had manually taken control, so she wouldn't be able to use the controls to fly away. And they were in space, so there was nowhere to go. The chances of her death were high, but if she was going out, she was taking as many of them with her as she could. A few feet in front of her, she spotted a wrench that must have been left by the maintenance crew. Uncurling her body, she rolled onto her stomach, inching forward and keeping her eyes on the men's boots. She reached for it. Only two more inches to go. There was a sudden jerk on her legs, and she let out an unintentional scream as she was dragged backward and out of her hiding spot.

"What do we have here?"

A hand wrapped around her hair and lifted her upward. The men gathered around, looking her up and down. Though she was in a panic, she noted that there were five of them.

"Let go of me!" she snarled.

"Well, aren't you a pretty one," Gruff Voice said with a nasty smile. He wore a baggy grey shirt that matched the stubble on his face.

"Look at those eyes, Mack. You ever seen anything like it?" another asked.

"No, I can't say I have," Gruff Voice, or Mack, said. "What's your name, pretty one?"

She spat at him.

"Oh, she's got a fire in her. The captain'll like that."

"He does like unique things," one man agreed.

She bared her teeth. "I'm not a thing."

He ignored her. "Why's a pretty girl like you heading to Earth in a cargo ship? You wouldn't have been trying to smuggle yourself in, would you?"

So they didn't know who she was. Good. Her mind raced for something to say. "I'm just a mechanic. I didn't have the money to pay for passage to Earth, so I'm sneaking in. I'm nobody special, I just want to get to Earth."

"Well, Nobody Special, I don't think you're going to make it there."

They pulled her toward the door, and like a cornered rabbit, she fought. She pulled on the man who held her, forcing him forward and over her body. Two more arms circled her, squeezing her arms to her side. She leaned against him and kicked the man directly in front of her. The power in her mechanical legs sent him flying back several feet. Using her bionic arm, she pried the man off her and turned to hit him. Before she could, however, there was a sharp sting on the right side of her neck. She reached up and pulled a small needle from her skin. As she did, the whole world tilted sideways. Someone caught her and lifted her into their arms. She wanted to fight back, to kick and scream and fight, but she had lost control of her limbs. Her head rolled around and landed in the crook of the arms that held her. She gazed up and saw a face that she hadn't noticed before. Dark green eyes stared down at her under a mop of dark red hair. Before she lost consciousness, she thought she heard him say, "It's OK, you're safe."

Darkness enveloped her. She wasn't sure how long she stayed floating in the dark, but when she came around, the first thing she noticed was the cold. There was a cool metal surface beneath her. She blinked and slowly lifted her head. The floor of a ship? Three metal walls and one made of bars suggested a cell, dimly lit, but clean at least. The attack on the ship and dart in her neck rushed back into her memory. How long had she slept? Her breathing became labored as the panic set in. They had taken her. The pirates. She was trapped in space with a bunch of murderous pirates! And then before she had lost consciousness, for one strange moment, she had thought she had seen...

"It's OK."

She spun around at the voice. She was sure, in that moment, she had lost her mind. Because sitting across from her, outside the cell, was Allen. The handsome redhead that had been on her mind for the past couple days watched her with his eyebrows drawn together. She shook her head slowly, trying to force her mind to understand.

"I-I don't... What are you doing here? Did they take you too?"

He swallowed and looked down. "No, Andy, they didn't."

Realization slowly crept up on her, like a tendril sliding up her back. Her chest began to rise and fall quickly.

"You. You're a pirate?" She spoke in barely more than a whisper. It felt as though the walls were closing in on her.

He leaned toward her, his hands up as though he was trying to placate her. "Andy, calm down. Take a deep breath."

She wanted to shout at him to not tell her what to do, but her throat was too tight, and her mind raced too fast. She leaned back against the cold wall and dug her fingers into her hair, each breath coming in a gasp. It was too much.

"Andy, please, let me explain. This isn't what you think it is. I didn't plan any of this."

She didn't want to listen to him.

"Go!" she gasped out. "Leave me alone!" She didn't want anyone present while she was in this state, least of all him.

He was silent for several moments before he stood. "OK, fine. I'll come back when you're ready to talk. I'll make sure nobody bothers you." He made his way to the door, then looked over his shoulder. "I'll be back later, Princess."

Her breath caught in her chest as she looked up at his disappearing back. He knew who she was. He would tell the rest. And then she would be dead.

CHAPTER FIVE

ANDROMEDA WASN'T SURE HOW LONG she sat with her head in her hands. It could have been minutes or hours. All she knew was that, eventually, her mind calmed enough to make some sense of what had happened. The story wasn't difficult to put together. Allen was a pirate. He had been undercover in her garage. He'd tricked her into trusting him and had then sold her out to his crew. He'd likely planned the kidnapping long before he'd even met her. Andromeda realized she was biting her lip hard enough to taste blood. She forced herself to calm down and think. She was trapped in space with a bunch of murderous pirates, and she needed to get out.

With a final breath to steady her nerves, she rose to her feet. The cell was about eight by eight feet. The three walls that were solid metal were a dead end, but the wall of bars was promising. She walked to them and looked for the lock. A keypad sat about a foot away on the wall. She could reach it but didn't have the code to open her door. Unless... Andromeda looked around the cell for what she knew wouldn't be there. They had taken all her tools from her, of course. If she had a thin, flat piece of metal, it could be possible to pop off the panel and hack the wiring. The empty walls and floor mocked her. She paced, racking her brain for an idea. After a moment, she froze.

Her eyes darted down to her left arm. It was possible. She glanced back at the closed door through which Allen had left and listened. Not just with her normal hearing—with the advanced upgrade of her left ear. The buzz of the ship, the engine rattling floors below her, a distant banging. But no voices outside her door. Now may be her only chance. She rushed back to the bars.

With a rattling breath, she brought her wrist to her mouth. Her mind protested the action, but now wasn't the time to get queasy. She sunk her teeth into the synthetic skin. The pain that her mind insisted should be there never came, as she knew it wouldn't. She tugged at the skin until there was a wide enough hole and then used her fingers to tear it wider. The shiny inner mechanisms of her bionic arm gleamed up at her in the sharp light. She twisted her arm in different directions, trying to determine which piece would be the best to take. After a moment, she decided on a metal bracket between two veins. The removal of it wouldn't hinder the use of her arm, and she could always replace it later.

Without giving herself the chance to second guess what she was doing, she pinched it between two fingers and snapped it off. She stopped to listen once more. Still no voices.

It took twisting her arm at a weird angle to get the bracket in between the panel and the wall. She wiggled it in deeper. There was an amount of care needed to ensure she didn't snap it in half. She could take another piece from her arm, but she would rather not. After a moment of maneuvering the thin piece of metal, there was a pop, and the screen swung forward. It hung by several wires still attached to the wall.

Now was the difficult part. She needed to know which wire to cut to open her cell. Cut the wrong one and the entire system might shut down, leaving her trapped in here. Or worse, an alarm would go off that alerted the pirates. At the angle she was at now, she was unable to see into the components.

Andromeda bit her lip and considered her options. Either she could make a wild guess and risk being wrong, or she could sit here and wait for the pirates to come back. She knew her choice. The wires slid along her fingers as she felt along their base. There was no hint which one would be best. At random, she pinched one between her fingers and took a deep breath. It was now or never.

The door to the room flew open and Allen strode in. Andromeda let go of the wire and wrenched her arm back through the bars, a strangled gasp escaping her lips. Allen looked with wide eyes from the panel and back to Andromeda, then slammed the door behind him and rushed forward.

"What the hell are you doing?" He spoke in a hushed voice, as though he didn't want anyone outside to hear. He grabbed the panel and refitted it to the wall.

She narrowed her eyes. "If you think I'm just going to sit here quietly and be your prisoner, you have another thing coming."

He rolled his eyes. "All you were about to do was fry the system. A mechanic like you should know that."

Something that sounded like a hiss shot from between her bared teeth. "Ah, that's right. You found that out about me on your little scouting mission. You must feel immensely proud of yourself."

A crease formed between his brows. "What are you talking about?"

"I'm not stupid!" she spat. "I know that's what you were doing in the garage in Celestine. Did they send you there to get intel on me so that you could kidnap me?"

Allen slid down the wall opposite her, sitting on the floor, and pinched the bridge of his nose. "Andromeda, you have it all wrong. That's not what happened."

"*You*," she snapped, "may address me as Your Highness."

He raised an eyebrow. "I think once you hear me out, you'll see why that's a bad idea. Will you let me explain?"

Andromeda ground her teeth. She didn't want to hear anything this pirate had to say, but at this point, what did she have to lose? She crossed her arms and nodded for him to continue.

He gave her a small smile. "You're partly right. I was in your garage hanger doing intel, but not on you. They sent me there to put trackers on the ships that would carry valuable cargo to Earth in the coming weeks."

"You mean like me?" she asked with a sneer.

"Well," he scrunched up his mouth, a look of guilt crossing his face, "sort of. The ship you were on was scheduled to be taking something valuable, but I had no idea it would be you! I assumed jewels or information. I never would have thought they would send the crown princess to Earth in a cargo ship!"

"Uh-huh, sure. And you expect me to believe that it was just a coincidence that I met you in the garage?"

"It was!" he cried, leaning forward. "Think about it. If I was there to get closer to you, why would I go as a mechanic? I had no idea you would be there that night. I would have gone as a guard if it was you I was after."

This caused Andromeda to pause. It was true that nobody would have known she went to the garage, as it had been a last-minute decision. But that still left a question.

"But you knew who I was. When you saw me in the garage, you knew I was the princess, but you pretended like you didn't."

He shrugged. "Well, yeah."

"So how did you know what I looked like if you had never seen me before?"

His teeth dug into his lower lip as he seemed to consider his answer. "I'm from Earth. A long time ago, I saw a picture of you. You were only a child, but I never forgot your face."

Andromeda shook her head. "There are no pictures of me in the media."

He smiled. "I didn't see it through the media."

She crossed her arms. "I look different now than I did as a child."

"Not too different."

Andromeda stared at him in silence. She was normally good at knowing when someone was lying. Her mother had always said it was uncanny how she could tell if what someone said was the truth or not. At the moment, it appeared Allen was indeed being truthful. His wide green eyes seemed to search the depths of her own.

"I'm serious, Andromeda. I never intended for this to happen. So, while I guess this is technically my fault, know that I had no malicious intentions toward you."

"Then let me go."

He let out a slow breath. "It isn't up to me."

She wanted to slam her head back in frustration, but knew the only thing that would get her was a headache. "Then who's it up to?"

"The captain. Captain Bran."

Andromeda felt a twinge of fear in her chest. She had heard of him. Back on Celestine, soldiers told stories of run-ins with pirates, and Captain Bran was the most infamous. As a child, she had often snuck into the kitchens to listen to the men tell stories of gruesome battles and horrible monsters. The men had said the name Captain Bran with reverence and fear. She would always go back and tell the stories to Emmi and Korra. They used to make a game of it, where Andromeda was a fearsome pirate queen who was in love with the beautiful damsel Emmi. Korra would play a rival captain who would try to steal Emmi away, and it would always end in clashing swords. Or in their case, hangers. But that was a long time ago. She had never imagined she would be on the ship of the actual Captain Bran.

"Let me speak to him."

"He's not here. He'll be back in two days. Besides, you don't want to talk to him."

"Why not?"

He looked at her like she was crazy. "Andromeda, surely you've heard about the hatred between your father and pirates. Now, at the moment, I'm the only one who knows who you really are, but—"

"Wait, what? You haven't told anyone?"

"No, of course I haven't."

She searched his face. "Why not?"

He pressed his fingers to his temples and shook his head. "Are you not listening to me? I didn't mean for this to happen to you. Right now, you're just some nobody we've found trying to sneak onto Earth. But if they knew who you were... well, I don't know what they would do. Most of the people on this ship are generally good, but not all of them. As for the captain, I've always known him to be honorable and fair. But he's still a pirate who hates your father."

"Why does he hate my father?"

"Do you really need to ask that Andromeda? He's a pirate. Pirates and royals don't necessarily mix well. Your father has been making life hell for a lot of people for a long time."

"That isn't true!" she snapped. "My father is a great king. The people love him."

He raised an eyebrow and tilted his head. "And who told you that? Your father?"

She wanted to snarl at him, but in the end she just looked away. Now wasn't the time to argue. This was bad. Incredibly bad. If the captain knew who she was, he would surely kill her. Or worse, he would use her to send a message to her father. She shuddered at the thought of all the vile things a horrendous man like Captain Bran would do to her.

"Give me some time. I'll try to find a way to get you out of here."

She stared at him, her brow furrowing. "Why would you help me?"

He sighed. "I really am just talking to a wall, aren't I? What aren't you understanding about me wanting to help you? You don't deserve this, and, as it's partially my fault, I'm going to help you get out of here."

She narrowed her eyes. "You don't act like a pirate."

"What does a pirate act like?" The corners of his mouth lifted in a slight smile.

She thought back to the tales she had heard her people tell. "Like a drunken, rude, selfish, murderer."

He raised his eyebrows. "Have you met many pirates?"

"I met your friends. They killed my pilots."

"No, they didn't. They shot them with the same thing they shot you with. Your pilots passed out for a few hours and woke up with their ship floating through space. They'll be fine."

Andromeda huffed and leaned back against the wall of her cell. "Good. They'll come looking for me."

"I know, that's the problem. I don't want the trouble we'll be in if we're caught with you."

Ah, so he was saving his own butt. Smart. "What will I do if you can't get me out of here before the captain returns?"

"You just have to hope he doesn't know who you are."

Andromeda chewed on her fingernail, an act her mother would scold her for if she ever caught her doing it. "OK, Allen, so what's your plan?"

"Tomorrow night, it'll be my job to guard the hall outside that door." He pointed to where he had entered the room. "When I do, I'll take you to the pod room. There are several single-seater pods you can take to the nearest station. From there, you should be able to get home."

"What if I'm seen?"

"I'll get a coat with a hood for you."

She paced, her stomach already twisting with nerves. "And if you get caught?"

"They'll be pissed, but they won't do anything. Like I said, to them you're just some girl. You don't have much value."

She closed her eyes. So much could go wrong, but it was the only chance she had. "OK. How can I trust this isn't a trick? How do I know you aren't just going to lead me out to a crowd of your friends?"

"Do you have another option?"

No, she didn't. "Fine. I don't trust you, but I'll go along with it."

"Smart girl," he said with a grin.

"Don't patronize me."

"Yes, Your Majesty."

Though he sounded serious, he still wore that lopsided smile that made her believe he was making fun. "I don't think I like you."

"What a shame, because I like you."

What a smug, self-assured bastard. "You don't know me."

"True. And it's a shame I'll not get the chance."

Andromeda rolled her eyes. "Yes, what a horrible shame."

"Maybe in another life."

Andromeda glanced at him. There was something in his expression, something that looked almost wistful. "Don't give me those googly eyes."

He raised his eyebrows. "Googly eyes?"

"You were giving me some kind of eyes, and I don't like it."

He laughed again, the sound deep and rumbling. "This is why I like you."

"Because I'm mean to you?"

"No, because you're honest. Honesty is important to me."

"Isn't honesty important to everyone? Does anyone *like* being lied to?"

"You'd be surprised."

She crossed her arms. There was something about him she couldn't put her finger on. It was the same something that had made her continuously think about him ever since she had first met him in her garage. He didn't tiptoe around her. He didn't hold her on a silk cloth, as though afraid she would shatter if applied with too much pressure. She hated that she liked that about him.

After a moment, he stood. "I'll be back tomorrow morning with your breakfast and an update on the plan."

She nodded and watched him go. He paused near the door and turned back to her. He pulled out a piece of cloth that was tucked into his pocket and unfastened his belt. She stepped back in alarm, but he only held them out for her.

"For your arm. You ripped it open pretty bad."

She glanced down at the ruined skin. "Oh, yeah. I mean, it's not real. It doesn't hurt."

He allowed his eyes to linger on the exposed metal of her forearm. "Still. I don't want you to be uncomfortable."

She reluctantly took the offered items and pulled them into her cell. He gave her one last smile, then walked out the door, leaving her in silence again.

She waited a moment and then sat down to fix what damage she could. Pinching the skin together, she wrapped the cloth around the open area and wound the belt around that. Once it was tight enough to hold everything together, she buckled it. It would do for now.

She laid back on the metal floor and dug her fingers into her hair. What the hell was she going to do? She was trapped here, and her only means of escape was a pirate who claimed he wanted to help her. She didn't trust him. She couldn't. But her options were limited. The only thing she could do was hope that he didn't betray her and plan to fight her way out if he did. Because she would. She would rather die in a fight than in a cage.

God, what must her parents be feeling? Surely they had found out by now. At the very least, they would know that her ship hadn't reached its destination. Her father would begin a search immediately, likely deploying the military. They had to find her eventually, right?

She tried to ignore the little voice that wiggled its way into her mind, the little voice that said her father had been trying to capture pirates for years now and was constantly evaded. It was a relentless thorn in her father's side that he couldn't catch any pirates of significance. So how would he find her now? He wouldn't even know which pirates had taken her.

She rolled over and pressed her cheek onto the cold metal, feeling horribly ill-equipped and out of her depth. Her entire life she had trained to deal with stressful situations, but in all the scenarios she had prepared for, it was assumed she would be safe and surrounded by advisors. Her father had never taught her what to do if she was alone in enemy territory. She didn't realize that she was crying until she felt the wet pool against her cheek. Sitting up abruptly, she raked the back of her hand over her face. Weakness was not something she would allow them to see. Her tears were not for them.

The fatigue hit her hard as she sat against the wall of her cell. The emotional toll of being forcefully taken from the only home she had ever known sat like a black hole in her mind, sucking the energy and life from her. She knew she had to get some rest if she was going to be prepared when Allen returned, but the thought of letting her guard down made her stomach turn. But soon, without her permission, her body slipped into a fitful sleep.

Her dreams were broken and more closely resembled nightmares. At one point, she ran through a complicated set of halls, all identical and pearly white. She wasn't sure why she was running; all she knew was the feeling of dread and the idea that if she stopped, she would die. Then the nightmare shifted, and she was in a throne room, but it wasn't her own. She spun to see a cruel king sitting upon the throne. His face hid in shadows, but the energy that rolled off him was pure evil. Her feet pulled her backward and away from him, but his voice rang out.

"Come here!"

The sound sent a tremor of terror through her. The voice was sharp as a razor and hard as steel, but somehow it sounded familiar. She tried to run, but then she was falling.

She woke with a start as the cell door was thrown open. The terror from her dream still permeated throughout her body, and she found herself gasping for air.

Allen paused beside her cell. "Hey, are you all right?"

She sat up and pushed her curls out of her face. "I'm... yeah. Yeah, I'm fine. It was just a nightmare." Glancing around at her surroundings, she let out a bark of laughter. "I mean, I guess this is a nightmare as well."

He sat down beside the bars and slid a tray beneath them. An apple and a sandwich. "Well, I can't do anything about your nightmares, but I'm doing what I can to help with the situation at hand."

She scrunched up her nose at the tray. "I'm not hungry."

Her treacherous stomach betrayed her by growling angrily at that statement.

He dropped his head to the side. "Yes, clearly. I'm sure you'll perish if you take a single bite."

She narrowed her eyes and glared for a moment, then dropped the expression with a sigh. "Fine. You win this time, but it's only because I don't want to pass out."

He watched as she pulled the tray toward her and tore a bite off the sandwich. His lips twitched up at the corners. "Very ladylike. Did your governess teach you those manners?"

"Shut up," she said around a full mouth.

He snorted. "As you say, Princess."

She wiped her mouth on the back of her hand. "Whom do I need to perform my manners for? You? I doubt you care about that sort of thing."

A shrug of his shoulders. "True, I don't care. You know, you said I don't act like how you thought a pirate would act. But you're not exactly the picturesque princess I would have imagined you to be."

"Sorry to disappoint."

He held up his hands. "I didn't say it was disappointing. Quite the opposite. I thought you'd be a spoiled brat."

She snorted, taking another bite. "Oh, I am. Just get to know me a bit."

His grin widened. "You're a real smartass, anyone ever tell you that?"

She tried to fight a smile, but when she couldn't, let out a small laugh. "You just did."

They lapsed into silence as she finished her sandwich and moved on to the apple. She knew that he was watching her but did her best not to acknowledge it. "So, is everything still going as planned?"

Allen folded his arms and leaned against the wall. "I hope."

She paused in her chewing. "Gee, your level of confidence is astounding."

"As is your level of faith."

"It's hard to have faith in someone you don't trust."

"I suppose it is."

Andromeda stared down at the now empty tray. "What do you think the captain will do if he catches me?"

Allen pursed his lips. "I don't know. He's always been a fair man to me, as far as pirates go. But then again, I'm not the daughter of his enemy."

"I've heard of Captain Bran. He doesn't sound like a fair man to me."

"You shouldn't believe every story you hear. The Lord Captain isn't so bad."

"Lord Captain? He's not a lord." She scowled at the idea of a pirate referring to himself as royalty.

"Yes, he is. Maybe not to you and your family, but your kingdom isn't the only one out here."

"What's that supposed to mean?"

Allen just smiled, a hint of mischief in his eyes. "That's need-to-know only. I'd get in a lot of trouble if they knew I was giving away valuable information to a royal."

Andromeda rolled her eyes. "Well, don't bring up subjects you can't talk about."

He shrugged. "Fair."

The door opened, causing Allen to straighten and jump to his feet. Two men entered, still laughing at something one had said. One looked as though he seriously needed a shave, while the other wore brightly polished boots.

"Allen, what are you doing in here?" Polished Boots asked.

"Come to look at the pretty girl?" Unshaven Guy chuckled.

Allen glanced at Andromeda. "I was just talking to the prisoner."

"Yeah, well, don't get too friendly. She's a gift for the captain."

Andromeda stood and flung her curls from her face. "Slavery is illegal in all kingdoms, and what you are doing directly violates the law. If caught, you could all face the penalty of death."

The men laughed, and Polished Boots said, "And who exactly is going to tell on us? You? You ain't anyone."

"I'm— " Andromeda paused, catching herself as she realized she was about to disclose her identity. "Not anyone."

"Yeah, that's what I said," sneered Polished Boots.

"Allen, leave the poor little thing alone. Isn't your guard shift about the start?" asked Unshaven Guy.

"Yeah. I'll be right out. Just give me a sec."

The men both cast one last look at Andromeda and then left. Allen slumped back against the wall.

Andromeda rolled her eyes at him. "Yeah, you seemed real casual, Popeye. Looked like you were about to jump out of your skin."

He frowned. "Popeye?"

"Yeah, you know. That ancient cartoon. He was a sailor."

Allen stared at her, a bemused smile creeping onto his face. She sighed and rolled her eyes. "Never mind."

"Right, well, just be ready. I'll be back for you."

She nodded and watched as he disappeared out the door. Sitting cross-legged on the floor, she waited. She couldn't risk falling back asleep. Her mind needed to be clear when the time came, not fogged up with sleep. Entertainment came in the form of running back through every piece of information she had learned so far.

This was the ship of Captain Bran. He was off-site at the moment. He fancied himself a lord. Allen was helping her out of a sense of guilt and self-preservation. She could use that.

For what felt like forever, Andromeda waited, staring at the door and willing it to open. Her nerves were on edge, and any sound outside the door caused her to jump with anticipation.

What if Allen didn't come back? What if he had been playing with her emotions? This could all be an elaborate game between him and the crew. Oh, wouldn't that be just great. A side of humiliation with her kidnapping. Just as she was beginning to think he truly had lied, the door opened, and Allen rushed in.

He held a keycard in his hand and pressed it to the scanner. Andromeda leapt up and rushed to the cell door. As he opened it, he threw a bulky green jacket at her.

"Put that on and pull the hood up," he ordered.

"Won't I be just as conspicuous with this on?"

"Not nearly. And here, take this." He pressed something cold and hard into her hand. She looked down in shock at the small knife. When she looked back up at him, he shrugged. "Just in case." He took her hand and pulled her to the door.

They stopped and peered out.

A gleaming white corridor stretched out in front of them. Not what she would expect of a pirate ship. Allen seemed to decide it was clear and, holding Andromeda's hand, tugged her out after him.

They walked at a brisk pace, not wanting to run in case anyone saw them and thought it suspicious.

"Where is everyone?" she asked as they traveled down one empty hall after another.

"Most of the crew are asleep, and those who aren't are working on the flight deck," he explained.

Andromeda's heart pounded. They could be caught at any moment. She could be killed, or worse. "How far is the pod room?"

"Just ahead. Be quiet."

Andromeda didn't argue. Allen pulled her around another corner, and she saw it. Several sliding doors with panels sat up ahead, each leading to what she assumed were pods.

"Can you fly one?" Allen asked.

"Psh, can I fly one? Of course. And why did you wait until now to ask? What were you planning on doing if I couldn't?"

Allen didn't answer.

Andromeda's heart leapt. She was almost there. Almost free. But a sudden loud hissing sound, and a massive door opening ahead to their right, caused Allen to stop.

"Oh no," he whispered.

"Allen? What are you doing? Let's go!" Andromeda insisted, pulling at him.

A voice spoke from behind them. "Allen, what are you doing?"

Andromeda turned and saw four men approaching.

"Let's go!" she said, trying to pull her hand from his grip.

"It's too late," he said, his eyes full of panic.

"No, it's not, don't say that!" she cried, ripping her hand from his and running for the pod doors. Before she got more than a few feet, however, several men entered through the large sliding door.

At the head of them, Andromeda knew, had to be Captain Bran. He wore a dark purple coat over a crisp white shirt with gold buttons, and black pants that met black and gold boots. For some reason, Andromeda had envisioned him with black hair. Instead, gold curls hung almost to his neck and a blond beard covered the lower part of his face. Green eyes stared back at her.

Andromeda glanced frantically at the pod doors and knew she would never make it. She gripped the knife in her hand. She would kill this man before she let him touch her. Before she neared him, however, hands gripped her arms and shoulders, and one man from behind wrenched the knife from her hand.

She thrashed, trying to get free. She glanced at Allen, pleading with her eyes for help. Instead, his eyes focused on the captain. It figured. He was a coward.

Andromeda stopped struggling, realizing her last hope was gone. She looked at the captain, whose eyes were wide with surprise. She knew that look on his face.

He recognized her.

"Lord Captain, you're back early. We didn't expect you until tomorrow," one man from behind said.

Captain Bran didn't respond and continued to stare at her.

"We found this girl on a cargo ship to Earth. We thought you might like her," said another man.

Rather than look at his men, the captain spoke directly to her. "What's your name?" His voice was deep and demanded respect.

She clenched her teeth and shot venom with her eyes. "Andy."

"Andy. Are you all right?"

That was a strange question. Instead of answering, she glared.

"He asked you a question," the man holding her snarled, giving her shoulder a shove.

"Don't!" the captain's voice boomed. His eyes never left hers. "Jaquen, Allor, take Andy to my room and make sure she stays there."

Two of the men to her right took ahold of her and pulled her down the hall. Andromeda looked at Allen once more, hoping for his help. He met her gaze, and she noted sadness in his eyes. He wasn't going to help her. She was on her own.

CHAPTER SIX

THEY PASSED SEVERAL DOORS AS they dragged Andromeda down the halls. She tried several times to shake the men holding her, but it was no use. Even if she got free, there was nowhere to go. Any chance of escape now would be impossible.

They finally stopped in front of a door that had a keypad just to the right of it. After pushing a few buttons Andromeda couldn't see, the door slid open, and they shoved her in. Before she could even turn around, the door closed behind her. Andromeda swallowed hard and tried to calm her pounding heart. Being trapped had always been a fear of hers, and she had never been as trapped as she was now. She looked around the room. It was lavishly decorated and looked like it belonged in a mansion on Celestine rather than a pirate ship. A large bed that was draped in purple and gold bedding sat in the middle of the room, with a wooden desk against one wall and a hammock against the other. Gold and marble statues were postured around the room, giving the feel of an ancient home. Captain Bran's wealth was on full display.

Andromeda's mind kicked into gear. She had to protect herself. If he truly knew who she was, he would likely expect her to be a gentlewoman. But if he thought she would just sit idly as he did what he liked... She looked around for a weapon and spotted a heavy-looking candle holder beside the bed and grabbed it. There was an ornate clock on the wall, and though she wasn't sure what time zone it was set to, it read 11:23. Every nerve in her body was on high alert. She bounced the candle stick against her leg, knowing if she couldn't fight him off, if he overpowered her... She wouldn't think about that. At 11:31, she heard footsteps approaching and muffled voices on the other side of the door.

"I wish to be left alone for the rest of the night. Keep two guards at the end of the hall."

"Yes, Lord Captain."

The door opened, and the captain walked in. Andromeda held the candle holder in front of her like a sword. He glanced at her as he walked in, looking from her to her makeshift weapon, then closed the door behind him and pulled off his coat. She narrowed her eyes, turning her whole body to follow him around the room. He walked to the chair in front of his desk and sat down, not looking at her as he pulled off his boots and socks. Andromeda's breath was sharp and ragged, her nerves frayed. He leaned back in his chair and took a deep breath.

"You can put that down."

She glared. "I don't think so."

He looked up at her. "I'm not going to hurt you."

"Yeah," she said with a laugh, "I really believe you."

He smiled, making his eyes crinkle. "Don't be afraid."

"Can you blame me? Your crew took me prisoner, locked me in a cell, and kept me as a gift for you. If you participate in slavery, what else do you take part in?"

He frowned, a troubled crease forming between his brows. "We do not participate in slavery. Some of my crew were misguided in doing what they did."

"Then let me go," she demanded.

"I can't do that."

"Why not?"

He looked into her eyes and she knew why. He knew who she was. She had value to him. She wanted to ask, to know for sure, but she couldn't risk it. The captain leaned back in his chair and selected a piece of fruit from the bowl on his desk. He took a bite and looked at her.

"Are you hungry? Have they fed you?"

"I'm not hungry."

"I'll have some food brought up."

This was a power play. "I won't eat it."

"Please, Andy, don't be difficult."

"I'll be how I want."

He smiled. "Why don't you lie down and get some sleep. The bed is very comfortable."

"Do you think I'm stupid? I can only imagine what you'll do to me the moment I fall asleep."

He reached into his drawer and pulled out a gun. Andromeda's eyes widened, and she took a step back. Was he going to hold her at gunpoint? But he only tossed it onto the bed in front of her.

"Take it. It's fully loaded."

She snatched it off the bed. With a quick flip of the barrel, she saw he was telling the truth. She threw the candle holder onto the bed and pointed the gun at him.

"Why shouldn't I kill you right now?"

"Well, there are two reasons. The first one is that killing me would only get you in a worse situation. Sure, you could shoot a few of my crew, but you would never make it off the ship. They would catch you and kill you."

"And the second reason?"

"You aren't a killer."

"You know nothing about me," she sneered.

A strange look crossed his face. "That's true." He got up and walked over to the hammock. "I'm going to get some sleep. Feel free to do the same."

He flicked the light switch off, climbed into the hammock, and closed his eyes. It was so sudden Andromeda could do nothing but stare and point the gun. After a moment of standing in darkness, she lowered it. What was she supposed to do? She sat on the bed, not taking her eyes off the captain. As time passed, she felt sleep pulling at her. The dark, cool room lulled her into calmness, tempting her to lean back against the pillows as they sank beneath her, welcoming her like a cocoon. She continued to hold the gun, laying it against the pillow. She closed her eyes for a second, trying to rest them.

When she opened them, artificial light streamed in through the window. She sat up abruptly and looked at the clock: 10:34. She had fallen asleep. As she tried to stand, she realized there were blankets covering her, and the gun was still in her hand, though the safety had been turned on. What had happened after she fell asleep? She felt confident that she would have woken up if he touched her, but then she hadn't felt this blanket being laid on her. Maybe he had drugged her? No, that made little sense. She would have remembered that. Was it possible he had left her alone?

She stood and stretched, bending her metal joints, then noticed a dress and a note hanging near the door.

I thought you would like some clean clothes. Feel free to come out and join us for a meal when you are ready.

She glanced back at the dress. It had a floral pattern and hung to the knee. She threw the note to the floor in disgust. Like she would ever wear his clothes and join him for food. Her stomach growled angrily at her in protest. She sighed and bit her lip. She couldn't go forever without eating, not if she wanted to get out of here. But she would *not* wear his clothes. She would rather writhe in her own filth. But maybe a shower.

She pushed a side door open and sure enough a bathroom was on the other side. It was simple, comprising a shower, a toilet, and a sink. After a quick search for hidden cameras turned up nothing, she undressed and climbed into the shower. She had to admit, the hot water felt good on her sore back muscles. Once she finished showering and drying off, she put her old clothes back on. They were stiff with overwear, but they were still comfortable enough. Then she rewrapped her arm in the cloth. She didn't need everyone on the ship knowing about her enhancements.

Before she walked out the door, she ran to the bed and grabbed the gun. She tucked it into the waistband of her pants and pulled her shirt over it. If anyone tried to mess with her, they would get a bullet in the head. She walked to the door, but before she could open it, she heard voices.

"Did you get a good look at her?" a deep voice asked.

A higher voice answered. "Only when Allen carried her in."

Was that a woman? Andromeda was surprised, though now that she thought of it, she shouldn't have been. Why wouldn't there be female pirates? Andy leaned forward and pressed her ear to the door.

"What did she look like?" the deeper voice asked eagerly.

"Asleep."

"Ha ha, hilarious. I mean, is she pretty?"

"Beauty is a spectrum that varies by opinion."

"Oh my god, Mars!" the deep voice cried. "You're so annoying! Is she conventionally attractive?"

The woman, Mars, laughed. "You're so touchy, Arlo. Yeah, I guess she's conventionally attractive."

"Man, I wanted to get a look at her, but Joc and Peter wouldn't let me in."

"Yeah, because she isn't an animal in a zoo."

"I wouldn't treat her like an animal! I'd take her to a nice dinner. No! I'd make her dinner. Then we could go for a delightful walk on the beach and—"

The woman cut him off. "Aren't you dating Don?"

"Psh, we went on like one date! And he wouldn't stop talking about taxidermy," Arlo said. "I don't want to date someone who's obsessed with taxidermy. But this girl—"

"You've never even seen her!" Mars interrupted again.

"That's not the point."

Andy leaned harder against the door, and to her shock, it slid open. Arlo and Mars spun around, their eyes wide. Andy mirrored their reaction and quickly straightened up.

"Oh, hello." The woman, Mars, said with a smile. "The Lord Captain asked us to wait here for you to wake up."

Andy didn't respond. Her throat seemed to have gone dry. She hadn't yet had a pleasant experience with any of the pirates. Both were young, no more than a couple years older than herself, she thought. Arlo was tall, at least six feet, though quite thin. Short black curls sat atop their head, with dark eyes only a few shades lighter than their skin. Mars was similar. Tall, with long black braids, and warm, bright eyes. They were both stunning. Arlo held out their hand for her to shake.

"My name's Arlo, resident thief."

"Aren't all pirates thieves?" Andy asked, against her better judgment.

Arlo smiled like this was the best thing they'd ever heard. "Technically, sure. Some of us are just better."

"And I'm Mars, their older sister."

"Psh." Arlo rolled their eyes. "Stop telling people that! You're older by three minutes. That doesn't count."

Mars shrugged as Andy looked back and forth between the two. "Right, well, I was just going to head down to the kitchen. "

"Oh, of course!" Mars smiled. "We'll walk you down."

Andy considered telling her that wasn't necessary, but she realized she had no clue where the kitchen was. So, instead, she nodded and let them lead the way. Arlo blabbered on, though Andy didn't pay attention. The halls were all sleek metal with white floors, and doors every so often. She looked everywhere she could, trying to find an escape. She had wasted too much time here already; she had to find a way out. Her family would have already begun to search for her, but their chances of finding her were incredibly slim. Pirates knew how to hide from the authorities. She would have to save herself, though she couldn't imagine how.

"What's this?" Mars asked as she reached out and lifted Andy's arm.

Andy flinched back against the touch. "Oh, that's—that's nothing."

Mars narrowed her eyes. "It looks like you tried to wrap up a wound. You don't need to put on a brave front, I'm a doctor."

Andy looked over at the other woman with some skepticism. "Aren't you a little young to be a doctor?"

"Eh, I started my training when I was thirteen, so not really." She pulled up the cloth at the edges. "I don't see any sign of blood. You should let me check it, so you don't get an infection."

Andy tried to yank her arm away, but Mars's grip was firm. "It won't get an infection."

Mars raised one of her delicate eyebrows. "Are you a medical professional?"

"Well, no, but—"

"Then let me see."

Andy swallowed as Mars pressed her thumbs along the inside of her forearm. She saw Mars's eyes widen a fraction and then dart up to meet hers. Andy knew what a doctor would feel beneath the synthetic skin. Rather than the soft give of muscle and tendons, she would feel the hard press of metal.

They held eyes for a long moment, and in that time, Andy saw several expressions flick across her face. The surprise faded into a look of curiosity and then seemed to settle into a look of amusement.

"Well, aren't you full of surprises."

Andy licked her lips and looked down to where Mars was still holding her arm. Mars glanced down as well, and a flicker of mischief danced in her eyes. She ran her hands down until she was only holding her hand and ran her fingers over Andy's palm.

"Truly exquisite work."

Andy felt heat rise to her cheeks. "Thanks."

Arlo snickered. "God, Mars, tone it down. You'll give the girl an aneurysm."

Mars smiled but dropped her hand. Andy clenched and unclenched her fist, but reluctantly returned the smile. "I don't know about that. I'm fairly resilient."

Mars threw her head back and laughed. "What's your name?"

"Andy."

"Well, Andy, it's lovely to meet you."

The cell port on Mars's hip went off with a ding. She lifted the screen to her eyes.

"Crap. I'm needed in the infirmary. Doc says he needs you too, Arlo, to help restrain a patient." She turned to Andy. "We have to go, but the kitchen is right at the end of this hall. Just go straight down and you can't miss it."

Andy looked to where she was pointing and nodded. When she looked back, Mars was still eyeing her shrewdly.

"Really, it's been great to meet you. I look forward to seeing you again." Mars took Andy's hand once more and pressed a kiss to her knuckles. With a final wink, she turned and rushed down the hall, Arlo following behind her, trying to hide a grin.

Andy watched them go. So far, these pirates weren't turning out to be anything like what she had thought they would be. Andy turned and continued cautiously to where Mars had indicated. As she approached the door, voices could be heard laughing and talking within. She peered around the corner. It was a kitchen, sure enough, and it was filled with men. They laughed and ate loudly, joking and pushing each other around. As she watched, the captain entered through another door. There was a general cheer and commotion as the crew welcomed him.

"Captain! How are you feeling this morning?" one man shouted.

"Probably pretty good after spending the night with that lass," another chuckled.

Andromeda noticed Allen standing near the back wall. He wasn't engaging in the conversation and was instead staring dejectedly into his cup.

"Come on, Captain, give us some details!" a black-haired man said.

Captain Bran didn't answer as he poured himself something to drink and got a plate of food. He sat down and took a drink. "She is a lovely young woman."

"Yeah, we gathered that. Did you enjoy yourself with her?" the black-haired man asked.

The captain looked at him. "She is special. That is why no one is to touch her besides me."

"Aww, come on, you can't expect us to keep our hands to ourselves."

"If you wish to keep your hands, you will. And you can all refer to her as Lady Andy."

"*Lady?*" the black-haired man frowned. "Captain, you can't seriously be telling us you're taking her as your lady?"

"I am," he confirmed.

There was a murmur around the room. Andromeda didn't understand what that meant. Allen was frowning.

"Lord Captain," said Mack, "are you telling us you have decided t-to take a wife?"

What? Andromedas eyes widened, and an icy chill ran down her back. Marry him? She reached down and felt the gun in her belt. She would not marry him.

"No," he said, shaking his head, "I'm not going to marry her. But she is mine and is under my protection. Is that understood?"

There was a general murmur of agreement. Andromeda narrowed her eyes at the captain. What sort of game was he playing? She leaned forward to get a better look at the room.

"Lady Andy?"

One man had seen her. The entire room turned to look, including the captain. She froze as all eyes fell on her. Captain Bran stood.

"Lady Andy. Come, have a seat." He motioned to a chair beside him.

Andromeda straightened and smoothed out her shirt. She would not let them see her fear. When she made eye contact with Allen, she didn't understand the way he was looking at her. There was desperation in his eyes. She looked away. He had failed her, and she was furious with him. As she sat down, she noticed that the room had gone quiet. The captain slid a plate of food in front of her.

"You must be starving. Are you thirsty as well?"

She cleared her throat and held her head high. "Yes, I am."

"You heard her, get her something to drink!"

One man scrambled to pour her a drink from a pitcher. He sat it down in front of her and retreated. She hadn't realized how thirsty she was until she began to drink. She downed the whole glass in one go.

"Get her another," the captain demanded.

Again, a man filled her cup. The rest of the men stood and watched her as she ate.

"Which one of you men were responsible for locking Lady Andy in the cells?" the captain asked, looking around.

The men shuffled around, looking at each other uncomfortably.

"It was me," Mack said, stepping forward.

"And why did you do that? You know our policy on slavery and captives."

Mack looked grudgingly at Andy. "We… I thought it was a good idea at the time."

Captain Bran leaned back in his chair and pointed to her. "Apologize to the lady."

Mack pressed his lips together, and for a moment Andromeda thought he would refuse. "I'm sorry, Lady Andy. Can you forgive me?"

She knew what she should to do as a Celestine princess. But she wasn't on Celestine anymore.

"No."

There was a tense silence around the room. Mack shifted, his expression growing sour.

"What would you like his punishment to be?" the captain asked.

It took her a moment to realize he was still speaking to her. "Excuse me?"

"His punishment. For locking you up."

Andromeda looked between the captain and Mack. She hadn't expected this. To be honest, she didn't want to give him any punishment. She had no clue how long she would be stuck on this ship, and she didn't need enemies.

"I desire no punishment for him."

Silence range heavy. Captain Bran looked at her for a long time before looking back at Mack.

"The lady is too kind. But I am not. You are to receive five lashes, and you are on cleaning duty until further notice."

Mack tightened his jaw but nodded. "Yes, Captain."

Andromeda tried to go back to eating without appearing nervous but found it almost impossible when there were dozens of eyes on her. The one time she looked up, she met Allen's eye and immediately turned away.

The captain leaned forward on his elbows, watching her intently. "Right, I'm sure you would like to look around and get used to where you'll be staying from now on."

Andromeda wanted to say no, she didn't want to look around, because she wouldn't be staying long. But then again, she had no idea how to get out of here and getting a look around would help.

"Um, yes. How kind of you."

"Allen, would you mind giving Lady Andy a tour?"

Allen straightened up, looking surprised at being addressed. "Of course, Lord Captain."

"Very good. I have tasks I must see to now, so I will leave you in Allen's hands."

He walked to Allen and leaned in, whispering something she couldn't hear. She stood and followed Allen out the door, watching as the captain left through another. Allen was silent as they walked, and he looked like something was on his mind. They passed several doors before Andy spoke.

"Allen?"

He looked back at her like he had just realized she was there. "Yeah?"

"Usually with tours, the person giving it actually talks."

"Oh, right. I'm sorry," he apologized, turning away. "That door there leads to one of the public restrooms. The doors we passed lead to the crew's quarters. Up ahead and to the right is... " He slowed down until they were fully stopped.

"Allen?"

He spun toward her suddenly, and she took a quick step back.

"What the hell is wrong with you?" she asked.

"Andromeda, just let me talk, OK? I'm sorry. I really tried to get you out of here, and that I couldn't has been destroying me all night. I know the captain is a good man, but he is a pirate all the same. Did he hurt you?"

Andromeda stared at him. For a moment she considered lying. It might make him more willing to help if he thought she was being hurt. But as far as she could tell, he had been nothing but honest with her since she had arrived on this ship.

"No, he didn't touch me. He slept in his hammock and gave me the bed."

Allen's shoulders visibly relaxed, and he let out a breath. "Thank God. I didn't think he would, but... you never know."

She nodded. "But that still changes nothing! I'm still being held captive here."

"Don't be ridiculous, of course this changes things! He clearly doesn't know who you are."

Andy frowned and looked away. She wasn't so sure. When he had first seen her, recognition had been all over his face. But perhaps she had been mistaken and it had just been surprise. If he did in fact know who she was, why was he being so casual about it? Regardless of what he said about slavery and captives, he was still a pirate and would understand the monumental payday ransoming her could bring.

"Maybe. But I still need to be careful. Unless... " She glanced at him. "Unless you plan on telling him."

He threw his hands into the air and slumped against the wall.

"Seriously? After everything I've done, you think I'm going to run and tell him?"

She crossed her arms and raised her eyebrows.

He sighed and shook his head. "I won't. I promise."

She sucked her teeth, then shrugged. "All right, I believe you. But what about helping me to escape?"

Allen pushed off the wall and walked away, so she rushed to keep up. "Andy, I can't betray him. I would lose everything I've built here."

"But you were willing to betray him before!"

"Yes, but he would have never found out."

She scoffed. "Oh, so it's only OK for you to betray someone when they won't know you've done it?"

"Yes! I mean, no! Look. " He stopped and turned to her. "You're safe here for now. He thinks you're just some stray we've picked up. Eventually he'll grow bored and let you go on your way."

She opened her mouth to argue, but he cut her off.

"And when that happens, I promise I will help you get back to where you need to be. But until then just calm down and enjoy your vacation from royal life."

"*Vacation?*" she practically screeched. "Are you serious? I am being held here against my will by a bunch of pirates! I need to get home to my family! I can't just sit around waiting for the captain to get bored. Besides, what if you're wrong? What if he has more sinister plans for me? Am I just supposed to sit around and wait?"

Allen tossed his hands in the air. "What else are you going to do? There is no way of getting out of here unless the captain wants it. And at the moment, he does not want it. I will protect you while you're here. You can do whatever you like on the ship."

Her lip curled into a sneer. "Oh, how truly kind of you. Will you be walking me around on a leash as well?"

His eyes rolled all the way around in his head. Honestly, he was way too good at that. He could give Rosetta a run for her money. "You are so damn dramatic, do you know that? You're not some caged animal."

"Then stop treating me like one!" she snapped.

"What do you want me to do, Andy? Huh? I'm doing the best that I can with the situation we've been dealt."

"Yeah, you could have fooled me. And if I'm such a problem, then why even help me?"

"Is it so hard to believe that I'm a genuinely nice person who doesn't want anything to happen to you?"

She crossed her arms. "Yeah, kind of."

"What could I have possibly done to show anything of the contrary?"

"You let him take me!" she cried.

He frowned. "I already told you, I didn't know you were on the ship."

"No, not then. Last night. You had no idea what he was going to do to me, and you let them take me away. You wouldn't even look me in the eye."

He flinched at the vitriol she spat. "Andy, I'm sorry about that. But what could I have done? Pulled a weapon on eight of my crewmates and my captain?"

"Yes!"

"Don't be stupid. All that would have done was get me killed and put you into more danger. I'm doing everything in my power now to help you. So, can you just relax and trust me?"

For several seconds Andy said nothing, her anger a bright spark in her chest. But after a few moments, the fury faded into something that just felt tired. "Do I have another choice?"

He shook his head. "No, I don't think so."

She looked into his eyes. "Fine. But I swear, if he lays one finger on me, I will bite it off."

A small smile pulled at his lips. "Oh, I don't doubt that for a second. I honestly wouldn't be surprised if I found out you were actually raised by wolves in a jungle rather than as a princess in a palace."

She couldn't help but smile at that sentiment. "Wolves are native to forest habitats, not jungles."

He threw his head back and laughed, his eyes full of mirth. "Why doesn't it surprise me that you know that?"

She straightened her shoulders and smoothed out her shirt. "A monarch must know a great variety of information."

"Uh-huh, sure," he said with a smirk. "Come on, Olive Oyl, let's finish that tour."

Andy scrunched up her face. "Olive Oyl?" She gasped, running up beside him as he moved away from her. "You looked up Popeye!"

His expression remained aloof. "I have no idea what you're talking about."

Without her permission, her face transformed into a wide grin. "You did. Admit it."

His eyes remained on her beaming face for several seconds before he looked away. "Yeah, maybe I did."

She fell into pace beside him, still smiling. "Wait! If you're Popeye, then don't go around calling me Olive Oyl. Don't flatter yourself."

He groaned. "Great, now you're going to read too much into it."

"Hey, you said it."

As they walked, she noticed a large sliding door. "What's that?"

"Oh, that's the elevator that will take you down to the engine rooms. I work down there sometimes."

Andy had only ever dreamed of working on engines of this magnitude. Back home, the best she could get were pod engines.

"Well, you said I could do whatever I wanted while I was here . . . "

He raised an eyebrow. "You can do whatever you want, and the first thing you can think of is manual labor?"

"It's fun!" she insisted. "I love working with tools and figuring things out. I don't really get the chance to at home."

He just shook his head and smiled. "Well, I'll have to ask the captain, but I don't see why not."

She tried to tamp it down, but for the first time in a long time she felt a trill of excitement. This might be her only opportunity in her life to get her hands on engines of that size.

Later that evening, after touring the entire ship, Allen escorted her back to her room. Or rather, the captain's room. She glared at the door.

"He isn't in there."

She looked back at Allen. "How do you know?"

He shrugged. "He's always in the main control room at this time of day."

"So where exactly are we going?"

"What do you mean?"

"Well... " She swept her arm out to indicate the ship. "We're clearly moving. So where are we going?"

Allen stuffed his hand into his pocket. "We don't always have a set destination unless we have a target, or if the captain needs to meet with someone. He will probably announce where we're going in the coming days."

She nodded. She would feel better if she knew what was coming next. Despite what Allen said, she would be looking for the first opportunity to escape.

"Right, well, good night then. I suppose I will see you tomorrow?"

Allen leaned against the wall. "If you want to work in the engine rooms, then yes. The captain doesn't want you left alone while not in your quarters."

She let out a deep breath and reclined her head back. "Yes, not a caged animal at all."

"It's for your safety."

"I'm not as breakable as you think."

"Trust me," Allen said with a snort, "I believe you. But there's no need to put you into senseless danger. Besides, wouldn't you rather be left alone? As long as I'm there, that'll be the case."

She couldn't argue with that. She would put up with Allen if she had to.

"Very well. Good night, Allen."

She didn't look back as she pushed open the door and walked in. Sure enough, it was empty. Once she was alone in the room, she paced back and forth. Despite what Allen had said, she needed to find an escape. Her family was probably worried sick about her, and Eden would likely lead a charge from Someron to come after her. At least, she hoped so. While she didn't find him particularly interesting, he was a good man.

From what she had gathered during her tour, the pod ships were her only bet. But getting near them while alone seemed an impossibility. Since the captain had gotten back, there had been a guard stationed outside the pods at all times. She supposed he expected her to try to escape. A headache was building behind her temples, and she knew if she let it escalate, it could become debilitating. She pressed her knuckles into her temple and massaged in short, tight circles. She would kill for some pain medication but doubted she could get any here. After a moment, the pain dissipated. Once it was under control, she decided to go to bed. Rest was the best thing for her right now.

She pulled open the drawers of the ornate dresser beside the bed and rummaged through it. There were several large button-up shirts, but nothing more. Next, she looked in the bottom drawer for something to cover her legs, but as it was a man's dresser, she found nothing. She wouldn't wear the captain's clothes, in case it gave him any ideas. Looking around the room, she noticed a black and red trunk pushed against one wall that she hadn't seen before. It was partially hidden by a hanging tapestry.

She walked to it and pushed the tapestry off. It was latched shut but not locked. Andy undid the fastenings and lifted the lid. The first thing that lay on top was a white lace dress. Andy lifted it and examined it in the light. It smelled of dust, like it had been stored in there for quite a long time. For some reason she couldn't quite place, the old, dusty dress left a feeling of sadness in her heart. Like a happy memory that had been locked away after a lifetime of disappointment and pain. A thought of hope that had been discarded, no use to a man that had become jaded by the cruelty of the harsh reality he lived in. Andy set the dress aside and pushed those thoughts from her mind. The next thing in the trunk were several articles of clothing, one of which, Andromeda saw with relief, was a long purple night gown. She pulled it out. It too smelled of dust, but it would have to do.

Why would the captain have a trunk full of women's clothes? Curiosity took hold of Andy, so she picked out the rest of the clothes to see what else was in the trunk. Only three things remained at the bottom. The first was a ring. It had a band of white gold, with a single green emerald set into it. Andy ran her finger over it but didn't pick it up. The next thing was a letter. She turned it over and saw that it wasn't sealed. The initials on the envelope were A.C.C.

Andy's eyes slid to the last thing. It was a single baby's onesie. She lifted it out of the trunk and ran her fingers over the material. The cloth had stiffened with age, so she knew it must be quite old. It gave her an uneasy feeling, even more so than the dress. She put it carefully back into the trunk and replaced the clothing except for the nightgown.

She put it on in the bathroom and looked at her reflection. It was an exceptionally fine gown, made of high-grade cloth. She made her bed and was about to climb in when the door opened. Captain Bran walked in, looking at a screen in his hand. He froze when he saw her. His eyes moved from her face down, taking in the gown. Andy pulled at the side of it and clenched her teeth.

"You went through my things." It wasn't a question.

She lifted her chin in defiance. "Yes. I needed something to sleep in."

"You could have asked. I could have gotten something from one of the female crew members."

"Well," Andy said, annoyed that she hadn't thought of that, "I didn't have time for that. I wanted to sleep now. If it's such a big deal, I'll take it off."

"No, no, it's fine," he said, though he was still frowning.

"It doesn't seem fine."

"It is. It's just, I haven't seen that gown in a long time."

Andy climbed into the bed and pulled the blankets up to her chest, still sitting up. "Why do you have a bunch of women's clothes in that trunk, anyway? Kidnap women often?"

He gave her a small smile. "No, not too often. Those belonged to someone I knew a long time ago."

"Your wife?"

Captain Bran looked up, almost looking alarmed. "Why do you say that?"

She shrugged. "There was a ring in the trunk as well."

"Oh, right, I forgot. Yes, they belonged to my wife."

Andy considered asking more questions but realized she really didn't care enough. She slid down into the blankets and pulled them over her shoulders. The captain changed into his sleeping clothes in the bathroom and walked to his hammock. Before he turned off the light, a question struck Andy that she couldn't resist asking.

"Do you have a child?"

The captain froze once more, his hand reaching for the light switch. He didn't turn to look at her, but there was a noticeable change in his mood.

"Why would you ask me that?"

"The trunk. There was also a onesie in there."

The captain closed his eyes, as though forcing back something in his mind, then looked at her.

"Yes, I had a child."

"Had?"

"Yes. They were taken from me a long time ago. Good night, Andy."

He switched off the light, and Andy laid in bed, silent. She refused to feel sorry for him, but losing a child would be incredibly difficult. Was that why he was being kind to her? Did he see his own child in her? She considered this. If that were the case, she could use that to her advantage. She had never been good at manipulating people, but now was her chance. If she could get the captain to feel for her, then perhaps she had a chance of getting home after all.

CHAPTER SEVEN

THE SOUND OF THE ENGINE overhead was a constant thrumming in Andy's ears. She could feel the vibration of it from where she currently lay on her back beneath one of the enormous valves, the sensation rattling the breath from her. The heat was edging toward uncomfortable, causing beads of sweat to slick along her hairline. She loved it. Even doing something as simple as fixing an oil leak, as she was doing now, made her feel alive. She thrust her hand out from beneath the valve.

"Torque wrench." She had to practically shout it over the sound of the engine, but Allen must have heard, because a moment later the proper tool was placed into her hand.

Once the bolt was tightened to her satisfaction, she slid out from beneath the valve. Allen stood a couple of feet away, watching her with a small, amused smile.

"You know, I've never seen someone so thrilled to be doing work."

Andy pushed her stray curls out of her face. She had done her best to tie it all back into a bun, but her hair had never been one to cooperate. "Speaking of work, aren't *you* supposed to be doing something?"

He smirked. "I am doing something. I'm babysitting you."

She glowered at him. "I do not need to be *babysat*. I'm clearly a more capable mechanic than you are."

"Mmm, yeah, I won't argue that. But you aren't exactly alone down here."

As though to prove his point, two men, dirty from their work, walked past, each casting a curious glance at Andy. She had noticed the crew doing that ever since she had begun working in the engine room a few days ago. They didn't seem threatening, just curious, but she had to admit she was glad to have Allen watching her back so that she could focus on her tasks. Of course, she could never admit that to him.

"Yeah, much good you'll do."

He pressed his hand to his chest in mock offense. "I will have you know I am one of the best warriors on the ship. Why else do you think the captain assigned me to look after you?"

"Oh, I just assumed this was some form of torture. Why else would he stick me with the most annoying pirate in existence?"

He let out a bark of laughter. "Yeah right, you like me."

She scrunched up her nose. "I do not like you."

"You know, I thought princesses were supposed to be sweet and diplomatic."

"The world is full of disappointment. You should get used to it."

He scoffed. "When have you ever had to deal with disappointment? I doubt you've ever had to want for much in your comfortable life."

She looked up in surprise at his sudden harsh words. "You know nothing about me, or my life. You think because you've read about me in articles that you know a damn thing about what I've been through?"

Allen chewed his bottom lip, looking her over. "So, tell me then. Tell me the things I don't know about you."

Great, another headache was coming on. She began to pack up the tools that were lying about. "I don't owe you anything, and I don't care what you think of me."

He still wore a small smile on his face. "I don't think that's true."

"Again, you seem to be missing the point that I don't care what you think."

"Oh, come on!" he said, his voice thick with exasperation. "If we have to spend time together, we may as well try to get along."

She stopped and looked up at him. There was a hint of amusement in his eyes, as though he was sure she would turn him down.

"Fine. What do you want to know?"

He looked her over. "How many relationships have you had?"

Andy crossed her arms. "That's personal."

"How else am I supposed to know more than what the tabloids say if I don't ask personal questions?"

Andy ran her tongue across her teeth before she let out a huff. "Two. How many have you had?"

He held up his hands. "Whoa, I thought we were talking about you."

She shrugged. "It's only fair that I know you just as well. So?"

He huffed, rolling his head along with his eyes. What a drama queen. "A few." He motioned to her legs. "Do those hurt?"

Andy shook her head. "No, not anymore. When it first happened, the sensation was so strange. It was as though I could feel them just the same as I had felt my real parts, but I couldn't. They moved and worked the same, without even a thought, but at first, I was slower. I would take a step and it was as if my other leg just forgot it was supposed to move too. I fell down more times than I can count. I cried every night for the first few months." She stared at her left hand, and only after a few minutes realized Allen was staring at her. She cleared her throat and straightened up. "But then my mother told me that if I just kept crying about it and did nothing, it would never get better. She was right. I was the only one who could improve my situation. After that, I trained every day. I trained until I was just as good at everything as I had been before my accident, and eventually until I was better."

She looked up and met his eyes. Though he still wore a small smile, his eyes were serious. She swallowed hard and looked down at her hands again. "So, what *do* the tabloids say about me?"

He raised an eyebrow. "Have you not read them?"

She shook her head. "I tried once, but my father had put a block on all media about me. I guess he was trying to protect me. So, tell me."

He leaned back against a metal pipe, looking as though he was trying to be nonchalant. "Oh, you know, this and that."

Andy frowned. "Allen, tell me."

He sighed. "Well, it depends on which one, really. When you first got into your accident, they all said that you had been horribly disfigured. They speculated you would be removed from the line of succession and have to live a life as a recluse. Luckily, they were wrong about that."

"Not entirely." Andy twisted her fingers around each other. "The doctors had to work for days to reconfigure my face. It was a miracle of science, they called it."

Allen nodded. "Well, I must say, they did an excellent job."

Andy glanced back at him and couldn't help but smile. "Flattery will get you nowhere."

He returned her smile. "Oh, I disagree with that. I can't tell you how many unfortunate situations it's gotten me out of."

She rolled her eyes and stretched, lifting her arms high above her head. "You don't think it could get me out of this one, could it?"

His smile slipped. "No, unfortunately I don't think it could."

"Right." It had been worth a shot. "Besides, that was never something I cared much about. What I looked like was more for them. For the family, which I'm supposed to be the face of. I couldn't be anything less than perfect."

Allen frowned. "That doesn't seem very fair."

"Yeah, well," she said with a shrug. "You know what they say about life."

Just as she finished gathering up her tools, the sound of footsteps made her look around. Mars was sauntering toward them, her hands in her pockets and her dark braids swishing against her back. She smiled when she reached them.

"Hey, Allen, Rio said you were down here."

Allen quirked an eyebrow and crossed his arms. "Well, he was right. Why were you looking for me?"

Mars's eyes darted to Andy for a moment. "Am I not allowed to hang out with my friend?"

Andy looked back and forth between the two and saw something unsaid pass between them. Allen looked as though he was trying to hold back a smile.

"You know, if you wanted to see Lady Andy, you could just say."

Mars threw her head back and laughed. Andy noted she had perfect straight white teeth. "I admit, the view is much nicer than when it's just you. Much less arrogant, at least."

Allen snorted. "You clearly don't know her very well."

Andy swung at his shin, but he dodged out of the way. "You're an ass, Allen, you know that?"

"Oh, I knew I would like you," Mars said with a wink.

Andy tried to push herself to her feet, but there were suddenly two hands reaching out in front of her. She blinked up at the both of them. They both seemed to ignore the fact that the other had reached out, neither wanting to back off. She placed her hands into both of theirs and with little effort, they helped her to her feet. She immediately let them go and rubbed her hands on her pants, feeling a bit awkward.

"Right, well, there are a few more leaks I wanted to fix, so… "

When neither of them said anything, she picked up her bag and made her way down the row between the pipes. Both Allen and Mars followed. Andy crouched beside the place she had marked for a leak.

"So, Mars, you work in the medical field?"

Mars pulled herself up to sit on one of the metal components. "Yep, ever since I came here when I was thirteen."

Andy nearly dropped the tool in her hand. "You—you've been here since you were thirteen?"

"Mmm," she hummed. "Arlo and I both have."

"Captain has a thing with taking in strays," Allen said as he sat down beside Andy.

"Oh, is that what you call yourself?" Mars said with a smirk. "And I would hardly call us strays. More like legacy members." At Andy's confused face, she continued. "My father has been with the captain since the beginning. When my mother died when I was thirteen, this was the only place for us to go. We had to earn our keep, so I helped in the medical bay."

Andy supposed she understood, though when she compared her ideas of what pirates were and the image of two children being a part of that, it didn't seem compatible. Though she had to admit, her idea of what pirates were was being constantly challenged. Especially by these two. Allen was almost… nice. And as for Mars, she didn't seem so bad. She ignored the part of her brain that mentioned that they were both rather attractive. That was certainly not a helpful thought.

"And what about you?" Mars asked. "Where do you come from?"

Andy stilled. She had thought about what she would say when asked this. Allen had also gone still beside her.

"I'm from Celestine. My parents were workers in the palace, a maid and a cook."

"Any siblings?"

"Yes, two sisters." As close to the truth as possible would be best.

"So why were you trying to smuggle yourself onto Earth? Sounds like you had it all made for you."

Andy bit her lip. "It wasn't all as good as it sounds. Yeah, I had a good home and enough money to get by, but I was trapped. I didn't get much of a choice in what I could be. I would be just like my parents. I had to get out of there before I suffocated."

She wasn't sure why her chest was aching so painfully until she realized that wasn't what she had planned to say. The truth had just been too strong, sitting on the tip of her tongue, waiting to make itself known. She swallowed and looked over at Allen. He was watching her, a look of such understanding on his face. She wanted to snap at him to not look at her like that. He didn't understand. He had no right to pity her.

"Wow," Mars said quietly. "That sounds rough. I would have left as well. What about your family? Did you tell them you were going?"

Andy opened her mouth and then shut it again. "They... no, they don't know where I am. I meant to message them when I got to Earth, but well, obviously that didn't pan out."

"Ah." Mars looked down at her lap, and then back to Andy. "Well, I'm sure everything will work out and you'll see them again."

Andy didn't respond. What was she supposed to say to that? Mars didn't know the whole truth. She didn't know that Celestine's crown princess was kneeling in front of her working on the ship's engine. She didn't know that Allen knew, or that the captain possibly knew.

They all looked up when they heard footsteps and saw a man approaching. His head was shaved bald, and he was at least a couple inches shorter than Andy. Mars waved.

"Hey, Ruger, what's up?"

"Hey, Mars, hey, Allen," Ruger said when he was close enough. "The captain has requested Lady Andy eat with him in his study. He wants her there now."

Andromeda narrowed her eyes and wiped her grease covered hands on the rag at her hip.

"And if I don't want to join him?"

He frowned, eyes darting from her and back to Allen. "I'm sorry, my lady, but you don't have much of a choice."

She straightened up and crossed her arms. "I disagree."

"We can argue logistics all day, but one way or another you are coming with me."

"You can try to make me," Andromeda challenged. "But I don't guarantee you'll walk away with all your parts."

The man clenched his jaw.

"It's fine," Allen said. "I'll take her."

Andromeda looked at him furiously. "Excuse me?"

Ruger frowned but didn't argue. "You better hurry; the Lord Captain doesn't like to wait."

"I know that," Allen said.

They watched the man walk away, and then Andy rounded on Allen. "I'm not going."

He sighed. "Look, you can either go on your own with your pride and your head held high, or he can send a group of men in here and drag you to him. Which would you prefer?"

"Right, well, I better get going," Mars said as she hopped down. She shifted awkwardly on her feet for a moment. "I'll see you both around."

Allen nodded, his eyes still on Andy. "Yeah, of course. See you later, Mars."

Mars looked back to Andy for a moment, and then turned and made her way the same way Ruger had gone. Once she was out of earshot, Andy shook her head in disgust.

"So much for protecting me," she sneered.

He shook his head. "I can't protect you from him. What do you want me to do, tell him I won't allow him to be near you? How do you think that would look? I've already explained this to you. The best thing we can do for now is play our parts."

She snorted. "Yes, well, you're playing your role of coward perfectly. Bravo."

He clenched his teeth. "You know, you really act like a child sometimes. Life isn't so black and white. Sometimes you have to do what you need to in order to survive, even if it's unpleasant. This is one of those times."

Rather than respond, she shoved past him and speed-walked down the aisle toward the elevator. She didn't need another lecture from him about doing what needed to be done. She knew enough about that.

Once on the main floor, she continued on to the captain's office with Allen on her heels. She stopped outside the door and took a deep breath.

"I'll be waiting right here if you need me," Allen said.

"A lot of good you'll do," she snapped before opening the door.

The office was decorated similarly to his bedroom. A dark wood desk took up the middle of the room and matching bookcases lined the walls. Gold and purple banners hung on the walls, giving the impression of royalty. He sat behind his desk with his hands folded in front of him, as if he had been waiting on her. Two plates of food sat on the desk. She closed the door behind her and sat in the chair across from him.

"Thank you for joining me, Lady Andy," he said with a smile.

She gave him her coldest glare. "Like I had a choice."

"Of course you did. I told my messenger to ask you if you would like to join me."

"Then why did you already have two plates set out?"

A half smile pulled at his cheek. "I was hopeful."

"Mmm, sure."

He laughed. "You really don't trust me, do you?"

She raised her eyebrows. "Trust you? How could I trust you? I was kidnapped, and you are now keeping me prisoner!"

"You are a guest, not a prisoner."

"The difference between the two is that guests can leave whenever they want. Since I cannot, the only reasonable explanation is that I am a prisoner."

He smiled again. She wanted to smack it off his face. "Please eat. I had this made special."

She glanced down at the food and saw that it was some kind of pasta. Using her fork, she twirled some up and ate it. She would never admit it, but it was good.

"Do you like it?"

She shrugged.

"It's a dish my mother used to make me. She always said the most important ingredient was love. Cliché, I know, but it was important to me."

She swallowed and wiped her mouth before speaking. "I doubt this was made with love."

He raised an eyebrow but didn't offer a response. "I was raised on Earth, you know."

She fought the urge to roll her eyes. "Fascinating."

"Have you ever been to Earth?"

She looked at him. "No."

"That's right, you were going there when my crew found you."

"Found me," she laughed, humorlessly. "That's one way of putting it."

"Once again, I apologize for that. But as I was saying, Earth is quite a wonderful place. At least where I grew up, it was."

He was silent for a moment, as though hoping she would ask where that was. She wouldn't give him the satisfaction.

"I grew up in Ameriadia."

"What, were you some beggar? Are you going to tell me the story of how you went from being a street rat to a wealthy pirate lord? That story has been told plenty of times before."

He wiped his mouth and twirled up some more pasta, though his eyes never left her. "No, I was not a beggar. My father was one of the wealthiest men in the kingdom. He supplied weapons to the Royal Army. We were quite the loyalists."

Well now, *that* surprised her. "Then, how— "

"Did I become a pirate outside the law? That is a complicated story for another night. What I will say is that I grew up in a large house with expensive things and a father who didn't have time for his overly ambitious son."

Andromeda pouted her lips. "Oh, poor thing, did Daddy not approve of you?"

The captain looked down at his plate. "Something like that."

"Some people don't even have fathers. You should count yourself lucky."

"And where is your father, Andy?"

She pressed her lips together. He had led her into a dangerous conversation. "He's dead."

"Dead? How did he die?"

"There was a pod accident."

"How terrible. Was it that same accident that left you in your condition?"

Her heart thudded in her chest. "Yes, the same one. Though pod accidents are quite common on Celestine."

"Are they?" He asked it with an air of intense interest.

"Yes. Have you ever been there?" she asked, trying to change the subject.

"Many years ago, yes."

"How did you like it?"

"I didn't favor the king."

He knew. He had to. There was no other reason he would be saying these things.

She kept her eyes on her plate and her voice light. "I've never met the king."

"No? You aren't missing much. He's a pompous, self-centered egomaniac."

Andy gripped her fork tightly. He was trying to goad her into revealing herself, and she wasn't about to fall into his trap.

"Perhaps he is, but like I said, I wouldn't know."

"No, I suppose not. I am sorry your father died. A father should be there for his child."

"Sometimes they can't be."

"That's true."

"All right," she said, patience snapping as she set her fork down with force. "What is it you want from me?"

He furrowed his brow and sat back. "I beg your pardon?"

"What do you want from me? Why am I here? I'm no use to you, so why not just let me go?"

He was silent as he stared at her, only the sound of his index finger tapping on the arm of his chair to fill the silence. When he finally spoke, his eyes were on the window.

"It can become quite monotonous here, if we don't look for ways to entertain ourselves."

A flurry of anger and indignation swirled inside her. "So that's what I am to you? Entertainment? So much for being a guest."

He leaned back in his chair and folded his hands over his chest, regarding her with what looked like amusement. "As I said, you *are* a guest."

"Bullshit!" she cried, slamming her hand onto the desk. "You can pretend all you like, but I know the truth. You're holding me here against my will because you're a twisted man on a power trip. I have a family that I need to get back to! My parents are probably worried sick, and you don't even care!"

The only reaction this got from him was a single raised eyebrow. "I thought you said your father was dead."

Andy felt the blood rush to her face. Crap.

"My biological father is. I have a stepfather."

"I see."

A silence stretched out between them for several seconds, both staring down the other.

Finally, Andy stood. "Thank you for the dinner. I should go now."

"It was my pleasure. But the dinner wasn't why I called you here."

She stopped, half turned away. "Then, why?"

"Allen tells me you're feeling restless. That you feel trapped on this ship."

She would kill that damn spy. "Can you blame me?"

"No, I can't. That's actually why I wanted to have dinner with you. To discuss allowing you certain freedoms."

"Freedoms?" she asked, her eyes narrowed.

"Yes. I want you to be happy here." He almost sounded sincere.

"I highly doubt that's going to happen."

"Well, in any case, we will port in Station Fourteen tomorrow. If you wish, with the company of Allen, you may go ashore to stretch your legs and get some air."

She stared at him in disbelief. "You're going to let me leave the ship?"

"With the company of Allen, yes."

"What's the catch?"

"There is no catch," he said with a smile.

"What if I run away?"

"Station Fourteen is strictly a pirate port. If you think you'll find anyone there who will treat you better than us, you are mistaken."

Andromeda focused on his eyes as his words sank in. "Wait a second, there is no Station Fourteen! There are only ten stations."

He stood and walked to a bar set up along the wall, where he poured himself a glass of amber liquid the same color as her eyes. "You are misinformed, Lady Andy. There are only ten stations under the direct protection and rule of Celestine. There are in fact twenty stations. The other ten are all run by thieves, merchants, and pirates."

"If the royal family knew about this—"

"They do. The king keeps it a secret. He would rather pretend they don't exist than acknowledge that he and his ancestors lost their hold over them long ago. It would be far too expensive for him to try and take them back, with little reward."

"That's not true."

"How would you know?"

She huffed and bit back an angry remark. "Why would the king lie to all of his people?"

The captain took a sip of his drink. "Not a good look, is it? Telling people that there's another way to live outside of his rule? Granted, most of the people out here live in poverty and under the rule of other men who would call themselves kings."

Her lip curled up in a sneer. "What, like you?"

He inclined his glass toward her. "I don't rule over anyone who does not wish it."

"I beg to differ."

This finally drew a frown from him. "Is it truly so horrible here?"

She opened her mouth to say yes, it was, but stopped. Honestly, ever since the captain had returned, it hadn't been bad at all. She could do far more than she was allowed at home, including working on the engines. But she supposed that was the problem. She was *allowed*.

"That isn't the point. I'm not free. You tell me what I can and can't do."

"And if you could do anything you wanted, what would you do? Would you go back home?"

Again, she paused before answering. Of course, she had to go home. But if she had the choice to do anything… If she could go anywhere and become anything, would she really choose to go back and marry Eden? She shook the thought away.

"Yes, I would."

The small smile on his lips told her he didn't believe her. "Well, I'm sure you'll get back to them someday."

Andy suddenly felt weary, as though she had been awake for days without rest. "If you'll excuse me, I'm feeling tired."

"Of course. Good night, my lady."

She walked to the door, but before she could leave, he called out to her.

"Lady Andy, if you are going to port tomorrow, you will need money. Here," he tossed her a small flash screen, "you'll find there is more than enough money on there to buy whatever you may need."

She stared down at the small, clear piece of glass. "I don't need your money."

"Of course you don't, but it's nice to have. There are no strings attached."

"There are always strings attached."

"As I said, I just want you to be happy here." He held her gaze and took another drink from his glass.

She stared at him for a moment more before leaving. Allen sat in the hall with his head resting against the wall, and he leapt up when she came out. She didn't speak to him as she walked past.

"Hey, slow down! What happened?"

"Nothing happened."

"Then why are you walking like you're being chased?"

She rolled her eyes. "Because you're chasing me."

He caught her by her elbow and pulled her to a stop. "Well, hold on, I wanted to show you something."

She glanced over her shoulder at him. "What?"

He smirked, his green eyes twinkling with a hint of mischief. "Come with me to find out."

She shook her head, not in the mood to play games. "No. I'm tired."

"Oh, come on, it's really cool!"

"That fact that you think it's really cool makes me believe it isn't."

"OK, smartass, fine. But you're seriously missing out."

She let out a deep breath. If she didn't go with him, he would never leave her alone about it. "Ugh, fine! What is it?"

"Come on," he urged.

He took her by the hand and pulled her after him. He raced down the hall, and she kept up, knowing if she got lost, she probably wouldn't be able to find her way back to her room on her own. Eventually, he stopped at a ladder that led up to the ceiling.

"You're taking me to an attic?" What the hell was he playing at? Honestly, she didn't believe he would do anything to hurt her, but her stomach still twisted with nerves.

"Just come on," he said as he climbed the ladder. When he reached the top, he pushed a button, and the ceiling slid open. Andromeda followed him cautiously. As she reached the top, he bent and offered his hand. She grudgingly took it because he was in the way. When he pulled her through the opening, her eyes went wide. She wasn't sure what she had been expecting, but it wasn't this. They were surrounded by a glass dome, at least twelve feet tall at its highest point. Beyond that was space. It stretched out in every direction, broken up by the distant light of stars. She walked to the glass and placed her hand against it, finding it cold. She had seen space before, but never like this. When she turned to Allen, he was watching her.

"What do you think?"

"It's incredible," she breathed.

He smirked. "Better than sleeping?"

"Definitely." She kept her hand on the glass, and soon it became numb. She glanced back at him. "Why are you being so nice?"

"I thought we had already established that I'm a pretty nice guy."

"Can you not be sarcastic for once?"

They were silent for a few moments before he spoke. "Maybe it's because you deserve someone to be nice to you."

"You don't know me."

"I know enough. I know you cared enough about your pilots to still be worrying about them even after you were locked up on a pirate ship."

"That's just being human."

"No, it's not. I've known enough humans to know that being kind and selfless aren't common traits."

"I'm not selfless," she sighed.

"Maybe not." He shrugged. "But you are kind. Sometimes that's enough. Besides, it's not as if I haven't done my fair share of selfish acts."

Andy sat on the floor, leaning her back against the glass. Allen remained standing, looking out at the stars. A silence stretched between them before Andy spoke quietly.

"You tried to get me off this ship. You could have gotten into a lot of trouble. That wasn't so selfish."

Allen closed his eyes. "Of course that was selfish. I can't think of many things I haven't done for selfish reasons. Even helping you."

He dropped down beside her. His dark red hair fell over his brows and he pushed it aside. Up close, Andy could see features she hadn't noticed before. His eyelashes were long, longer than hers. His skin was even and smooth, though if she looked hard enough there was just a trace of freckles that had once likely covered his cheeks and nose. He made eye contact with her, and she saw that his right eye had a single black spot, like an island in a green sea.

The corner of his mouth lifted. "Why are you looking at me like that?"

She turned away; her face warm. She hadn't meant to stare so hard. "Sorry," she muttered.

Now he stared at her, though she did her best to not look back. Instead, she looked up through the glass and saw something that made her heart lurch. Another ship could be seen, flying far off in the distance. It was only a small dot, but she had no doubt it was another ship.

"It's not part of the royal fleet."

Andy turned to look at Allen. "What?"

"I know that's what you're thinking, that they've come to save you. But it isn't them."

Andy's heart sank, but she tried hard not to show it. "How do you know?"

"Because if that were a part of the royal fleet, every alarm in this ship would be going off before they got that close."

She turned back to look at the ship, wishing desperately that he was wrong. But she knew he wasn't. Expert pirate ships were never caught by the royal fleet, which meant her family would never find her. As tears welled in Andy's eyes, she fought against them. She didn't want to cry.

"Andy? Are you OK?"

"Of course I'm not OK! Why would I be OK? I want to go back to my family! And my fiancé!" That last bit was a lie, but it felt necessary to add.

Allen stared at her. "You're engaged?"

She nodded, wiping her eyes. "Yes. How did you not know that? You were on Celestine."

He shrugged. "Other things distracted me. I didn't hang around and gossip. Who's the lucky guy?"

She pressed her palms into her eyes. "The prince of Someron."

Allen was silent for a long time, so Andy peeked up at him.

He was staring away from her, his mind seeming to be somewhere else.

"When's the wedding?"

"It was supposed to be a week from now, but somehow I can't imagine that happening." She wanted to sound angry and bitter, but her words came out empty. She found, with a bit of horror and uncertainty, that she wasn't all too sad about her impending wedding being pushed off.

"Do you love him?"

The question caught Andy off guard. She wanted to say yes, to dissuade any doubt. But she couldn't force the words out.

"I... no. No, I don't. I wish I did. It would make everything so much easier. He's a good man, kind. But when I was with him, I felt nothing. It's not fair to him."

"It's not fair to you, either!" Allen said it with such intensity that Andy blinked at him in surprise.

"What?"

He huffed out a breath and ran his hand through his hair. "You keep talking about everyone else, but what about you? How is that fair? Why should you have to marry someone who you don't love or even really know? For all you know, he could be a complete monster!"

"He's not—" she began, but he cut her off.

"That's not the point! They force you to be something you don't want just because it benefits them. How is that love? You don't have to do something you don't want, you know."

Andy crossed her arms tight over her chest. "What do you mean?"

"I'm sure as a royal you're told that you don't have a choice in the matter, that you have to marry who they say and do what they say. But you don't."

"Of course, I do. I'm the crown princess of Celestine. I have to make choices that are beneficial to my kingdom."

"I'm sure that's what they told you. But if you can't decide for yourself, how are you supposed to make decisions for an entire nation?"

His words gave Andy pause. He wasn't wrong. Andy had always wanted to make her own decisions but had never been afforded that opportunity. She shook her head. "That just isn't how things are. Besides, I could do worse than to marry Eden. He's a good person."

He snorted. "What a glowing sentiment. You shouldn't marry someone just because they aren't the worst option."

Andy clenched her jaw and looked away. She absolutely hated that he was right. She had been having those same thoughts from the beginning, but she had no choice. Going against the will of her father wasn't an option.

"So, what about you? Have you ever been in love?"

His eyes darted to her. He clearly hadn't been expecting her to ask that. "No, not exactly. There were times when I thought I might be, but I had to learn the hard way the difference between lust and love."

"So, who was she? The girl you thought you were in love with, I mean."

His brow furrowed slightly, as though he was trying to remember something. "It was a long time ago."

"What was her name?"

"Geovine."

"Do you miss her?"

Allen blinked several times, looking like he was coming out of a memory. "What? No, of course not. That was five years ago. I was barely sixteen. I think she's married now."

Andromeda nodded. "And what about your family? Where are they?"

Allen's jaw tightened, and he stood. "Come on, it's getting late. You better get to bed."

He helped Andy to her feet. "Did I hit a sore spot?"

"No. My family just isn't something I enjoy talking about." He didn't meet her eyes.

He walked to the door, but Andy grabbed his arm and pulled him to a stop. He had gotten into her life, why couldn't she get into his? "Is your family disappointed you're a pirate?"

He closed his eyes. "No. They're dead."

Andy let go of his arm. "I'm sorry," she said, and she meant it. "How did it happen?"

"I don't really want to talk about it."

She was silent for several moments. "OK."

They stood together, looking out of the dome for a while. Andromeda couldn't help but feel bad. His family had died, and he came to work on this ship as a last resort. She couldn't really blame him for that.

He looked at her and gave her a tired sort of smile. "Come on, let's get you to your room."

He helped her through the hole and led her down the halls.

"Hey, can I ask you something else?" she asked.

He seemed cautious, but he nodded.

"What does 'Lord Captain' even mean, anyway?"

He smiled, seemingly relieved she hadn't asked a question about him. "Well, you know how Earth and Celestine have kings and queens?"

"Yeah."

"A lord captain is basically a king out here. They rule over their own sectors and usually have massive armadas of ships to protect their territories and people."

"How does one become a lord captain?" She couldn't imagine it was easy, or else everyone would become one.

Allen shrugged. "By amassing power and wealth. Lord Captain Bran has taken down dozens of other rising captains. Eventually, he got to a point where his power was too great to deny, so the high pirate council crowned him lord."

"High pirate council?" Andy questioned.

"Oh, yeah," he said. "Out here they're the ones who help keep order."

Andromeda frowned. "Why would they make Captain Bran a lord? Wouldn't they just be giving power to their enemies?"

"No, not necessarily. They still need laws and order out here, at least to some degree. By naming the most powerful people lords, they essentially make them peacekeepers."

Andy didn't understand how that could work. "But what if the lords break the law and do horrible things?"

"What if kings break the law and do horrible things?"

His words made Andy stop. "Those two aren't the same thing."

Allen stopped too, turning to look at her. "How are they not the same? They're both given power and support. They both rule over large masses of people. They can both get away with doing horrible atrocities if they wish."

Andy looked at the floor, considering his words. She hadn't thought of it that way before. Though it had been a long time, there had been horrible kings in both Earth's and Celestine's past. Just around two hundred years ago, her great-great-great-grandfather King Buron had ruled Celestine with an iron fist. She had heard the horrible stories of how he had innocent people brought in off the streets and convicted of crimes they hadn't committed, all so he could sentence them to slave labor. If he saw a beautiful girl on the streets, whether she were married or not, he would have her brought to his concubine house and force her to be his mistress. Concubines had been strictly forbidden, but he overturned that during his rule. He had done many horrible things, and nobody had stopped him. As she thought of this, Allen watched her calmly.

"You see? Not so different."

Andy sighed. "I suppose not."

They continued to walk side by side. "How many pirate ships would you say there are?" he asked.

Andromeda thought about it. "I have no idea. A thousand?"

"That's a good estimate. Our lord captain owns over two hundred. He's notorious for his power and everyone from Station Eleven to Station Twenty respects him."

"How many lord captains are there?"

"Six."

"Why so few?"

"It's incredibly difficult gaining that much power, especially with so much competition. Captain was one of the youngest people to ever be crowned a lord captain. He was twenty-five. He's been building his fleet ever since."

She considered this as they walked to her room. If he had so much power, how was she ever going to escape? Nobody was going to help her. They had finally reached her room, so she turned to say good-bye to Allen.

"I'll see you tomorrow?" she asked.

"Yep, I'll be the one escorting you."

"Right. Well, good night, Allen."

He was still smiling at her when she turned to close the door. "Good night, Andromeda."

The door slid shut between them, leaving Andromeda alone in her room. She realized, with a bit of surprise, she wasn't completely against seeing him again tomorrow.

CHAPTER EIGHT

ANDROMEDA AWOKE TO KNOCKING. SHE rolled out of bed and stumbled to the door, all while she raked her fingers through wild curls.

"Who is it?" she called

"It's me," Allen said from the other side.

"Give me a minute!" She yawned and stretched as she walked to the bathroom.

"I'm just dropping something off for you. We'll be docking in a half hour, so I'll leave this outside your door. I'll be back in thirty minutes."

"OK."

She heard him walk away, his footsteps retreating down the hallway. When he was gone, she opened the door. A large box sat at her feet. She picked it up and carried it to the bed. Inside was a blue dress with a full skirt, like one she would wear on Celestine, but it hung only to her knees. It had the appearance of an upside-down tulip. A pair of white short-heeled shoes lay beneath the dress, with a coin and a note beside them. She laid the dress on the bed and picked up the note.

Lady Andy,

This dress should help you blend in. I hope it is to your satisfaction, and I hope you enjoy your time at the station.

Lord Captain Bran

She scoffed in disgust. He really thought she would dress up like his little pet? She flung the dress to the floor and hastily yanked on her usual outfit of loose brown pants and white button-up. If he thought she would just take this slight against her honor sitting down, he was delusional.

She threw the door open and marched out into the hall. Thankfully it was empty, so she made her way to the captain's office. She was halfway there when she rounded a corner and saw someone she recognized. Mars was leaning against the wall typing away on a screen. She looked up when Andy came into view and smiled.

"Lady Andy, good morning."

Andy forced a smile, not wanting to take her anger out on Mars. "Please, just Andy. I'm not a lady."

Mars raised an eyebrow. "All right, if that's what you want. What's wrong?"

Andy stopped a short way from her and shifted on her feet. "Wrong? Why would something be wrong?"

Mars laughed and tilted her head. "When you walked around that corner, you looked like you were out for blood. Wouldn't blame you if you were, mind you."

Andy chewed on her lip for a moment before letting out a breath. "It's the captain. He had this horrible little dress sent to me to wear on the station."

Mars hummed and nodded. "Oh yeah, that's the height of fashion for upper-class women on Station Fourteen."

"Well, I'm not his doll to dress as he likes! He doesn't own me."

Mars's smiled softened. "No, I don't think anyone could ever own you."

Andy didn't understand why her heart fluttered in her chest at those words. Perhaps it was the way Mars was looking at her, like she really *saw* her.

Mars pushed off the wall and motioned with her head for Andy to follow. "Come on."

Andy did, practically running to catch up. "Where are we going?"

"My quarters. My clothes should fit you just fine, and I should have something that will let you blend in while still feeling like you."

They reached a smaller hall that branched off the main one, and Mars opened the third door down. The room inside was much smaller than Andy's, only a third of the size, but she found she liked it much better. A bed that looked like it could snuggly fit two sat against one wall, and it was draped in a fluffy black comforter. The walls were decorated in everything from landscapes of Earth and band posters to tapestries and intricately woven cloth. It was a clash of colors, and Andy loved it. She would have loved to decorate her room like this but had never been allowed. "Not becoming of a princess," her father had said. She walked to a woven rug and ran her hand over it. When she turned back to Mars, she found she was watching her with a small smile.

"Do you like it?"

Andy nodded and smiled back. "It's beautiful. Where did you get it?"

"My mother. She made it for me just before she passed."

"It's lovely."

Mars stared for a moment more before moving to a closet that was set into the wall. "Maybe I could make one for you while you're here."

Andy's eyes widened in surprise. "You would do that?"

Mars shrugged, not looking at her. "Sure. My mother taught me how, but I haven't had the chance to make one for anyone in a long time."

"Thank you. I would like that."

Mars peeked over her shoulder, her eyes crinkling at the corners. "That settles it then. Here, try this on."

She tossed a burgundy shirt and black pants at her, which Andy caught with ease. Mars turned back around and faced her closet. Andy stood still for a moment, then placed the clothes on the bed and removed her oversized button-up and pants. The burgundy shirt was also a button-up, though it was made of silk and had buttons of gold. The jeans were tight and black, their grip on her hips just right.

"All right, you can turn around."

Mars did, and when her eyes fell on Andy, a slow smile pulled at her lips. "I was right. A perfect fit."

Andy examined herself in the mirror. "Will I blend in?"

"I would say so. Here, try this on." She picked up a gold chain from a dish on her desk and stepped close to loop it around Andy's neck. Andy held her breath, with Mars's face only a few inches from hers.

"There," Mars said, running her fingertips across Andy's collarbone. "It matches the color of your eyes."

Andy looked down at herself. "You don't think I'll look too—"

Mars stopped whatever she was going to say by curling her finger beneath Andy's jaw and lifting her face, so they were eye to eye. Andy inhaled, the floral scent of Mars filling her senses.

"You look beautiful."

Andy swallowed. "Thank you."

Mars kept her finger pressed to Andy's chin for a moment more before stepping back. "It's no problem."

Just then Mars's cell com pinged loudly. She lifted it to her eyes and smirked. "Allen's freaking out because he can't find you."

Andy huffed a laugh and rolled her eyes. "He worries too much."

"Not normally. Actually, he's typically petty chill. I guess it's just the effect you have on people."

Andy felt her face warm at Mars's compliment. "That's... no, that's not... "

Mars laughed, brushing her long braids over her shoulder. "Relax, I'm joking. Sort of. Not really."

Mars typed out a message onto her screen. "OK, let's go. He's going to wait for us outside your room."

Andy followed Mars out of the room and into the main hall.

"So, are you excited to go on your first excursion in an outer station?"

"I suppose. A little nervous, actually. I've never been anywhere outside of Celestine."

"Ugh, that sounds horrible," Mars said with a grimace. "Being trapped in one place your whole life with no option of escape? Nah, I'd choose to live free out here rather than in one of those gilded cages any day."

Andy looked down. She couldn't openly disagree, and honestly, she couldn't disagree in general. She had always dreamed of having the freedom to be her own person.

Mars seemed to sense her shifted mood and rushed on. "Not that there was anything wrong with your life!"

Andy gave her a small smile. "No, you're right. I lived a wonderful and privileged life, but it wasn't one that I chose for myself. I always wanted to be a mechanic or a programmer, but that wasn't an option for me."

Mars tilted her head. "But you know, it could be. This could be, I don't know, a fresh start for you."

A tightness settled in Andy's chest, and she shook her head. "I'm no freer here than I was there. The nature of my captor has just changed."

Mars looked like she wanted to say more, but just then they rounded the corner and came face-to-face with Allen. He was pacing back and forth, his arms crossed over his chest. He let out a breath when he saw them.

"There you are!"

Andy raised her eyebrows. "Yes, here I am."

"You can't just go running off like that."

Andy stopped in front of him, crossing her arms to match his stance. "Actually, I can go anywhere I like. Why? Were you worried?"

"Of course I was worried!" he cried. "I came back and found the package I had brought strewn across the floor, and you were nowhere to be found! You could have at least left a note."

Mars raised a placating hand. "Calm down, Allen. Lady Andy didn't appreciate the wardrobe the captain sent to her, so I lent her some of my things."

Allen finally let his eyes move over Andy's body. He sighed. "You still could have messaged me."

"She was perfectly safe while she was with me. There's no need to throw a hissy fit."

Allen narrowed his eyes at Mars. "I am *not* throwing a hissy fit."

"Mmm, seems a bit like a hissy fit to me."

Andy snickered, which earned her a glare from Allen. He threw his hands into the air. "Fine, if you both are going to gang up on me. We need to get going, Andy, if you still want to go. Will you be coming, Mars?"

"Eh, maybe," she said with a shrug. "I might head out a little later when the pubs get good."

Allen snorted. "Just don't let the captain catch you bringing anyone on board for the night. You know the rules."

"Of course not. I never let him catch me." She gave Andy one last wink and then made her way back down the hall.

Andy pushed past Allen and walked toward the docking doors. He kept up with ease, falling in line beside her.

"So, you and Mars are getting to know each other?"

Andy glanced at him out of the corner of her eye. "What, am I not allowed to have friends?"

"Of course you are."

"Good, then leave it alone."

Thankfully, he did. "We're about to dock, we'd better hurry so we can be the first ones out."

"I'd actually rather wait until everyone else is gone."

"It's customary for the lord captain or the lady to exit first. Since the captain isn't going, that leaves you."

"That is a stupid rule."

"Perhaps, but a rule, nonetheless. Now let's get a move on, Princess."

She rolled her eyes. They reached the docking doors, and Andy saw that some of the crew were already there.

"All right, out of the way, lady of the ship coming through!" Allen called.

"Would you shut up!" she whispered furiously.

Everyone turned to watch as they pushed their way past. She could feel their eyes moving over her, and she felt as though she might as well be naked. She subconsciously reached out and took Allen's hand. He glanced down at her in surprise, and she released him immediately.

"Sorry," she mumbled.

"You on babysitting duty?" one man asked Allen.

Allen winked at Andy. "Yeah, unfortunately."

"That sucks. No fun for you this time."

He smiled. "Oh, I'm sure I'll be able to find a bit of fun."

The man chuckled. "You always do."

Allen positioned her in front of him so that she was directly in front of the doors. There was a rumbling and a jerk as the ship latched on to the dock.

"You ready?" Allen asked.

Her mouth felt incredibly dry. "Sure. It'll just be a bit of exploring."

The truth was, she was quite afraid. She hadn't been in a large crowd for years, and the last time she had been, she was a princess with guards and a private seat. Crowds had always been overwhelming for her, the noises a cacophony that frayed her nerves.

The door opened, and light streamed in as the space grew. As she stared out into the station, her eyes widened. She had been to Station One before, as a child, and remembered it well. She recalled the tall, elegant buildings with clean lines and even cleaner streets. The ceiling, which had seemed miles up, had projected a clear blue sky, just like on Celestine. The shops had been organized, all set an even distance apart with clearly labeled signs. Everyone had been dressed in the latest fashions, all with polite smiles and quiet voices. This was nothing like that.

Men and women rushed around the loading docks, carrying crates and boxes into ships. They were dressed in a hodge-podge of fashion, with everything from form-fitted shirts and jeans to long flowing robes. People shouted over each other from every direction. Beyond that, she could see buildings and roads. There was a gentle nudge on her back from Allen, urging her forward. She took a deep breath and stepped out. As she walked, people stopped to look her up and down.

They made their way farther into the station. The buildings rose on either side of them, each made from a mismatch of materials. Tall cement buildings were pressed against shorter wooden structures. A rickety shack stood alongside a sleek metal four-story, with a thin brick shop that leaned a bit to the left beside them. While the ceiling seemed just as tall as it had been on Station One, the projections appeared to be broken. They were black and empty, with the odd panel flashing a white screen. Andy looked around, trying to take everything in. If the buildings were eclectic, then the people were even more so.

On one side of the road, a mother dragged her two children by their hands, each child crying to go into a different shop. A tall man in a top hat and purple coat pushed past them, while a group of loud teenagers played a game of kickball, weaving their way through the crowd of shoppers. Andy noticed several children dressed in rags. She had a sneaking suspicion they were homeless, given the poor state of their attire.

"Are there any shops you want to go into?" Allen asked.

She scanned the signs before she found what she wanted. "There, that one."

He squinted at the sign. "Antiques? Don't you need clothes?"

"There's plenty of time for that. I just want to look around."

She pushed her way through the crowd to the store without looking to see if he was following. As she pushed the door open, a bell jingled overhead. The room was warmer than outside, and a heavy smell hung in the air, like a closet that hadn't been opened in a while. Allen walked in behind her and stood with his back against the wall. Andy strolled among the shelves, examining artifacts and old bits of machinery.

"May I help you, madame?" a voice purred from the back counter.

Andy looked up and saw an elderly man leaning against the register. His face was scrunched up and puckered, as if he spent a great deal of time peering through a microscope. She smiled at him.

"I was just looking around. I wanted to see if you have anything interesting."

"Oh yes, I have many interesting things. Come see," he beckoned.

She approached the counter cautiously. He pulled something from beneath the shelf and placed it on the counter.

"This is a rare piece indeed, over two thousand years old."

She peered down at the object. It was rectangular and flat with a black glass surface and white bottom. She ran her fingers along it and found that it had small buttons along its side and a circular button on the front.

"What is it?"

"It is believed to be some sort of ancient telecommunicating device. Terribly rudimentary," he whispered, making her lean in to hear.

"I would be interested to see what it looks like on the inside," she marveled, turning it over in her hand.

"And you can. For the small price of three hundred pics, it can be yours."

"Three hundred pics!" she exclaimed "That's outrageous."

The man's face turned sour. "If you cannot afford it, you may leave."

"That's not a decent way to treat your customers," she said with a frown.

"I don't give a damn about customers who aren't buying," he growled, and pulled a gun from beneath the counter. Allen was beside her so quickly, she hadn't even heard his footsteps. He pointed his own gun at the man's head. The old man seemed extremely surprised, as though he hadn't even noticed Allen until that moment.

"Lower your weapon from the lady, or you will find yourself a head shorter," he said in a low tone that she hadn't heard before.

The old man's eyes shifted between the two. "What sort of girl has a bodyguard?"

"The lady of Lord Captain Bran," Allen said.

The shopkeeper's eyes went wide, and he dropped his gun as though it had become hot. "My God, please forgive me, my lady! I meant nothing of it! Please forgive me! Take anything you want from the shop!"

Andromeda stared in complete confusion. Everything had happened so suddenly she was having trouble understanding.

"I-I don't want anything," she stammered.

"Let's go," Allen said as he pulled her by her hand out of the store.

Once outside, Andy turned to Allen. "What the hell was that?"

"What do you mean?" he asked, looking as if nothing had happened.

"That was completely bizarre! Why did he pull a gun on me?"

He shrugged. "That's just how it is out here. The farther out you get, the rougher the conditions of the station."

"That's insane," she said, wiping sweat from her forehead. "And why is it so hot in here?"

"Outer stations are known for their mechanical issues, one of those being their heating and cooling systems. Don't worry, you'll get used to it."

They spent the next few hours going shop to shop, buying clothes and other items Andy thought she might need. She was much more careful now, staying close to Allen in case anyone else pulled a gun on her. As the day went by, sweat beaded its way along her brow. After a while, Allen stopped her.

"Hey, let's go over here." He dragged her under a shady overhang where a vendor was selling drinks. He bought two and slid her one. She took a sip.

"Coconut?"

"Yeah, it's one of my favorite drinks," Allen said.

"Mine too!" she said brightly.

He smiled back at her.

Andy ran a finger over the edge of her cup. "Hey, thanks for defending me back at that antique shop."

"Well, it is kind of my job," he said, looking off into the distance. "We should probably start heading back. The captain will worry if you aren't there before night. This place turns into a whole other beast after dark."

She raised her brows. "In what ways?"

He shrugged. "People start drinking and the streets turn into one big party."

"What if I want to stay and see that? It sounds like it could be fun."

Allen threw a disbelieving look at her. "Trust me princess, it wouldn't be your kind of party. No tiny finger sandwiches or crystal glasses of champagne here."

A rush of anger hit Andy. "Just because I'm not from this world doesn't mean I'm some spoiled porcelain doll."

"Hey, I never said you were. But you don't know this world or the things the people in it would do if you let your guard down. That shop owner was nothing compared to the things I've seen."

"Well then it seems the easy solution for that is for me to not let my guard down."

Allen pinched the bridge of his nose. "Andy, don't fight me on this."

She stepped away from him and threw her cup into a nearby trash chute. "Why not? I'm sick of being treated like a child or a pet. What could it hurt for me to have a little fun?"

"A lot actually! Don't test the captain's patience."

"Oh, no, I wouldn't want to do that! I wouldn't dare do anything your precious captain didn't like."

"You're being a real brat, you know that?"

"Excuse me, love, are you all right?"

Andy turned to see a woman in a nearby doorway watching her. "Oh, yes, I'm—"

"We're fine," Allen snapped.

Andy glared at him, but the woman acted as if he hadn't spoken. "Would you like to come in for a drink and to sit down?"

Andy felt her spirits lift at the kindness of the stranger. "Actually, yes, I would."

Andy took a step toward the woman, but before she could get closer, Allen had taken her wrist and was dragging her away.

"No, we're leaving right now."

"Let go of me! What's the matter with you?" she shouted.

"What's the matter with me? What's the matter with you?"

"That woman was just trying to be nice!"

"Oh, nice was she? That woman was a madame and that place was a brothel. She was trying to recruit you."

Andy's mouth fell open. "What? But she... Well, so what? Just because that's her profession, that doesn't mean she had bad intentions."

He scoffed and shook his head. "Wow, you really are naive."

"And you're an ass!"

"OK, I can't handle this right now."

As they walked, Andy fumed silently. She glanced up at one of the shops they passed, and her heart leapt. With its sign shining like a beacon in the growing darkness, was a cell port store. If she could get a cell port, she could let her family know where she was. She could be saved. She had to get away from Allen, but the crowds weren't thick enough here. If she tried it now, he would catch her quickly. He pulled her down side streets and through small alleys, winding their way through the station. Once they neared the loading docks, the crowds thickened, and Andy knew she had to take her chance. She waited for a large group of people to push through, then ripped her hand out of his.

She turned and ran, her hair flying behind her as she did. Allen shouted, but she didn't look back to see if he was in pursuit. She ran down alley after alley, trying to remember which way they had come. The streets were darkening now, and the farther she ran, the fewer people she saw. Her heart pounded in her chest. She had to find that store! She turned a corner and slid to a stop. Two men stood at the end of the alley near the street, and they were facing her. She couldn't see their faces in the shadows, but their clothes suggested they weren't the sort of people you want to meet after dark. She straightened up and walked toward them.

"Excuse me, I need to get past."

"You're excused," one man said with a laugh.

She didn't have time for this. "Not trying to be rude, but can you get out of my way?"

"Oh, the lady has demands," the other chuckled.

"What's a pretty lady like you doing wandering these streets?"

Andy tried to step around them, but they blocked her. "I'm not wandering, I'm running somewhere with purpose."

"And what would that purpose be?"

"Look, can you just get out of my way?"

"Say please."

She gritted her teeth. "Move, asshole!"

The man chuckled and nudged his friend. "The lady has a mouth on her."

"I'd like to get a closer look at that mouth," the other nodded.

There were footsteps behind her, and she turned to see three more men advance from behind her. Shit. Genuine fear prickled up her spine. She could handle two men, but five? She was too far out-numbered. They advanced on her.

"Get away from me!"

"Oh, get away!" one mocked.

She tried to push her way through, but they grabbed her roughly and shoved her against the wall.

"Let go of me!" she screamed.

"Why should we?" one of the men asked with a chuckle. "I'm sure eyes like that would sell for a pretty penny on the market. Same with this nice hair of yours."

She'd heard of people like this, who killed and sold parts in the underground markets. Andy tried to scream, but a hand pressed firmly over her mouth. The adrenaline kicked in then, her mind going blank as her body reacted on instinct. She kicked out at the man in front of her. The power behind her mechanical legs sent him flying backward against the opposite wall, his head hitting the bricks with a satisfying crack. She reached with her left hand to the man nearest and dug her fingers into his eyes. He shrieked and shoved her back. Two sets of hands grabbed her by her arms and pinned her to the wall. She bared her teeth and practically snarled at them as she wrenched her left arm free. With a hard, upward swing, she caught him in the jaw. But the man she had clawed was back, and now three sets of arms held her down. Her blood ran cold when she saw the knife he pulled from his belt. She was going to be stabbed.

But then the hands disappeared, and she stumbled to the ground, her fingers gripping at the wall as her head spun. She looked up in confusion and saw why they had drawn back. Allen had flung them off her and now stood between her and the five men, his body like a shield and his gun drawn and ready. He was taller and wider than any of them, but they were still outnumbered, and they all had guns drawn as well. She couldn't see his face, but she could tell by his rigid shoulders that he was furious. Her thoughts were confirmed when he spoke.

"Walk away now, before I kill you all," he growled.

"In case you haven't noticed, mate, you're outnumbered. Now, we can kill you both right now, or you can walk away and leave the girl with us."

Allen turned and glanced back at her. She wanted to glare at him but didn't have the energy. Not to mention, she was actually glad to see him. So instead, she smiled.

The tiniest smile pulled at the corner of his lips for a second, but then it was gone the next. He turned back to the men. "No deal. I'm charged with keeping her safe."

"Charged by whom?"

Allen reached into his pocket and pulled out a coin. It was the same one that had been delivered with the dress the captain had given her. There was a murmur from the men as they all looked nervously at each other.

"You've just assaulted the lady of Lord Captain Bran."

Fear arose in their eyes. "Hey, we didn't know!"

"No, you only thought you were assaulting a normal girl, which doesn't make it better."

"Let's go!" one man cried, as they all turned and fled.

Once they were gone, the adrenaline drained from Andy's body and weariness set in. Allen holstered his gun and slowly turned to face her, then knelt down, so he was at her level. Here it comes. He was going to tell her *I told you so*. Or he was going to mock her for not being strong enough to fight them on her own. He would call her Princess and roll his eyes.

"Are you OK?" he asked quietly.

Any sarcastic or defensive remark she had been ready to say fled her mind, and all she could focus on were his sincere eyes that held so much concern for her. The gentleness of the question broke down all the walls she had put up. Tears welled in her eyes and a sob bubbled up from her chest. She wanted to wipe them away, to hide any ounce of weakness from him. But in that moment, she found she didn't care. He wouldn't judge her. Allen sat beside her, his shoulder pressed to hers, and after a moment he lifted a cautious arm and wrapped it around her. He was solid and warm, yet somehow also unbearably gentle.

"Is this all right?" His voice was low and coarse.

She nodded, and then reached up and gripped his hand. He let out a slow sigh. They sat like that for a while, both seeming to enjoy the comfort of the other.

Allen was the one to speak first. "You scared me."

"I'm sorry," she whispered.

He shook his head. "No, I'm sorry."

She frowned. "What do you have to be sorry about?"

"I should never have called you a naive brat. I know that's what made you run away."

She stared at him. He thought that was why she had run? He didn't know she had been trying to escape.

"If they had hurt you, if they had done what they wanted to—if I hadn't been here—"

"I know."

He looked at her. Even in the dark, she could see some unknown emotion battling in his eyes. "You do?"

"Yeah, the lord captain would have killed you."

He stared into her eyes with his mouth partially open, as though there was something he wanted to say. After a moment, he closed it and nodded.

"Yeah, he would have."

She took a deep breath, settling her heart and mind. "We should probably get back to the ship."

"Yeah, we should."

Though it was nearly dark inside the station now, she could still make out the worried crease between his brows.

"The captain's going to be angry."

He gave her shoulder a gentle squeeze. "Not at you."

CHAPTER NINE

As ALLEN GUIDED ANDY BACK to the ship, the stress and exhaustion of the day hit her with such force she could barely walk. She leaned against him for support and was sure that if it weren't for her bionic legs, she would have collapsed. As they reached the ship, a few crew members stood outside, though the one she noticed right away was Mars. She was leaning against several crates and had something dangling from her mouth that was emitting small amounts of smoke, but as soon as she saw Allen and Andy, she flicked it to the man beside her and ran toward them.

"Allen, Andy, what happened? Why do you look like you were in a fight?"

Andy balanced herself so that she was standing without Allen's support. "We were. Some thugs attacked us."

Fire blazed in Mars's eyes. "Who? Where are they?"

Allen held up a hand. "Calm down, Mars, we'll get to the bottom of it later. For now, Lady Andy needs to rest. She overexerted herself a bit."

Though the storm on Mars's face seemed to still for the moment, Andy could still see traces of lightning in her eyes. "Fine. But we're going to talk about this."

Without another word, she stepped forward and took the support of Andy's other arm. Andy wanted to protest, to say that she could walk on her own without their support, but she was just too tired. She let them lead her up through the doors and past the other crew members. Luckily for Andy, the halls were empty with many of the crew still out at the pubs. She didn't disentangle herself from them until they reached her room.

"I, um, I think I'll be fine from here."

Allen looked at her with concern. "Are you sure? Can I get you anything?"

Andy began to say no, but then stopped and really thought about it. "Something to drink, actually."

"I'll go get it," Mars said with a nod.

Once she was out of sight, Allen let out a sigh. "Andy, you don't have to be strong. That was pretty traumatizing for me as well."

"I'll be fine, Allen."

"Yes, I'm sure you will be. But you don't have to be right now. I won't judge you."

She looked to meet his eyes, so full of sincerity. "Yeah, I know you won't."

After a moment, he nodded. "OK. The lord captain will wish to come see you."

"No, please, not tonight," she begged. "I'll see him in the morning."

He looked uncertain for a moment, but then smiled. "OK, I'll talk to him. Here, take this." He handed her his ringer. "If you need anything, just type in my name and I'll come. Or type in the captain's, if you want him," he added.

"Thank you, Allen." She gave him one last tired smile and then closed the door. It took her only a few minutes to dress for bed, and as soon as her head laid on the pillow, she slipped into nothingness.

Andromeda blinked. She was in a room filled with light. Turning her head to the left, she saw two large windows that appeared to face out over a garden. The sound of something scraping against china caught her attention. She looked the other way and to her surprise saw Eden.

He sat behind a large desk and was drinking what appeared to be tea. On the table was a plate of lemon cakes.

"Eden?"

He didn't look up. He couldn't hear her. She tried again, stepping toward him, but was stopped as she hit an invisible barrier. She pressed her hands to the air around her and tried not to panic. It was as though she was trapped in an invisible glass box.

She hit against the barrier. "Eden! Eden, I'm here! Can you hear me?"

He looked up suddenly, right at her. Her heart leapt. He could see her! But then his eyes slid past her. A screen on the wall was showing the news, and the title caught her attention.

The Celestine Royal Family Still Under Lockdown

She leaned in closer and found that she could hear what the reporter was saying.

"King Alder has still made no statement regarding the reason for his postponement of the royal wedding. Some speculate that Princess Andromeda is too unwell to make the trip, while others believe Prince Eden has refused to marry her, due to her alleged disfigurement."

Confusion and panic took hold of her mind. What was going on? People didn't even know she was missing? She felt herself beginning to hyperventilate. What the hell was going on? Her vision blurred as the surrounding scene faded. Darkness enveloped her and her panic only increased.

Andy awoke abruptly, sitting up with a gasp and scrambling around for a moment before gaining her composure. She flopped back onto the bed with a sigh. What the hell had that been? Her dreams had never been like that before. It was as if she'd been looking in on a real moment of something happening thousands of miles away. She rolled over in bed only to leap up with a shriek. The captain sat in his chair watching her, twisting a ring around on his finger.

"What the hell are you doing? Why are you watching me?" she shouted.

"I was waiting for you to wake up."

"You couldn't have waited outside?"

"This is my room," he reminded her.

"OK, well, what do you want?" she demanded. It was an eerie feeling, knowing his cold blue eyes had been on her while she slept.

"To speak with you about what happened yesterday evening."

She sighed and brushed her curls out of her face. "OK."

"Are you hurt?"

"Not in any permanent way."

He nodded. "Allen says he only saw what happened when he got there, but he doesn't know what happened before. Did they... " he trailed off, asking the question with his eyes.

"No! No, they didn't. I think they just intended to kill me. They said something about selling my parts at the dark market. Luckily, they had no idea how valuable some of my parts truly are."

Again, he nodded. "Do you need anything? Any... girl stuff?"

Andy raised an eyebrow. "Girl stuff?"

"Yes. I don't know. I haven't spent too much domestic time with women in quite a long time."

"No. I don't need anything."

"OK, well if you think of anything, tell Allen and he'll get it for you. I just wanted to make sure you were all right. I have business I need to see to today, so I'll leave you with him."

He stood and began to leave but stopped near the door. "Unless you wished to be left alone today?"

Andy considered it. "No, that's fine. If Allen or Mars wants to come by, they can."

He nodded. "Very well, I'll let them know."

Without another word, he left, and she was alone. The captain was certainly a strange man. She still had no idea what his true intentions were. Somehow, keeping her for entertainment didn't seem a likely reason. For one thing, she hardly saw him. There was a strong possibility that he knew who she was, and this was all an elaborate trick. He could be taking her to be sold to the highest bidder. But again, this just didn't feel likely. The not knowing left an uncomfortable feeling in the pit of her stomach.

A short while later, there was a knock at the door.

"Yes, come in."

The door slid open, and Allen walked in. "Did I wake you? Captain said you were awake, so I thought..."

"No, yes, I mean I am awake. I was just resting."

He nodded, raking his eyes over her face. "Are you all right?"

She groaned and flopped back on the bed. "Yes, I'm fine! Will you all stop looking at me like that? Nothing happened."

Allen approached the bed and crossed his arms. "Andy, you don't always have to be fine. I wasn't."

She narrowed her eyes. "I'm sure you get into fights all the time."

"Well, yeah, but that's when it's just me. Yesterday, it was you I was worried for. I just want to make sure you're safe."

As though realizing what he had said a moment too late, his face flushed a soft pink, and he looked away. Andy, too, was struggling to look him in the eye.

"Oh, well, that's... thanks."

He rubbed the back of his neck. "Yeah, no problem. So, um, are you hungry?"

She shook her head. "Not really. I kind of just want to lie here today."

He stood beside the bed, his arms crossed over his chest, for several seconds before speaking again. "Do you mind if I stay with you?"

Glancing at him out of the corner of her eye, she watched as he shuffled a bit, looking unsure. She rolled her eyes and smiled.

"If you insist."

He looked surprised for a moment, then returned her smile and dropped beside her on the bed. She inhaled sharply at their sudden proximity. They had been close before, but this was different. They were in a bed, and she was in her sleeping gown. But he remained a foot and a half away and on the top of the covers. Slowly, Andy relaxed into the mattress. An awkward silence stretched between them until finally Allen turned his head to face her.

"But really, how are you?"

She let out a breath. "I'm... I don't know. Is Celestine under lockdown?"

Allen frowned. "When did you hear that? Did someone tell you?"

"I... no. I don't know. I dreamed about it last night. But it's true?"

He nodded. "Yes. Since the day after you came here. I suppose they don't want it getting out that you've been taken."

Andy chewed her lip. It made sense. If people knew, the public would panic, and it could put her in more danger.

"What are you thinking about?"

"Just my mom. I had a bit of a nightmare last night, and when I was young, she would always come to me when I had them. Even after the accident. She would stroke my forehead and sing to me. She wasn't exceptionally good, but that didn't matter. At least she was there."

Unbidden, tears sprung to her eyes. This was the first time she had really thought about her family and what they must be going through in all this. A warm pressure against her hand made her look over. Allen's fingers wrapped around hers.

"I'm sorry, Andromeda. For all this. It's perfectly normal to miss your family."

She wiped her cheek with the hand Allen wasn't holding. "Yes, but that's just it. I should miss them terribly, and I do! I miss them all and I want to see them again, even my sisters. But... I've hardly thought of them. This is going to sound strange and terrible, but these past couple weeks have felt like a relief. I mean, I know this is a bad situation, and it hasn't been at all relaxing, but for the first time in my entire life I'm not expected to be something I don't want to be. I haven't been paraded around or told to sit up and smile more, I haven't been chastised on how I eat or told I'm not allowed to work on machines. Nobody has made me sit on my hands when they're twitching too much or gotten angry when I wasn't paying attention. I know I'm not free, but this feels like what freedom could be."

Andy clenched her eyes shut. "And I hate myself for that. I'm being so selfish. My parents are depending on me, my entire kingdom is."

Allen squeezed her hand gently. "Andy, that isn't selfish. It's selfish of them to expect all that from you. Everybody should have a choice to be whatever they like in this life. You only get one, after all."

She shook her head. "You don't understand. I was born to do this."

A harsh scoff from him made her look up. There was an almost angry twist to his mouth.

"Nobody was born to do anything. Don't let them manipulate you into thinking differently."

"And how would you know anything about it?"

He turned his face away to look at the ceiling. "My parents had a family-run business. I was always told that someday I would have to take over from them. The business was my family's whole livelihood, including my younger siblings. I was never given another option, never allowed to explore what else was out there. It was a terrible stress and burden on me. When I tried to tell my parents about the other things I wanted, they would laugh or sometimes get angry."

Andy held his hand more tightly. Though her burden was on a greater scale, she could relate to what he was saying.

"Being a disappointment to the people who rely on you is terrible."

He glanced back at her. "Yeah, but it's even worse to be a disappointment to yourself."

"Is that why you came here when they died?"

His silence stretched on for a long time. "Yeah, I guess so. Didn't have anywhere else to go or anything else to do."

Andy let herself examine his profile. The strong curve of his jaw was softened by the bit of red stubble that just hinted at a beard. There was the slightest hint of a curve in the middle of his nose, possibly from a break earlier in life.

"You can tell me about your family, if you want. What was your mother like?"

He snorted. "Unfortunately, I don't have any stories of soft lullabies. My mother wasn't a cruel woman, she never struck me or said harsh words. But her love needed to be earned. Everything was a competition to her. Either you loved her the most, meaning you did whatever she said, or you didn't love her at all. It was difficult to come to terms with the fact that it was her with the problem and not me."

Andy realized she was rubbing a gentle circle against the back of his hand and immediately stopped. "I'm sorry. That doesn't sound easy to grow up with."

"No, it wasn't." He looked at her and smiled. "But hey, I think I turned out all right."

She nodded. "Yes, you turned out all right despite her, not because of her."

His eyebrows twitched. "How can we know which is which?"

She didn't have an answer for that. Before she could continue the conversation, the door slid open, and a man walked in. Allen leapt out the bed as though it had caught fire, ripping his hand out of hers.

The man stopped in the doorway and looked between the two. She realized this probably looked odd.

"Yes? May I help you?"

He cleared his throat. "Lady Andy, the lord captain wishes for you to join him in the observation chamber. He said Allen can join you."

Andy glanced at Allen and saw that he looked confused, but he nodded.

"Very well. I need to dress, but I will be there with haste."

The man nodded and left. Andy climbed out of bed and gathered a few articles of clothing she had purchased the day before.

Allen shifted on his feet. "Er, do you need me to leave?"

She waved a hand. "No, that's not necessary. I'll change in the restroom. Just wait here for me."

She changed quickly and washed her face. When she emerged, Allen was still waiting patiently.

"All right, we can go."

They made their way out of the room and down the hall.

"So, what's the observation chamber?"

"Think of it being the equivalent of a throne room. It's where the lord captain meets with outsiders. And sometimes where he holds public punishments."

Andy frowned. Why would the captain want to meet with her in there instead of his office? They reached two doors that slid open as they approached. The room they entered was large, with one entire wall made of glass that looked out into space. Allen had been right; it resembled a throne room. A large, comfortable-looking chair sat on a raised platform overlooking the room, and two smaller chairs sat beside it. When they entered, Captain Bran turned from the window.

"Lady Andy, Allen, please take a seat." He stepped up the dais and settled into the largest chair.

The two glanced at each other before doing as they were told. They each sat on either side of the captain.

"Lord Captain, may I ask why we were summoned?" Allen asked.

"You will see in a moment."

Concern prickled at Andy's senses. She had never seen him in such a serious state, and there appeared to be a storm brewing behind his eyes. He snapped his fingers and a side door slid open. Five men were led through, each of them bound and hooded, and shoved to their knees. Pirates filed in, standing to the sides and filling the room. They all looked just as confused as Andy felt. When the room was full and silent, the captain stood.

"I have gathered you all here to explain a grievous and unforgivable crime that was committed against one of our own. I told all of you upon my return that Lady Andy was off limits and any hand laid on her would result in death."

There was a murmur around the room as each of the men looked at one another. Andy felt her pulse quicken. She knew where this was going.

"Now, these men," Captain Bran said, pointing to the hooded figures before them, "have done something horrible. Yesterday, these men attacked your lady and laid hands on her without her permission. These brutes believed they were above my law, above you, and believed they had the right to touch her."

Angry shouts came from around the room. Andy saw Mars standing near the door with her arms folded across her chest. They made eye contact, and Andy saw the same fury that had burned in her last night. Andy's breathing became labored as she looked around the room in shame. Why would the captain embarrass her like this? Now they all knew. Now when they looked at her, all they would see was a helpless girl who hadn't been able to protect herself from street thugs. Her hands began to flutter at her side, her fingers twitching as they grabbed absently at the cloth of her pants. The captain stood and strode toward the prisoners. He walked behind them and ripped each of their hoods off. Hatred radiated off him as he looked at the men. Andy didn't want to look at them, but there didn't seem to be anywhere else for her eyes to fall. Their faces were red and sweaty, their eyes bloodshot. Some of them cried, while others stared in terror. She gripped her armrest, images of yesterday's attack playing in her head. Andy didn't want to admit it, but a small part of her was happy to see them suffer. The captain walked around so that he stood in front of them. None of them would look at him. Instead, they focused on his boots. He pulled one of them to their feet.

"Have you heard of me?" he asked in barely more than a whisper.

Rather than answer, the man burst into sobs. The captain pulled a knife from his belt and pressed it to the man's throat.

"I asked you a question. Have you heard of me?"

"Yes! Of course I've heard of you!" the man sobbed.

"Who am I?"

"Lord Captain Bran," the man whimpered. His legs shook so badly it was a wonder they could hold him up.

"So, if you had heard of me, why would you think it a good idea to assault and brutalize my lady?"

"We didn't know, I swear we didn't know who she was! If we had known, we never would have touched her!"

"No, you would have found another victim."

"Please, please, let us go! Please, I'll do anything, whatever you want!"

"Oh, shut up," the captain said with a sneer. In a movement quicker than Andy had ever seen, he slammed the knife up through the man's jaw into his skull. She had to press a hand to her mouth to stop herself from screaming. She had never seen someone die before. Captain Bran pulled the knife out, and the man slumped to the ground, blood pooling around him. The other prisoners looked like they were about to faint from fear as the captain pulled another to his feet.

"Tell me, why did you attack my lady?"

"It wasn't our fault! We got a quota to fill with our boss! We were only following orders!"

"Just following orders?" Bran drawled. "When orders are evil, and you follow them despite their immoral nature, that makes you just as responsible as those that give the orders."

The man shook his head frantically. "Any of your men would have done the same!"

"Do you think so? Allen," he said, turning to look up at him "if I told you to ignore my previous order and to ravage Lady Andy right now in front of everyone, would you do it?"

Andy couldn't take her eyes off the pooling blood beneath the dead man's head, its slow spread covering the floor, but out of the corner of her eye she saw him shake his head.

"No, I wouldn't."

"That's the correct answer. You see, I believe you did what you did because you wanted to. Certainly, you had been ordered, but when you saw Lady Andy alone, I don't think there was any part of you that believed what you were doing was wrong. Do you disagree?"

"Please, I don't want to die," the man sobbed.

"That's what I thought." With a flick of his wrist, he cut the man's throat.

Once again, Andy watched in horror as he slumped down beside his friend. Blood covered the bottom of the captain's boots, red footprints following behind him as he walked.

"Do you have anything to add?" he asked the third prisoner.

"Plea—" He didn't even have time to speak before the captain shoved the blade through his eye socket. The man fell back, still twitching. Andy clenched her jaw. She hated these men, but she didn't want to watch them die. The captain looked up to where she and Allen sat.

"Allen, would you join me down here?"

There was only a moment of hesitation before Allen stood and walked to him.

"You were the one who saved Lady Andy and stopped these men from doing much worse than they did. So, I would like to give you the honor of killing this man any way you wish."

Allen looked from the captain to the man before him. "Thank you, Captain."

"Is this something that you want?"

"Yes, Captain. This is something I've thought of since last night."

A chill ran down Andy's spine. This wasn't the Allen she had come to know. There was none of the gentle kindness she had seen since she met him. She watched as he walked around the man like a shark eyeing its prey. The normally happy, sarcastic Allen was gone. This was a pirate. He had no weapon, so Andy wasn't sure how he intended to kill the man. He answered that question almost before she could think it.

Like a cobra, his fist struck out, hitting the man square in the jaw. The man fell onto his back with Allen on top of him. His fists struck again and again, beating into the man's bloody face. She heard bones cracking and wasn't sure if it was the prisoners or Allen's. Allen continued to hit him for several minutes after she was sure the man was dead. When Allen finally stood, his fists and shirt were covered in blood. He looked up into her eyes, and when he saw her looking at him he turned away.

"Lady Andy?"

She turned to look back at the captain. "Lady Andy, would you join me down here?"

Oh God, she didn't want to do this. She knew what he was going to make her do, and she didn't know if she was capable. Her legs shook as she descended the steps.

"This is one of the men who hurt you. He likely would have killed you. What do you want to do to him?"

She looked at the man before her and knew what she wanted to do to him. She wanted him to feel the same fear and pain he had caused her. She wanted to be strong enough to do it herself.

"I want him dead."

The captain nodded. "That is completely in your power."

He pulled a gun from his belt and handed it to her. She stared at it for a moment before taking it. Her hand shook so badly she was afraid she would shoot herself.

"Go ahead, do it," he urged.

She lifted the gun and pointed it at the man before her. He was still on his knees, and he stared at her with pleading eyes. "Please, my lady, don't do this. Please don't kill me. I don't want to die."

"Shut up," she whispered, tears pricking the back of her eyes. When she thought about killing someone, especially someone who had hurt her, it sounded like it would be easy. She could even see herself pulling the trigger. She imagined she would like it even. But standing there with a man begging for his life was not what she had imagined. The fear and horror of what she was about to do was not expected. She lowered the gun and shook her head.

"I can't do it."

The captain stared at her for a moment before nodding. He pulled another gun from his belt and fired it directly into the side of the man's head. Andy jumped at the sound and stared as the man fell at her feet, his eyes staring lifelessly up at her. Captain Bran turned and walked to the door. When he reached it, he looked back at her.

"It will get easier."

CHAPTER
TEN

ANDY LAID IN BED AND stared at the ceiling. The image of the bodies and the blood was etched behind her eyelids, those lifeless faces staring back whenever she began to doze off. She doubted they would ever go away. Despite trying to sleep several times throughout the night, sleep refused to come. The morning light now streamed through her window, and she didn't know if she had the strength to get out of bed.

Andromeda had been born to fine things, in a court that dealt in secrets and guarded smiles. But she was no longer in her court. In the realm of pirates, they had no use for whispered words or false niceties. No, in this world, the only currency they understood was the severity of your violence and the ease with which you could wield it.

The captain's words echoed through her mind, a warning dressed as reassurance. "*It will get easier.*"

The door to her room opened, and the captain walked in. He stopped at the foot of the bed.

"Why are you still in bed?"

She remained lying down but looked to him. "Could you just leave me alone? After what you did, I'd rather not talk to you."

"What are you talking about?" he asked, walking around the side of the bed.

"I'm talking about yesterday!" she cried as she pushed herself into an upright position. "I'm sure you feel like a big man now, putting on that show! Bravo, you're still a big scary pirate captain, huh? All while simultaneously making me look weak."

He remained where he was, seeming to consider what she said. After a minute, he sat on the edge of the bed. "None of them think you're weak."

She ran both of her hands over her eyes. "All right, seriously, what is going on? You've had me here for weeks, and for what? What are you going to do with me? Why don't you just let me go? You said that you are keeping me around for entertainment, but I've hardly seen you. So cut the bullshit."

He didn't say anything for several moments. Finally, he let out a breath.

"I'm trying to do what's best for you."

Andy's mouth fell open in disbelief. "What's best for me? You honestly believe keeping me here against my will is what's best?"

"Yes!" he shouted.

Andy jumped at the outburst. He closed his eyes and rubbed his fingers against his temples.

"I'm not a good man, Andy. I know that. I've done horrible things. But I'm trying. The world out there is terrible and cruel. So, while you might not like me, I'm the best chance you have. You admitted to me you were trying to escape the life you had. Well, I'm trying to give you that chance."

For the first time, Andy was speechless. He was trying to help her? He thought he was doing what was best for her?

"Wait, so let me get this straight. You're keeping me here because you want me to have a better life?"

The corner of his mouth quirked up. "Is that so hard to believe? I've done this for many people, though I admit not quite like this. They usually want to be here."

Andy felt like her brain was working in slow motion. "Yes, but that's the difference! Those people wanted to be here! I don't. I can handle myself."

He laughed. "Oh, really? Yes, you really did a superb job yesterday and the day before. You wouldn't last out there."

Blood rushed to her head, and she felt her face flush with rage. She forced her voice to remain calm. "How dare you? I did just fine. Just because you can kill people doesn't make you better than me."

"Out here, it does. This isn't the cushy life you led on Celestine. People will kill you."

"Why do you even care?"

"Despite what you believe, I'm not a complete monster. You're a good kid, but you're naive. You don't know what's best for you."

Andy leapt from the bed, her voice rising despite her efforts. "And you think you do?"

"I know more than you might think. You might hate me now, but someday you'll thank me. I'm doing this for you."

She let out a humorless laugh. "Well, now you sound just like my father."

She spun away from him. Her heart was pounding away in her chest, and her head was fogging up. A panic attack was coming. She did her best to get her breathing back under control, but it was already happening. Without waiting for the captain to say anything else, Andy ran into the bathroom.

Her back hit the wall, and she slid to the floor while her hands shook violently. The doctors had healed so much of her, why hadn't they been able to heal this? This terrible panic that overtook her at the worst moments and debilitated her.

"We can fix the body, but the mind is complicated."

That's what they had told her. It was nearly twenty minutes before her mind slowed, and she could climb to her feet. She splashed cold water on her face. When she walked out of the bathroom, she froze.

She had expected the captain to leave while she was in there, yet there he sat in the same place she had left him.

"You have panic attacks?"

She shrugged. "Yeah, sometimes."

He looked her over slowly. "They can be a bitch, can't they?"

Her eyes flicked up to his. "You get them?"

He gave a quick nod. "Yes, since I was a teenager. I've gotten them under control, somewhat. Can't exactly be a terrifying pirate captain if you break down in front of your crew once a week."

Andy walked to the hammock and flopped down onto it. She'd often worried about her condition affecting how she ruled. "How did you get them under control?"

He let out a slow breath. "Time. Practice. Focused breathing. And this."

He held up a hand to show a gold ring with a small blue stone set in it.

Andy frowned. "I don't understand."

"It's a focus object. Something to keep me grounded," he said as he took it off and twisted it in his fingers. "My wife gave it to me. When things start to feel like too much, I take it off and rub it between my fingers. It helps. Of course, I still get them. Only now I'm able to keep them contained to when I'm alone."

Andy watched him as he turned his ring over in his fingers. "You shouldn't have done what you did yesterday."

He didn't look up. "You deserved to get your revenge."

"I don't think that's what that was. You were sending a message. You're the biggest dog in this fight, and you don't want anyone getting any ideas about who's in charge."

Captain Bran leaned back and smiled. "That was part of it, sure. Do you think I got to where I am by playing nice?"

"So, your empire is built from blood."

"Every empire is built from blood."

She met his eye for a moment, then looked away. "Still, killing shouldn't be easy."

"You're right."

"But it is for you."

He let out a huff of breath. "Yes. But only because I've been doing it for over twenty-three years. After a while, they just sort of blend together."

Andy wrapped her arms around her knees. "Who was the first person you killed?"

He pressed his lips together and looked away. "That's not something I wish to discuss."

"You can't expect me to talk to you when you won't even tell me one thing about yourself."

He didn't answer. The silence stretched on, and she realized he wasn't going to answer. She began to turn away.

"My brother."

She blinked. "What?"

"The first person I ever killed."

A cold tendril of disgust rolled down her back. "Your brother? Wow, I was right. You really are a monster."

"I don't blame you for thinking that. I did, for a long time, until I realized what I did was necessary."

"How can killing your own brother be necessary?"

A shadow passed over his face. "All I'll say is that my brother was a bad person. Always was, from the time we were children. He was only two years younger than me. I would catch him hurting small animals in the woods behind our house when we were young, and it only got worse the older we became. Sometimes he would have this look in his eye, like deep, empty pools with no life in them." He glanced at her, as though checking to see if she was still listening.

"He was horrible to our mother. Always cursing at her and making her life more difficult. He wasn't that way when our father was around, which wasn't often. He acted like a saint with him. It was only those weaker than him he preyed on. I came home early from working with our father one day when I was nineteen. I heard crying from upstairs and went to investigate, and when I opened the door I saw him. He was—he was hurting my sister… " The captain closed his eyes, as though warding off a terrible memory. "I went a little crazy. I walked back to my parent's room, pulled my father's gun out of his drawer, walked back to my sister's room, and shot him."

Andy's pulse raced, her eyes wide, lost in his story.

"After I killed him, I panicked. My parents would never have understood, even if they found out what he did to our sister. They would have sent me to prison. I worked for my father, you see, as his apprentice to take over his business when he grew old. I stole all the money from my father's account, bought a small ship with a few crew members, and got out of there as quickly as I could. I suppose you can say that was my first act as a pirate."

Andy sat in silence once he had finished. If she put herself in his shoes, would she have done the same thing? If she discovered Rosetta was a monster, that she hurt Eleanora in an unforgivable way, would she be able to kill her?

"What was his name?"

His eyes were distant. "Astor."

"And your sister?"

A smile pulled at his lips. "Annamora."

"That's a nice name," she said quietly.

He sighed. "Yes, it was."

Her heart dropped. "Was?"

He swallowed hard and closed his eyes. "After I killed Astor and ran away, things became exceedingly difficult for my family. My father threw himself into his work, my mother began to drink, and my sister got into things she shouldn't have. She was so young, only thirteen when it happened, and she needed someone. But I left her, and my parents couldn't help themselves, let alone her. She became pregnant when she was fifteen and died in childbirth."

"My God," Andy whispered. "That's horrible."

"It was. When I found out I was a wreck. I couldn't even attend my own sister's funeral. As for my parents, they had to attend their second child's funeral within two years. They divorced shortly after."

"How did you get through that?"

"For a while I didn't. I drank, slept around, and stopped caring. Meanwhile, my crew and wealth grew by the day. Finally, one day I decided to take on a bigger scheme than normal, one that would quadruple my already substantial wealth."

"What did you do?" she asked, her curiosity piqued.

He blinked, as if coming out of a trance. "That's a story for another day."

She slumped back in disappointment, realizing she had been enjoying the story. The captain stood and walked to the door. "You should get dressed. Maybe go to the engine room. Just do something to busy your mind."

Once he was gone, Andy leapt out of the hammock. She didn't want to admit it, but he was right. She needed to do something with herself. Throwing on an old pair of brown pants and a black fitted shirt, she headed out to the engine room. She didn't expect to find Allen standing at the screen panels within the first doors. He looked up when she walked in, and an expression of guilt crossed his face.

"Andy, is everything OK?"

She shrugged as she tied her hair back from her face. "The same as always, I suppose."

"Oh." He frowned. "Were you... looking for me?"

"Um, no, I actually just came here to do some work. You?"

"Ah, yeah, there was some loss of pressure in one of the valves. It's all the way down in sector three."

"Do you need some help with it? I could come with you and take a look."

He shook his head. "No, that's all right. Actually, I wanted to talk to you."

Andy looked up from where she had begun packing her bag of tools. "About what?"

"Well, about yesterday. About what I did."

She looked away, a crease forming between her eyebrows. "You did nothing wrong, Allen."

"Yes, I did. Andy, I had no clue the captain planned that, you have to believe me."

"I do believe you."

He looked as though he had planned on more to say, but stopped. "You do? Oh, I thought it would take more convincing. Nevertheless, I'm sorry."

"For what?"

"For what... Andy, I killed a man in front of you! I didn't want you to see me like that."

"Allen, look," she said as she stopped and turned to face him. "I know who you are. I'm not under any impression that you're some gallant knight. You're a pirate, and I'm OK with that."

"But Andy—"

"No, really. You don't have to explain anything to me. I'm not going to try to change you or try to make you out to be some golden prince. I'll be completely me as long as you're completely you. Deal?"

Allen was silent for a moment as he mulled over what she said. Finally, after a few seconds, he nodded. "Fine. But what if you don't like what you see?"

"Then I'll get over it," she shrugged.

A small smile pulled at his lips. "It's just that easy?"

"It's just that easy," she agreed. "Now if you don't mind, I have some work I would like to get to."

She picked up her work bag and walked away down the aisle between the engines. Truly, she didn't think Allen had anything to apologize for. Just because she hadn't been able to pull the trigger didn't mean those men hadn't deserved to die. They would have killed more people and caused more harm. Though, really, they were a symptom of a much larger problem. Her family had abandoned these outer stations to run wild with crime and poverty. But it seemed as if these people didn't wish to be ruled at all, even if it would help them. She sighed and dropped her bag onto the floor. There was no simple solution for it.

Thankfully, the monotonous work of repairing the oil leak took her mind off it. After an hour under the machine, she slid out and wiped her grease-covered hands onto her pants. She was just about to pack up her bag when a bang and shock wave sent her to the floor. A blaring alarm went off overhead, and the sound of running footsteps made her look up. Crew members were running past toward the doors.

"Hey!" she called. "What's going on?"

One man spotted her and skidded to a stop. "Lady Andy! I need to get you out of here. Come on."

He took her by the hand and led her toward the doors. "But what's going on? Why do we have to leave?"

"There was a rupture in sector three. There may have been a minor explosion because the oxygen levels are dropping. I hope nobody was down there, because it's going to be closed off."

Andy came to an abrupt halt, forcing him to stop. Her eyes went wide as horror filled her mind. "Sector three? Allen was down there!"

The man frowned. "Shit. OK, let's get out of here, and then we can figure it out."

"No!" Andy cried, trying to pull her hand away. "By the time we do he could be dead! We have to go help him."

"Absolutely not. The captain would be furious if he found out I let his lady run into danger."

"I don't care! Let me go!"

When he only held on tighter, anger and panic took hold. Lifting his arm to her face, she bit down.

"Ah!" he cried, releasing her arm.

Immediately, she spun and took off in the other direction toward sector three. *Please,* she thought, *don't let me be too late.* She ran down aisle after aisle and through several bay doors until she saw a sign overhead that announced she had reached sector three.

As soon as she ran through the bay doors, smoke filled her vision. She coughed and waved her hand in front of her face, trying to clear it as much as she could.

"Allen! Allen, are you down here?"

"Andy!"

His voice came from the left, where she could just make out a venting valve that was on its side. The explosion must have knocked it over. She ran around the side of it and found Allen crouched down on the floor.

"Allen! Come on, we have to get out of here! They're going to close this place off."

"I can't! She's stuck."

For the first time Andy looked down. A young woman was lying on the floor, her legs trapped beneath the fallen valve.

"Shit. OK, let me help you."

"Andy, no, get out of here! You can't be here!"

She rounded on him. "I'm not leaving you down here, and I'm not leaving her. So, you can either help me or waste more time arguing."

Conflict flashed across his face for a moment, but then it settled into resolve. "All right. This beam seems to be what's holding her down. If we lift it enough, I think I'll be able to drag her out. On three."

Andy grabbed ahold of the place he indicated, allowing her left arm to take most of the strain.

"One, two, three!"

They both lifted, Andy using her legs to bear most of the weight. It lifted a few inches, and Allen began to pull her out with one hand while lifting with the other. She slid out slowly until her boots caught against the metal beneath the machine.

"Crap," Allen grunted. "We need to lift it more."

But just then, the sound of grinding made Andy turn her head. The metal door separating the sector from the rest of the ship was sliding down, about to lock them in. They would run out of oxygen in minutes.

"Allen! The door!"

"No, no, no!" A look of panic crossed his face as he looked down at the unconscious woman and then back at Andy. "Go! Save yourself! I can't leave her."

Andy looked to the door, which was now halfway down, and made a decision. She let go of the beam and made a run for the door. She slid beneath it, but rather than going all the way through, rolled onto her back just below it. Lifting her legs up, she placed the soles of her feet against the bottom of the panel. The metal of her legs was far stronger than any human bones, meant to hold up under intense pressure. But as soon as the panel pressed down against her, she knew they wouldn't hold for long.

"Allen!" she screamed. "Hurry! I can't hold it!"

As she lifted her head, she was able to see Allen give a hard yank. The young woman slid out, sans boots. Andy dropped her head back as a sharp pain shot through her body. The creaking of her metal joints left no question of the source of the pain. She couldn't hold it anymore. It was going to snap her legs. A scream ripped through her, a mixture of frustration and pain. She didn't notice the woman being slid past her. It wasn't until she felt two powerful hands grip her shoulders and pull her out from beneath the door that she opened her eyes.

Allen collapsed beside her, his breathing labored, and one arm still slung over her body. They lay there for several minutes, catching their breath. After what felt like a long time, Andy turned her head to look at Allen. His eyes were open, and he was watching her.

"Andromeda, you saved me."

She let out a broken laugh. "Well, I guess that makes us even then."

But Allen didn't look like he was joking. "You could have died. You never should have come down here. Why did you?"

"Someone told me there was an explosion in sector three. I knew you were down here. I couldn't leave you."

Emotion welled up in his eyes. "Andy..."

She looked away and tried to shrug it off, as though it didn't mean what they both knew it did. "You would have done the same thing if it were me."

He rested his forehead against her shoulder. "Yeah, I would have."

CHAPTER ELEVEN

Mars had looked Andy over and determined there would be no lasting damage, but that didn't stop the captain from insisting she rest for several days, just in case. He had been furious at first when he found out what she had done, but that hadn't lasted. In the end, he had even seemed impressed.

The other woman, Lorlee, Andy had learned, hadn't been so lucky. Both of her legs were broken. She would need to stay in a medical pod for several days until her vitals stabilized.

Currently, Andy sat on the edge of Mars's bed, watching as she danced around her room to the beat of some song Andy had never heard. Mars had switched out her long dark braids for hair of white silk, and Andy found herself mesmerized by the way it wound between Mars's fingers as she swayed to the beat.

"You've really never heard of this band?" Mars asked.

"Nope."

"Huh, weird. They were all over the stations a few years ago."

Andy shrugged, trying not to stare at the sway of Mars's hips. "Guess I was busy."

Mars peeked at her from beneath her lashes. "Don't you ever get tired of being busy? Don't you just want to go wild sometimes?"

Andy laughed. "I suppose. I just don't always have the chance."

"Well," Mars held out her hand. "You have the chance right now."

158 K. M. WATTS

There was only a moment of hesitation before Andy took Mars's hand and allowed her to pull their bodies flush together. Andy inhaled sharply. The smell of jasmine and clean clothes flooded her senses, and it took some self-control for Andy to not press her nose to Mars's neck and inhale. Mars began to lead them around the room in a dance, and Andy knew her face was flushed.

"You look quite cute when you get blushy."

Andy snorted and rolled her eyes. "Shut up."

"I mean it. Not to say you aren't always cute, but it's a nice bonus."

"You're a shameless flirt."

"So?" Mars asked, dropping Andy into a dip. "You don't seem to mind it."

Andy laughed as Mars spun away from her, only to twirl back and take Andy's hands once more. And no, she admitted to herself. She didn't mind it. Mars flashed her a smile, her eyes far too knowing for Andy's liking.

"How many times have you been romanced in your life?"

Andy scoffed. "Romanced? I haven't had much time for that."

Mars raised her eyebrows. "Well now, that's just a damn shame. Don't you think you deserve someone who wants to spend all their time with you? Someone who looks at you and knows without a doubt that you're the reason the sun continues to shine."

Andy lowered her eyes. "It's not as simple as that. Back home, I can't do things just because I want to."

A frown creased Mars's brow. "Why would you want to go back to that?"

"Because I have to. I can't stay here forever."

"Are you not happy here, Andy?"

"How can I be happy if being here isn't my choice?"

"And if you had the choice, what would you do?"

Andy opened her mouth, expecting to be sure of her answer. But when words didn't come, she closed her mouth again. Did she not know what she wanted? If someone had asked her even a week ago, she would have told them, with absolute certainty, that she wanted to go home. She wanted to be queen and marry Eden. It was what she had been told she would do all her life.

"I should want to go home and do my duty. I should follow the plan my parents set out for me."

"But can you ever be happy if that isn't your choice?"

Andy eyes widened, hearing her own words thrown back at her. "But it doesn't matter. I must do what's best for the majority. I can't just think of myself."

Mars's eyes drifted over Andy's face, her expression softening. "Who told you that?"

"I don't know, my parents, I suppose. But it's true. I can't put myself first."

"Andy," Mars said, lifting Andy's chin with the tips of her fingers, "I don't know your life. But I know what I've learned. And I've learned that if you don't take care of yourself first, you can't take care of anybody else. It's like trying to build a house from the roof down. Once you're happy, then you worry about others."

Andy stared at Mars in silence. Nobody had ever told her anything like that before. It had always been "for the kingdom," "for the future," "for the family." She couldn't recall anyone ever saying, "for you."

"So, Andy," Mars smiled. "What do you want?"

Andy sighed, looking away. "I don't know."

"That's good."

She scoffed. "How is that good?"

Mars released Andy's chin and took a step back. "Because, not knowing can open up so many wonderful possibilities that you never would have thought about if you were sure of yourself."

Later that evening, Andy stood at the window in the medical bay.

They had stopped at Station Twelve the day prior, but she had been forbidden from leaving the ship. The captain "didn't think she was ready." She hated being cooped up and was desperate to get out there again. They orbited Station Twelve, its enormous mass taking up the window she now looked out. She didn't hear Allen approaching from behind her.

"What are you thinking about?"

Andy turned and saw him standing near the door. "Nothing. I just—I miss my family. My mom especially."

He nodded. "I understand. I miss my family sometimes too."

"You must think me stupid. My family is at least out there waiting for me. Yours is gone."

He walked to her side and looked out the window. "I don't think you're stupid. The strange thing is, when I think of my family, I don't miss all of it. My mother, for instance. She was a difficult woman to please. I don't really remember her ever telling me she loved me. I think she saw me as more of an investment. My birth secured her the life that she wanted. And my brother, he was… difficult. An entitled little ass, I always called him. We never got along. But my father was great, always so happy. Nothing ever bothered him. I remember once when I was nine, I knocked over a bottle of red wine onto an expensive white rug that had been given to us as a gift. My mother was furious. She screamed at me. But my father just laughed. He said that spilling things was part of growing up, and it wouldn't matter ten years down the line."

"What happened to them?" Andy knew she shouldn't ask, but her curiosity was overwhelming.

Allen swallowed, his eyes distant. "There was a shipwreck. It killed everyone on board. I was the only one who wasn't there."

Andy's heart broke for him. "I'm sorry, Allen."

"Sometimes I-I wish I had been on that ship."

"Don't! Don't say that!"

"It's difficult to not blame myself."

"How can you blame yourself? It's not your fault."

"I just think if I had been there, maybe I could have done something. Maybe things would have gone differently. Nobody knows why it exploded. If I had been there, I could have saved them, I could have—"

"No. Stop it. Take it from someone who has been in a shipwreck and almost died. There was nothing you could have done. It happens so fast. The only thing that would have changed is that you would be dead too."

He nodded. "I know that you're right. And I try. Sometimes I don't think of them at all. Sometimes I go months without giving them a single thought. When that happens, I feel like the worst person in the world. But, when I don't think of them, I'm also my happiest."

Andy gave him a gentle smile and placed her hand on his arm. "That's understandable. Look, I've never gone through what you're describing, so I can't truly understand. Maybe you'll never fully get over it. But moving on is important."

He nodded, still looking out the window. "I know. What do you think I'm doing here on a pirate ship? Do you think I ever would have come here if something drastic hadn't happened in my life? That's why we're all here. Mars came here when her mother died. Her father came here when he discovered his wife was having an affair. Hell, even the captain came here after he killed his brother."

Andy looked at him in surprise. "You know about that?"

"Yeah, and he probably wouldn't be happy if he found out I knew. I overheard him talking to his first mate once." He leaned forward and gripped the wooden banister in front of the window. Andy turned so that her back was against it and watched his face.

"If you ever had the chance to leave, would you?"

Now it was his turn to look at her in surprise. "What?"

"I mean," she paused, thinking of how best to word what she was going to say. "If you and I were to get out of here, you could take me back home. We could go together. My father would reward you beyond measure. You could be named a lord, or you could ask for whatever you want."

He was silent for a moment, staring out the window. Before he spoke, he took a deep breath. "Andromeda, I—"

A loud crash from out in the hall interrupted whatever Allen was about to say. He straightened and rushed to the door, pulling it open and peering out. Andy leaned over his shoulder to get a look. Mars and Arlo both stood in the hall, Mars wearing a shin-length black trench coat and Arlo wearing slim-cut pants and a thick jacket. Mars had gold freckles drawn across the bridge of her nose and cheeks. Arlo had two large diamond earrings hung from their lobes, and they too had gold flecks sprinkled across their face. A large brown bag lay open at their feet with some sort of metal device sticking out from it.

Allen narrowed his eyes at them. "What are you two doing?"

"OK, OK, you caught us," Mars said, rolling her eyes. "We were coming to find you two anyway."

Andy raised her eyebrows. "Why are you two all dressed up?"

Mars looked down at her trench coat. "How could you tell?"

"Who just wears a trench coat around?"

Mars scrunched her lips to one side. "Huh, true. Anyway, like I said, we were looking for you."

"Why?" Allen asked.

"We're going to a party," Arlo said with a shrug. "We wanted to invite you."

This piqued Andy's interest. "A party? Where?"

"On Station Twelve. Baron Augusto is throwing his yearly birthday bash. We've never gone, but we've heard it's amazing. All the best people will be there."

"I'm not sure if you haven't noticed," Allen remarked, "but we aren't docked to Station Twelve right now."

Arlo rolled their eyes. "Of course, we've noticed. We're going to take a pod ship to port."

"Sorry, guys," Allen said, shaking his head, "but we can't go. Andy isn't allowed to leave the ship, captain's orders."

Andy shoved his shoulder. "Allen, come on! I'm so sick and tired of being on this ship!"

"I know, Andy, but if the captain found out—"

"He wouldn't," Mars cut in. "He's gone off-ship and won't be back for two days. We're just going for a few hours."

"Please, Allen. I know you can't help me escape, but you can at least try to make me not miserable."

Allen sighed, still looking unsure. "I don't know… "

"She'll be with you, Allen, and us," Arlo said. "She'll be completely safe."

Allen exhaled. "OK, fine. But only for a couple hours!"

"Yes!" Andy cried, leaping up and down. "Let me run to my room so I can get something to wear."

"Gotcha covered," Mars said, pulling something from the inside of her coat and throwing it to her. Andy caught it and held it up. It was a dress, but not like one she had ever worn. It had no full skirts or tight corset top but was instead slender and shimmery and the color of lavender. It was long, looking like it would hang to her ankles, but with a slit along the side.

Allen crossed his arm and tilted his head. "What about me?"

Arlo kicked the bag at their feet. "We're all set."

"And how are we going to get a pod ship?" Allen asked. "There's a guard watching over them, and I doubt he'll let us through if Andy's with us."

Mars flashed a smile. "Don't worry about that. Corbin was on duty, but we told him he was needed for an emergency in the lower engine rooms. We'll be gone by the time he gets back."

Sure enough, when they reached the pod ships there didn't appear to be anyone around. Mars snatched a key from a row of rings on the wall and swung it around her finger with a pleased grin. The four of them climbed into the nearest pod ship, with Mars immediately taking the seat in front of the controls. There was a hiss and a loud clanking sound as they detached from the ship.

"Andy, you can change in the bathroom if you like," Mars said over her shoulder.

Andy did as she was told and closed the bathroom door behind her. She took her clothes off and threw them into the corner, then pulled on the dress. It fit her body perfectly, though the neckline dipped down further than she was used to. The slit showed off her left leg, in all of its man-made perfection. She had no makeup, so her face was bare, and her black curls hung wild and free, falling just past her chest. She stepped out of the restroom to see that Allen had also changed. He wore a white shirt under a black coat with silver buttons on the collar, along with black fitted jeans. He looked up at her and smiled.

"Wow. You look great."

She gave him a wink. "You don't look half bad yourself."

He looked taken aback by her sudden flirtation, and to be honest, she was surprised herself.

"Here," Arlo said, pulling a round tin and brush from their pocket, "you both need a little something extra."

Arlo walked to Allen and dipped the brush into what Andy saw looked like gold paint and began tapping it onto Allen's nose and cheeks, giving him the same shimmery gold freckles the twins both sported. Allen remained still, allowing them to finish. Arlo then walked to Andy and did the same to her. When they finished, they took a step back and smiled.

"There, now you'll both fit right in."

Andy laughed. It was only now setting in what she was doing. The only parties she had ever been to were royal events, and even then she hadn't attended one since she was thirteen. Nerves twisted in her stomach, but she ignored them. She would be with Allen and Mars. She was only a little surprised when that thought comforted her.

"Andy, there are shoes in the bag for you as well," Mars said.

Sure enough, Andy found a pair of low black heels.

Mars flew the ship into the spaceport and landed. The doors of the port closed, and they were given the Ok to deboard. They each climbed out of the ship. Andy had expected the loud hustle and bustle from the first station, so she was surprised the find the place quiet.

"Where is everyone?" she asked, her hands beginning to flap in little aborted movements against her hips.

Mars took her hand and began leading them past the many parked ships. "They'll all be further in, where most of the pubs are. But don't worry, we'll skirt around and avoid the more unsavory parts altogether."

The deserted streets made Andy's stomach twist with unease. Somewhere far off she could hear music and voices, but where they walked there was nothing but tightly shuttered windows and locked doors. With each shadow, her mind made up a silent attacker. The flash of a blade in a dark alley, a cruel smile with wicked intentions. Without thinking, she squeezed Mars's hand.

Mars leaned in, her breath ghosting against Andy's ear. "Are you OK?"

"Hmm? Yeah, fine. Just a bit jumpy."

Mars pulled her a little closer. "Don't worry. We won't let anything happen to you. Besides, our destination is just up ahead."

Andy looked down the street and saw that the road was about to end. A wall that reached all the way to the ceiling, which rose at least a hundred feet above them, stood ahead. A large door, like that of an elevator, was right in the middle. Two armed guards stood to either side of it.

"What do you want?" one guard asked.

Mars stepped forward. "We're here to attend Baron Augusto's party."

"Invitation?"

Mars cast a look at Allen. "We, uh, we don't actually have one."

The guard glowered. "No invitation, no access."

Allen pushed past Mars and pulled something from his pocket. He held it up for the man to see, and Andy saw it was the lord captain's coin.

"I'm the first in command to Lord Captain Bran. He couldn't make it, so he sent us in his stead." Both guards frowned, seeming unsure. After a moment and a glace between the two, they shrugged.

"Fine."

One guard ran a card over a screen and the doors opened. The four of them piled in.

"Press ten," the guard instructed before the doors closed. Mars pressed the button, and Andy immediately felt a strong force propel them upward. A few seconds later, they came to a halt. When the doors slid open, Andy's senses were bombarded with a collision of sight and sound. The rest of her group seemed unfazed, each walking out of the elevator. Not wanting to be left behind, she hurried after them. They stood in a massive hall with marble and gold columns as tall as the towering ceiling. The light for the enormous room came from at least forty massive chandeliers, all of them dripping with diamonds.

The room thumped with music, with hundreds of people moving in time with it. Around the room, Andy could see men and women pressed against the walls. She had a tough time discerning where one person ended and the other began, and quickly pulled her eyes away from them.

"Well," Mars said with a smirk, "I see a whole lot of ways for me to get into trouble, and there simply isn't enough time. If you all will excuse me."

With that she was off, gliding away into the crowd.

"She's right. So much to do, so little time." Arlo gave them a wink and disappeared as well.

Andy and Allen were left standing alone. Allen shifted on his feet, then turned to her. "Do you want to get a drink from the bar?"

Andy shrugged. "Sure."

They made their way to the bar, where Allen ordered two drinks. He slid one to her and she peered into the cup. It was pink and bubbly, with a strong alcohol fragrance. She took a sip and wished she hadn't.

"Oh my God, what is this?" she coughed.

Allen laughed. "I don't know, I asked for their special."

"It tastes like ship fuel."

"It would probably be best to drink it in one go. On the count of three?"

She nodded, putting the cup to her lips, and wrinkling her nose.

"One, two, three." They both downed what remained in their cups. Andy shuddered and Allen grimaced.

Andy shook her head. "That was unpleasant."

Allen hummed in agreement. He turned to look at the dance floor. "Do you want to dance?"

She raised her eyebrows. "You dance?"

"Eh, when the occasion arises, I've been known to take a few spins through the room."

Andy hummed and held up her hand for him to take, a smile fighting for a place on her face. "Well then, by all means."

There was mirth in Allen's eyes as he guided her onto the dance floor. Andy had thought she knew how to dance, but she'd never seen people move the way these did. She could waltz circles around most, but the people around her certainly weren't waltzing. They wove their bodies in and out, circling each other with hands that roamed wherever they pleased. She spotted Mars a short distance away between both a man and a woman, and she danced in a way that was almost trancelike. Her hips did most of the moving, though her hands and arms also snaked around hers and the others' bodies. She twisted slowly, her eyes closed, and her head thrown back. The overhead lights glistened off her perfect skin, bringing out every rich tone. She was stunning. She glanced back at Allen and saw that he was watching her with a small smirk.

"You don't know what you're doing, do you?" he asked.

She grimaced. "I don't have much experience with this sort of thing."

"Here, this should be more comfortable for you."

He took her left hand in his right and pulled her hips toward him with his left. She was surprised for only a moment, before placing her right hand around his arm. They drifted back and forth, making their way in a gradual circle. He was right, this was more comfortable for her. She smiled up at him and realized they were quite close.

"Is that better?"

"Yeah, this—this is good."

The corner of his lip pulled up into a smirk, drawing her attention to the light freckling along the bridge of his nose, only noticeable in the right light. She was closer now than she had ever been. When she had first met him, she'd thought he was generally attractive, but now... His gentle, persistent kindness had chipped something inside her. A crack in the walls she had so carefully constructed. Her heart gave a hard thud in her chest and she looked away.

What was she doing? She shouldn't be thinking these things about him. Her heart shouldn't beat harder when looking at him. But it did. And sometimes when he smiled, she felt like he was really seeing her, not the façade she had spent so long building. As though he cared for her in the same way she cared for him. Her face burned as she stared a hole in his chest, refusing to look back at his face.

This couldn't be right. She'd thought she could develop feelings for Eden, but she certainly hadn't felt this way. This was different. The thought of kissing Allen made her feel a little queasy, but not in a bad way. Not in a way that meant she didn't want to kiss him.

"Andy?"

They had gone still, and he was looking at her with concern. She blinked several times, forcing herself to concentrate.

"What?"

"Are you OK? You look strange."

"Oh, yeah, I'm fine. I'm just feeling a little warm."

He looked away from her, toward one wall. "Here, come with me."

She frowned. "Why?"

He smiled and held out his hand. "Just trust me."

Andy took it. She did trust him. He pulled her through the thick crowd of people. They wound their way to the outer walls, where Allen led her to a curtained doorway.

"Allen, I don't think we're supposed to go in there."

He smirked at her over his shoulder. "Who's going to stop us?"

She looked around and saw that he was right. Nobody was paying them any attention, all too caught up in their own pleasures. She followed Allen through the curtain. Beyond the doorway was a long, high-ceilinged hall, like one she would find in her own castle. Allen led her down it quickly, then came to an abrupt stop outside a door to the left. He tried the handle, but found it was locked.

"Allen, where are you taking me?"

He pulled a metal lock pick from his pocket and began twisting and turning it. "You'll see."

Andy looked down the hall to make sure nobody was coming. "Have you been here before?"

The lock gave a click, and the door swung open. "Once."

He pulled her inside and closed the door behind them. Andy turned and saw with a shock that they were in a large, ornate bedroom. Why would Allen bring her here? Her stomach twisted uncomfortably again. Had she been wrong to trust him? But he didn't stop in the room, instead pulling her through it to a set of double doors. He pushed them open, and Andy stepped out into the night sky. It wasn't the real night sky, of course, just the ceiling of the station that had been designed to look like it, but it was still beautiful.

A large terrace stretched out in front of her, with potted plants that lined a banister, and green grass grew across the ground. She slid her shoes off and stepped onto it, finding it soft. She smiled at Allen.

"This is beautiful."

"I thought you'd like it. I found it the last time I was here, about a year ago."

She quirked one eyebrow. "Were you with a date?"

He laughed. "No, no date. The lord captain had a meeting with the baron, and I accompanied him. I found this by accident while looking around."

He kicked his shoes off as well and walked further onto the terrace. Andy followed him.

Allen looked up, the artificial stars reflected in his eyes. "I always found it fascinating how they can mimic the night sky. If I didn't know any better, I'd think we were outside on Earth."

Andy leaned forward, resting her arms on the banister. "We have something similar on Celestine." She inhaled deeply through her nose. "If I close my eyes, I can almost pretend I'm on my terrace over my gardens. I can almost smell the Andromedas."

She opened her eyes and saw that Allen had his closed as well.

A small, almost sad smile rested on his lips. He nodded. "And I can almost smell the orange blossoms that used to grow near my childhood home."

When he opened his eyes, he looked momentarily lost. As though for a split second he had thought he really was back at his childhood home. Andy placed her hand on his shoulder.

"Have you ever thought of going back? To where you grew up?"

He looked at her and gave her that sad smile again, shaking his head. "I can never go back."

"Would the captain never let you?"

He sighed. "It has nothing to do with that."

Andy waited for him to explain further, and when he didn't, she looked away.

"Well, enough with the depressing thoughts."

He dropped back onto the grass, resting one arm behind his head. Andy lifted the sides of her dress and joined him on the ground. They lay like that, together, for a while. Allen shifted beside her, and his hand brushed against hers. There went her heart again, pounding away. Part of her wanted to pull back, to remove the contact between them, but another, stronger part had gone completely still. Had he done that on purpose? She dared to turn her head slightly, to see his expression. He seemed to notice, as he turned to look at her at the same time. Their faces were only a few inches apart, and Andy found that once her eyes locked onto his, she couldn't look away.

Andy tried to ignore the insane part of her mind that was practically begging her to kiss him. If this was a normal situation and he was a normal guy, she would have no qualms. But this wasn't normal. He was a pirate, and she was a princess. She was engaged.

"To a man you barely know," her mind pushed. *"To a man you don't love. To a man you never have to see again, if you wish."*

She forced herself to look away. What the hell was she thinking?

She couldn't leave behind everything she had ever known. She couldn't give up her title of being queen. For what? A man?

"For something real. For something you chose. For freedom."

She closed her eyes. What was she doing? Why, out of all the people she had ever known, was her heart begging her to want this one? What was it about him that made every molecule in her body yearn to roll over and press her mouth to his? Why was her heart wanting something it could never truly have?

"Andromeda?"

Andy jumped a little at him calling her by her full name. When she looked at him, he was watching her with a pained sort of expression.

She wanted to sound normal, but when she spoke her throat was dry, and her voice came out hoarse. "Yes?"

He rolled over so that he was on his elbow, looking down at her. His head partially blocked out the stars. Having him over her, with his eyes roaming her face, made her head swim.

"Andy, are you afraid of me?"

She frowned. How could she ever be afraid of him? In fact, she had never been less frightened by anyone in her entire life.

"What are you talking about?"

"It's just, recently, every time you get close to me or look me in the face for too long, you look away like you're afraid."

Andy raised her eyebrows, realization dawning on her. He had misconstrued her sudden onslaught of feelings for fear. She couldn't help but laugh a little. His brow creased.

"What's so funny?"

Without thinking, she lifted her left hand to his cheek. Almost immediately, she wished she hadn't, but it was too late. Allen's eyes widened, and he sucked in a breath. She slid her fingers slowly over his cheekbones, her fingertips prickling with the sensation. Allen didn't move. He just stared down at her, a vast range of emotion showing on his face.

"I'm not afraid, Allen."

He swallowed hard. "That makes one of us."

"Why would you be afraid of me?"

He lifted his free hand to hers, pressing it into his cheek. "I don't think I've ever been as frightened as when I'm with you, Andromeda."

She stared up at him and knew this was her moment. This was when she should lean up and kiss him. She pushed forward, so that she was resting on both her elbows.

"Allen—"

Before she could say another word, a blaring alarm went off within the palace, causing Allen to leap away from her. He jumped to his feet and pulled her up with him.

"What is that?" she asked, concern making her pulse quicken.

Allen shook his head. "Nothing good."

CHAPTER TWELVE

ANDY AND ALLEN PULLED ON their shoes and raced back inside. Once out in the hall, they saw people running frantically past them.

"What's going on?" she shouted over the alarm.

"I don't know, but it must be bad. A lot of these people are likely on this station illegally, so it would take something big for the baron to set off the alarm and alert the station police. Otherwise, he wouldn't risk angering his wealthy illegal friends."

He took her hand and pulled her in the opposite direction of the main hall. "I need to get you out of here, and we need to find Mars and Arlo."

They reached the end of the hall and saw that it split into several others.

"Do you know a way out besides the front entrance?" she asked.

He didn't answer, but the concerned expression on his face made her think he didn't. "Allen, what are we going to do?"

"Don't worry," he said, touching the gun at his hip, "nobody's going to harm you."

"Give me a weapon. I can defend myself."

"I would if I could, but unfortunately this is the only gun I have on me."

"Allen, Andy!"

They both turned and saw the twins running at them from a side hall. "There you are!" Mars exclaimed. "We've been looking everywhere for you."

"Mars, what's going on?" Allen asked.

The twins exchanged a look, and Allen's face went from concerned to furious. "What the hell did you two do?"

Before they could answer, someone shouted behind them, "Hey, you four, stay where you are!"

Andy whipped her head around and saw five guards racing toward them.

"Run!" Mars cried, and they all took off. Mars, Arlo, and Allen were all quick, but not as quick as Andy. She pulled ahead of the others, her hair flying away from her face, and her dress whipping around her. Even though they were possibly running for their lives, for the first time in a while, Andy felt great. She smiled and turned to make sure the others were still behind her. They were, with Allen being the closest. He looked frightened, but when he saw her smile, a laugh replaced his look of fear.

"Turn left ahead!" Arlo shouted, and they did as they said. They raced down several long halls, with the shouts of the guards never too far behind them.

"Stop at the third door ahead!" Arlo instructed. They slid to a stop and Arlo pulled a set of keys from the inside of their coat. They jammed one key into the lock and shoved the door open. They all piled inside, and Mars shut it behind them. A moment later there was shouting in the hall, then several footsteps ran past. Andy's heart pounded similarly to how it had earlier, only now adrenaline also pumped through her. She looked around as her eyes adjusted to the dark and saw they were in a small storage closet. How were they supposed to get out of here? Allen turned on the twins and repeated his earlier question.

"What did you two do?"

Even in the dark room, Andy could see they both looked guilty and worried. "It wasn't supposed to happen like this."

"*What* wasn't?"

Arlo gave the bag on their shoulder a bit of a shake. "We had heard stories of the incredible and rare riches that belonged to Baron Augusto. We knew this was our opportunity."

Allen's eyes widened and he clenched his teeth. "This was a *job*? Why the hell did you invite Andy and me?"

When the twins were silent, Andy answered for them. "They needed your clearance coin."

Allen looked from her to them, understanding coming over him. "Oh my God. I cannot believe you two."

"We're sorry! But like we said, this wasn't supposed to happen this way!" Mars whispered.

"I can understand endangering me and yourselves, but Andy? What were you two thinking?"

"We knew you wouldn't leave her to come to a party, and we knew she would want to come. We were going to give you both a cut. From what we heard, it would have been enough for you to buy your own ship, Allen."

But Allen didn't seem to be listening. "You've put Andy's life in danger."

"Allen, just listen," Arlo begged. "We've been planning this for a month. We found out where the best of the baron's treasures were and what security measures protected them. Lorlee and I developed software that would allow me to get around all of them. And it did, it worked perfectly!"

"If it worked so perfectly," Allen snarled, "then why are we hiding in a cupboard?"

"Well, we didn't anticipate there being a second security measure. I accidentally triggered it when I took the items."

Andy raised her hands, trying to calm the situation. "So now what, we're just going to die in here?"

Mars rolled her eyes. "Of course not. We had a backup plan if something like this happened."

"And would you mind cluing us in to that plan?" Allen asked.

"Do you think we came to this specific room for its view?" Arlo asked.

They walked to the back of the closet and pushed boxes and cleaning supplies out of the way. Soon Andy noticed an unmistakable outline on the wall of a small door. It only came up to their hips, but it was still a door.

"This is an old laundry chute they used for the working staff. It was decommissioned years ago, but it should still lead out to the same place."

"Where does this one let out?"

Mars made a face like she'd rather not say. "On Level Two."

Allen's face looked stricken. "Level Two?"

"What?" Andy asked. "What's wrong with Level Two?"

"That's slum level. A massive city filled with the worst of the worst. It's heavily guarded, to not let the filth interact with normal people of higher levels. It'll be difficult to get out and back to our ship."

"Not to mention those guards saw us and will send scouts everywhere to find us. None of us have discreet looks," Arlo said.

Allen sighed. "Well, we have a better shot out there than we do standing in a closet."

Arlo opened the door to reveal a metal chute. "I'll go first." They sat down and slid their long legs through the door, then turned and lowered themself until just their hands and head were visible. "Drop my bag down after me." Mars nodded, and Arlo let go. They were gone in an instant. Mars went next, doing as Arlo had done. Now Andy knew it was her turn. She sat down at the chute's edge and peered down. It was an endless, dark hole. She turned and lowered herself, looking back up at Allen.

"It's OK," he assured. "I'll be coming right behind you."

Andy took a deep breath, then let go. Her stomach lurched into her throat as she free-fell straight down. She felt like she was falling for a long time before the metal of the chute pressed against her back and she realized she was sliding, though steeply. Eventually it flattened out, and before she was ready, she shot out into an open space. She skidded across the floor and landed with a thud against a wall. When she looked up, she saw Mars and Arlo were both on their feet. Mars helped her up and gave her arm a comforting squeeze. A moment later, Allen slid out of the chute and hit the same wall Andy had. Once they were all on their feet, Andy looked around.

They were in a small one-room house. There was one window against the far wall, though it was too dirty to see through. In fact, the whole room was covered in several layers of dust. There was no furniture, and just a single door.

Allen walked to the window and rubbed his sleeve against it, trying to see out. "It looks like this leads out to a street."

"The streets will be mostly empty at this time, since morning won't come for a couple hours," Arlo said.

"Should we try to get out now?" Andy asked.

Allen shook his head. "No, the four of us would stick out like a beacon. They'd catch us within minutes. We'll go once the streets fill up."

"Besides, we can't go out there dressed like this," Mars said, pointing to her and Andy's dresses. "Once the shops open, Allen can buy us all some common clothes. We might as well get some rest until then."

Arlo dropped the bag onto the floor and settled down beside it. Mars sat beside them, resting her head against the wall. Allen walked to the opposite side of the room and rested against the corner, where Andy joined him.

"I'm so sorry for this, Andy," he said quietly.

"It's fine, it's not your fault."

"No, it is. I should never have agreed to let you go off the ship. I knew it was dangerous."

"Allen, I asked you to let me leave. And I'm glad you did. I mean, I'm not glad we're in this situation, but I needed to get out."

He nodded. "You were never meant to be caged."

She huffed. "You make me sound like some sort of animal."

"Aren't we all?"

"You are seriously so dramatic." She rolled her head so she was looking at him. "We'll be OK, Allen. We'll get out of this. You'll be fine."

"I'm not worried for myself."

"You don't need to worry about me," she insisted.

"Of course I do. That's all I've done since I met you."

She shook her head. "Why?"

"What do you mean?"

"Why have you been worrying about me since you met me? You didn't even know me at first. I know that you said it was because you were covering for your crew, and you didn't want to get caught by the royal guard, but ever since we met, I've felt like there was something more. What aren't you telling me?"

He stared into her eyes for several seconds. "Andy, there are things I've done that you wouldn't understand. Horrible things that I will never be able to live down. When I first saw you, I was worried that my past would get dragged back up with you. I really did try to get you out for my benefit."

"And now?"

"What do you mean?"

Andy spoke quietly. "Do you still want to get me out of your life?"

His eyes crinkled at the corners. "No, Andy, I don't."

"What about your past?"

"It could still get dragged up, but… "

Andy waited. "But what?"

Allen looked away. "Nothing. Get some sleep, Andy."

She sighed. "I won't be getting much rest on this hard floor."

"You can rest your head against my shoulder, if you want."

She chewed her bottom lip, then nodded. "OK."

She leaned against his shoulder and took comfort in his warmth. The smell of his cologne filled her head, and soon she drifted off. When she awoke, she wasn't sure whether she had been asleep for minutes or hours. There was much more light in the room now, and she could hear hundreds of voices outside. Allen was also gone from beside her, and Arlo's bag was beneath her head. She sat up and pulled her fingers through her wild curls, then spotted Mars beside the window. She seemed to hear Andy's rustling and turned.

"Andy, good, you're up. Allen and Arlo just left to buy us some clothes."

Mars helped Andy to her feet. "How long have they been gone?"

"Not long. Don't worry," Mars said, wrapping her arm around Andy's shoulder. "This is pretty standard, nothing they haven't done before."

But as an hour came and went, neither could help but worry. After an hour and a half, Andy began to pace.

"They should have been back by now, shouldn't they have?"

Mars chewed on her lip but didn't answer. By the time two hours came, Mars was on her feet as well. When the door to the room finally opened, Andy couldn't help the loud sigh of relief at seeing Allen's face. He and Arlo slid into the room and closed the door behind them.

"What the hell took you two so long?" Mars snapped. "We thought you were dead."

"Psh, like those imbeciles could catch us," Arlo said with a wink.

"It's not funny, Arlo!" Mars shouted. "What happened?"

"We bought the items we needed and were coming back when we noticed at least twenty guards along this street. We had to circle back and wait for them to clear out," Allen explained.

Mars huffed, not seeming satisfied. She yanked the bag from Arlo's hands and began pulling out garments and throwing them to Andy. Andy caught a pair of brown baggy pants and a white tank top, as well as a black short sleeve button up that seemed to be missing all its buttons.

"Are you sure we'll fit in?" she asked.

Allen laughed. "Oh yeah. If anything, we'll be overdressed."

In the end, they were all adorned in similarly baggy and mismatched clothes. Mars twisted her hair into a bun and pulled a cap on to cover the rest. When they were finally ready to go, Allen stood in front of her.

"All right, before we head out, there are a few things you should know. Don't look anyone in the face for too long, it can draw their attention to you. But also, don't seem like you're avoiding attention, as that can also seem like you're hiding something. Just try to act natural and like you belong. OK?"

Andy wanted to point out that she didn't know how to act natural, since she had never been in this environment before, but decided they didn't have time for that. Instead, she simply nodded.

Allen sighed, still looking nervous. "Right. Let's go."

He opened the door, and they all stepped out into the light. The first thing Andy noticed was the heat. It was far warmer at this level than it had been higher up. Allen noticed her discomfort.

"The main engines are built around this level, so this is where most of the heat goes," he explained.

It didn't help that the street was packed with more people than Andy had ever seen. She had thought the shopping level on Station Fourteen had been full, but that was nothing compared to this. Thousands of people filled the streets, bodies pushing against bodies, all shouting over each other to be heard. She hadn't been able to tell from the inside of their room, but the buildings all seemed to have been stacked on top of each other. Rather than glass, some windows had been covered in cloth and blankets, while others stood open and empty. There were no gaps between the buildings, instead it looked like there was one massive wall with windows and doors all built haphazardly into it. Covered stalls lined the streets, their colored tarps offering shade to the disgruntled salespeople beneath.

Allen took her hand firmly in his as they made their way through the crowd. Andy kept her eyes down, not wanting to draw attention to their unique color. Though it seemed no one had the time to pay her any attention.

A group of men to her left argued loudly over the price of what looked like a pile of silver teeth. Several children darted through the crowd, all looking like they resided in a dumpster. A small girl who wasn't paying attention ran right into Andy's legs, causing her to fall backward onto the ground. The small girl looked up with wide, startled eyes. Andy smiled and reached down to help her up, but as she did, the girl flinched and raised her arm to protect her face. Andy stopped. The girl thought she was going to hurt her. Andy crouched, to not startle her.

"Are you OK?" she asked gently.

The girl opened her eyes and peered at her from beneath her arm. When she didn't answer, Andy slowly held out her hand. The girl stared at her hand for a moment before reluctantly taking it. Andy helped the girl to her feet and smiled. Before Andy could ask her any more questions, the girl turned and disappeared into the crowd. Andy straightened up and looked around. It took only a second for her to realize Allen and the twins were gone. She twisted in a circle, her heart pounding in her throat. She looked in every direction, panic seeping into her heart. They were gone. She was alone.

CHAPTER
THIRTEEN

She had stopped for only a moment, but the crowd seemed to swarm and shift around her. She stood on the tips of her toes, trying to see over the heads of the crowd.

"Are you all right?"

Andy turned and came face to face with a tall, handsome man. A dark, well-groomed beard covered the bottom half of his face, and his eyes were a cool green. When their eyes met, his smile widened.

"Wow, I've never seen eyes such as yours."

She smiled, trying to hide her panic. "Thank you."

"Sorry if I've bothered you, but you looked lost. You're not from here, are you?"

Andy stretched her neck, still looking around. "Uh, no, I'm not. I was with some friends, but they seem to have disappeared."

"Ah, I see," the man said and nodded. "Well, there's no need to panic. My name's Juper."

He held out his hand, and Andy shook it. "Andy."

"Lovely name," he said with a wink.

He was flirting with her, and she knew that flirting back was the best way to get him to help her. She smiled. "Thank you. I'm afraid I don't know my way around here very well. Is there any way I could get to the top of these buildings so that I might catch a glimpse of my friends?"

"Well, you'll need permission from the owner of the building to go to the top. But come with me, and I'll see what I can do."

Andy fell in step with him as he headed toward a group of buildings.

"So, lovely Andy, what brings you to the slums of Station Twelve?"

She thought quickly. "I came to visit some family."

Juper scoffed. "You must really love your family to pay to come here. Nearly everyone was born or brought here against their will."

"Yes, well, family is important."

"That it is," he agreed.

"Do you have any family here?"

He gave a quick tilt of his head. "Oh, you know, here and there. Here, let's go in this shop. I know the owner."

He led her into a dimly lit shop with a small front parlor. She couldn't tell from the décor what they sold.

"Take a seat there while I go ask my friend about using the roof," he said, motioning to a red velvet couch.

Andy did as he said and watched as he disappeared through a curtain. She looked around the small front room. A gold chandelier hung from the ceiling, and a matching red velvet couch sat across from her. The room smelled nice, if not a bit overpowering, like perfume. There were pictures along the walls of men and women throughout the ages. It seemed as if this were part of some organization or club. A minute later, Juper returned and gave her a warm smile.

"Right, it's all sorted. We can go up." He opened a door that led to a staircase and motioned for her to go ahead.

She stepped up to the door but stopped. A twinge of unease settled in her stomach. She didn't know this man. Allen would have told her not to trust anyone. But her only other option now was to push past him and go back out the front door, and then she may never find Allen and the others. So, she walked up the stairs. Juper followed and closed the door behind him. Andy's pulse quickened. She marched up the stairs and stopped at the landing at the top. Hopefully, this door led out onto the roof and she was worrying for nothing. Juper opened the door and bright lights momentarily blinded her. She sighed with relief. They were on the roof after all. But as she stepped through the door, her heart sank. This was no roof.

What looked like an examination room was set up in front of her. Metal panels lined the walls, and bright florescent lights were set into the ceiling. In the middle of the room sat a raised chair with manacles on the armrests and where the legs would go. She spun around at the sound of the door closing and a lock clicking into place. Juper dropped a key into his pocket and turned to smile at her.

"Thank you for making this so much easier for me."

Andy swallowed. "What the hell is this? What are you doing?"

He ignored her and walked to a counter along the wall where he removed his coat. When he turned back to her, he had a syringe in his hand. She immediately backed up, real fear and panic settling in. What the hell sort of sick things was this man into?

"So, tell me, how have you survived this long?"

She blinked. "What?"

He motioned to her eyes. "Your condition, moon sickness. How are you still alive?"

"I-I don't know," she answered honestly. Was that what this was about? He wanted to experiment on her?

"It's quite impressive, really. Did your mother hide you away? Have they come looking for you?"

Andy continued to back away from him as he circled her. He was looking at her as though she were a particularly interesting bug on his table.

"I have no idea what the hell you're talking about. Has who come looking for me?"

He acted as though he hadn't heard her. "What sort of things can you do?"

Andy moved to the other side of the chair. "I seriously have no idea what you're talking about. You have the wrong person."

"Ah," he said with a tilt of his head. "No, I don't think I do. Those eyes tell me everything I need to know about what you are."

"What I am? I'm human!"

He tapped a long, well-manicured finger against the arm of the chair. "Hmm, in a way, yes. Is it really possible that you don't know?"

"That I don't know what?" she shouted, anger and fear building inside of her.

"You would have to have led an extremely sheltered life, certainly not here. I admit, I am quite curious about you. You truly don't know what moon sickness is? What you are?"

She shook her head. "Nobody does."

He smiled now, as though incredibly pleased to have a secret. "Well, that's not true. I know, as do many others. I've never personally had an adult subject before, so this will be remarkably interesting for me. I thank you for that."

He advanced toward her, walking with purpose around the chair. Andy raced around him to the door, but that was no use. It was still locked. She spun back around as he approached.

"There is no need to be afraid. You won't feel a thing. I'll be gentle."

She clenched her fists. "Yeah? Well, I won't be."

As soon as he was close enough, she kicked out directly for his knee. When her foot made contact, he cried out and fell to the floor. She tried to run past him, but his hand shot out and caught her by the ankle. A harsh tumble to the floor nearly knocked the breath out of her, but she didn't let that stop her. She couldn't. It was clear that this was life or death.

Juper rolled over and grabbed her by the knee with one hand, the other fumbling with the needle. Andy surged away from him. If he got her with that needle, she was done. As she scrambled away, he moved after her.

He no longer wore a smile, his face instead twisted with fury. "Get back here, you little wretch!"

"Get the hell away from me!"

She tried to stand, but he took a handful of her hair and dragged her back down. He pinned her to the floor, his knees on either side of her and his full weight on her knees, rendering her legs useless.

"All right," he huffed, "I was going to be gentle, but not anymore. I'll only give you a half dose of this, so you'll be awake just enough to feel me taking you apart. There will be plenty of people who will be happy to own a piece of you."

He brought the needle down as she brought her left arm up. But rather than sinking into soft flesh, as he had expected, it clinked against the hard metal that lined the top of her forearm. A look of complete befuddlement crossed his face as Andy smiled widely. In a single movement, she knocked the needle out of his hand and struck him fully in the face. He fell off her enough for her to regain control. She flipped on top of him, the syringe now in her hand.

"Nobody's going to own me, asshole."

With a swift push, she stuck the needle into his neck and pressed the plunger. His eyes went wide for a moment, then his whole face went lax, and he collapsed back onto the floor, unconscious.

Andy fell off him and tried to regain her breath and get her racing heart under control. But she couldn't lie there for long. She had no clue if he was alone or if he had other accomplices waiting for him to give a signal. Once on her feet, she fished the key out of his pocket and ran to the door. She unlocked it and ran out onto the landing, locking the door behind her. She had no clue how long whatever had been in that syringe would leave him unconscious.

Andy raced down the stairs and into the sitting area, finding it empty. She ran to the door and threw it open, stepping out into the hot air of the midday crowd and pushed her way through the swarms of people, not thinking of where she was going. She just wanted to get as far from that place as she could. When she finally stopped to lean against a shaded wall, she had no clue where she was. The heat was making her feel lightheaded, and it didn't help that she'd had nothing to drink since yesterday. Her thick hair felt like a fur coat, wet and stuck to her skin. She piled it all on top of her head. A small breeze caressed her damp back, and she let out a sigh. She needed a plan. She had no doubt that Allen and the twins were looking for her. But how on earth were they going to find her?

Her only option was to do something drastic and showy. But that would risk the station security coming down on her. She could tell them who she was. Well, not who she *really* was, but that she was the captain's lady. Although, with all the corruption Allen had told her lived in these outer stations, there was no guarantee that would bring her safety. She leaned against the wall and closed her eyes. What the hell was she going to do?

A sudden explosion of sound made her eyes snap back open. A half mile down the road, from the direction she had just come, about a dozen fireworks seemed to have gone off at one of the shops. Allen? She took off in that direction. People shouted as she shoved them out of her way. She reached the firework shop but slid to a stop before getting too close. Several security officers already stood outside, guns drawn. A disgruntled old man, the shop owner she presumed, was waving his arms furiously over his head. She inched closer, trying to hear what he was saying.

"Stupid kids, thinkin' it's funny to ruin my livelihood! I tried to get my gun, but they were gone before I could reach it!"

"Shut it, old man!" one officer snapped. "We don't care about your damn shop. What did these kids look like?"

"There were three of them. Two guys and a girl. I guess they weren't really kids exactly, maybe in their late teen or early twenties."

"Come on, give us a description!" another officer shouted, becoming impatient.

The shopkeeper now looked nervous, realizing that these men weren't here to help him. "W-Well, one was tall with red hair and tan skin, a guy. Then there was another guy and a girl, both with dark skin and mismatched clothes, all at least six feet tall."

The officers turned to each other. "That matches the description of those thieves."

"But there were four of them. You sure you didn't see another one, old man?"

"N-No. Just saw the three."

The officers turned and walked away without another word. The old man, still looking flustered, turned and began making his way back into his shop. Andy needed to know which way Allen and the twins had gone. She walked toward the shop. Before she could reach the door, a hand clamped around her arm and dragged her into the narrow alleyway in between the shops. She spun around to fight, thinking Juper had caught up to her. Instead, in the dim light of the shadows, was Allen.

She let out a sigh of relief. "Thank God! Where did you go?"

"Me? Where did *you* go?" he whispered furiously. "We were walking, and I thought you were beside me. When I turned around, you were gone! I've been having a heart attack for the past hour!"

"I'm sorry! I stopped for only a minute."

"Don't do that! Do you know what could have happened to you?"

"Yes, I do, actually," she said. "There was a man. He said he would help me, but he didn't. He took me to this place that looked like a lab—and, Allen, he said some strange things. He said he knew about my moon sickness and something about people coming for me and that I shouldn't have lived this long. It was so strange."

Allen shook his head. "Andy, he was probably just crazy. There are a lot of people out here that aren't exactly in their right minds."

Andy frowned and looked away. She didn't want to argue, but she didn't think so. "I think he was going to kill me."

"I told you it was dangerous out here. You can't trust anybody. But there are more pressing matters, we need to get out of here."

Andy peered down the alley. "Where are the twins?"

"After we set off the fireworks, we couldn't all stand around and look conspicuous. They ran up the street to hide, and I waited here for you."

"Well, let's go get them so that we can get out of here."

She took him by his hand and led him back out into the busy street. Allen's eyes moved everywhere, looking for any sign of trouble.

"Where exactly did they go?" she asked.

"We didn't have time to talk specifics. They said they would go ahead and wait for us."

Andy looked up at each of the towering buildings they passed. Their mismatched materials gave the impression of a dollhouse made by a creative yet chaotic child. Some buildings leaned so much that the top halves pressed against their neighbors.

Andy brought her eyes back to the people on the streets. Those who were lucky enough to work in the shops and covered carts seemed well enough off. But for every one person she saw working a stall, there were at least five people sitting in the streets or against buildings who looked like they hadn't eaten in days. Their ragged clothes hung on their thin frames, some barely by threads. Children stood in the middle of the street, each with their tiny hands raised, dull eyes looking for someone who would help them. But as far as Andy saw, nobody did. People pushed past, their eyes never even dipping down to acknowledge them.

"How can people live like this?" Andy looked at Allen, realizing he likely didn't know what she was talking about, but he didn't look confused. His eyes were on the children as well.

"They know nothing else. They were born into a society that ignores their existence, while also relying on it. From the time they breathe their first breath they're told they have no place. But it's human nature to want more, to find a place to belong."

"Why don't they get out?"

The look Allen gave her was full of pity and anger, though she didn't feel like it was directed at her. "How? No kingdom even recognizes this place's existence. To buy legal papers and enter a society would cost more than these people will ever see in their lifetimes. Those that are wealthy here don't want to leave, and they don't want those who are poor to get out. They rule like kings, even though they hold no title other than the one they gave themselves. They thrive off the misfortune and squalor these people live in. None of them ever stood a chance."

Andy looked back at the children. "If the kingdoms know they're here, why don't they do something about it?"

Allen laughed humorlessly. "Because kindness isn't profitable."

Andy wished she could argue in the defense of her lineage, but he was right. They knew about this and did nothing. It was reprehensible. And if she were being truly honest with herself, would she have even cared if she hadn't seen this with her own eyes? She couldn't be sure.

"Hey! You two! Stop right there!"

They turned and saw four guards rushing toward them through the crowd. Without saying a word, Allen took her hand, and they ran. They moved through the crowd, Allen being surprisingly agile for his size.

"Where are we going to go?" she shouted.

Allen didn't answer. They came upon a crossroads between the buildings, and Allen immediately pulled her left. They rushed down this new street, though it looked an awful lot like the street they had just come from. The only noticeable difference seemed to be that several of the tall, haphazard buildings appeared to be abandoned.

"Allen, let's go in one of those!" she said, pointing to the empty-looking building.

He looked to where she pointed, but shook his head.

Andy frowned. "What, do you have a better idea?"

"Yeah, I do."

They continued to push through the streets, but as they went, Andy noticed fewer and fewer people. Andy hadn't thought it was possible, but the further they went the shabbier the buildings became. They had left the market setting, and these building looked like they could have once been apartments. They were all made from the same sheet metal, and it looked like someone had precariously stacked them on top of each other. But they weren't completely empty, as some of the buildings showed signs of life. Clothes hung out of windows and broken toys littered front stoops. A group of dead-eyed elderly people sat in spindly wooden chairs lined against a metal wall. Their resemblance to the broken toys made Andy shudder.

Andy twisted around to look behind them. "Allen, I think we lost them."

Allen slowed and looked back. The street was mostly empty, with only a few people wandering the worn road. "We need to find cover. If they spot us here, there won't be any way for us to hide."

He led her to an open door. It hung loosely on its hinges, swinging slightly despite the lack of breeze. He pushed her in ahead of himself, checking the street once more before he followed her in. The inside was filthy. A thick layer of dust and grime coated the floors and walls. The first room was empty but for an old couch frame that had been stripped of its cloth and cushions. Andy walked ahead of Allen to the next room. Here stood what looked like was once a kitchen. Old, broken-down cupboards hung from the walls, and a wood table missing two of its legs lay upside down on the floor.

"Let's go upstairs, we're less likely to be spotted there," Allen said.

Andy followed him to a narrow staircase across from the kitchen. Every step creaked as they walked up, each sound a threat that it would snap beneath their weight. They stepped onto a landing that led to a narrow hall with three doors. They walked down the hall, and Andy peered into the first door to see a bathroom. Someone had ripped the toilet out and stripped the tile from the shower walls. Allen kept walking, and she followed him. She looked into the second room and saw a sight that made her stomach twist. The room looked like it had once been painted pink, but that color had faded and peeled off the walls. A stripped-down crib stood against the wall. She moved on, not wanting to think about the strange, empty nursery. Allen walked into the last room and she followed him. She assumed this had simply been a bedroom, as it was empty but for an old, stained mattress. Light streamed through the open window, but Allen quickly pulled the tattered curtains shut. He dropped down and leaned his head against the wall. Andy remained standing.

"How long should we stay here?"

Allen lifted his eyes to her. "I'm not sure. Until I think it's safe to leave."

Andy sat beside him on the floor. "How are we going to find the twins now?"

He shook his head. "I doubt we'll be able to. We may have to find a way out and come back for them."

"I hope they're safe."

"I'm sure they're fine. They're survivors."

"How are you unbothered?"

"Oh, I'm definitely worried. But freaking out and losing my cool isn't going to do either of us any good. If you stick around with us long enough, you'll learn how to keep calm in desperate situations."

Andy chewed her lip, something in her heart trembling. "Allen, you know I can't stay here, right? I have to get back to my family. I can't stay on the ship forever. I don't know what the captain plans on doing with me, but I can't wait around to find out."

There was a long moment of silence before Allen looked away. "I know."

"I need to know that if I get the chance to send out a call for help to my kingdom, you won't stop me."

Allen didn't look at her for a moment. When he finally did, there was a certainty in his eyes. "I won't. I promise."

Andy smiled. "Thank you. I know we already discussed this, but you could come with me. If you returned me to my family, they would give you anything you wanted."

Allen twisted a ring around his finger. "I don't think your fiancé would appreciate that."

Her fiancé. Right. She had completely forgotten about Eden. "Why would he care if you came back with me?"

He raised his eyebrows. "Andy, what happened back on that terrace—"

She swallowed. "We shouldn't talk about that." She couldn't deny her feelings for him, but she couldn't let him know. The terrace had been a mistake.

Allen looked hurt. "What were you going to say before you were interrupted?"

Honestly, Andy couldn't remember, but she knew it would have changed things. Once he knew, once she told him of her feelings, things would be different. What if he tried to convince her to stay? What if she wanted to?

Andy shook her head. She couldn't compromise her kingdom and family for him.

"It doesn't matter."

"It does, Andy."

"No, it doesn't! Because no matter what I say or how I feel, I still have to go back."

Allen was silent for a moment. "How *do* you feel?"

She looked away, and she knew that was enough of an answer for him.

"Andromeda, I know they probably told you your whole life that what you want wasn't important. They probably told you that you need to do what's best for the realm and put your desires second, but that's no way to live."

"You know nothing about how I was raised!" she snapped, suddenly and unfairly angry with him. He was right, after all. But she couldn't admit that. Because once she did, she doubted she could do what needed to be done. "God, why can't you understand? I can't have feelings for you! I have honor and loyalty to my family! I can't just be selfish like you!"

Allen looked like she had slapped him, and he was angry now as well. "Yeah, well, you don't know a damn thing about my life before you met me either! At least I know who I am, and I know what I want! You're too afraid to even admit it."

"I don't owe you anything, and I certainly don't have to explain myself to you!" she cried, standing up.

Allen stood as well. "You're not fooling me, Andy. I can see in your eyes that you're torn. I know you want to do what's right, but God, for the first time in your life just do something for yourself!"

"Stop acting like you know me!" she practically screamed.

He walked forward so that he was only inches from her face. "What I know is that you're hard-headed, and bratty, and sometimes a little bit selfish."

Andy's face burned red with anger. "Oh yeah? Then why are you still here?"

"Because despite all that, I'm pretty sure I love you."

Andy fell silent, her mouth still hanging partly open in what was going to be a retort. He looked flustered, and a little surprised himself, but he set his jaw.

"You... what? No, you don't." There was no conviction behind her words.

"And if I do?" he challenged.

Nobody had ever loved her before. Not in this way. Not in a way that twisted her stomach into knots and made her feel like she was going to vomit, all while filling her chest with so much hope and a desperate desire to belong.

It took only a single step for her to be close enough to reach up and pull his face down to hers. His mouth was warm and soft, just as she had suspected it to be. Allen let out a desperate little sound, like he couldn't believe what was happening. He froze for only a second, but as soon as his brain seemed to catch up with what was going on, he surged forward. His hands slid up into her curls and gripped at her frantically. Andy's back hit the wall as her breath escaped her and poured into his mouth.

Kissing Eden had not been like this. That had been clinical and planned. This was like finally coming home to a place you hadn't even realized you want to be. When Andy opened her eyes to look up at him, she found that his were squeezed shut, as though he were in pain. That wouldn't do. She smoothed her thumb over his jaw, then trailed it up to his eyelids. Her thumb slid over his scrunched-up brow and it immediately relaxed. Allen opened his eyes and looked into hers.

"Well, isn't that sweet?" a voice said from the doorway.

Both Andy and Allen spun toward the door. They had been so lost in their kiss that they hadn't noticed anyone coming up the stairs. Four men stood in the doorway, guns drawn. The man in front had a scraggly gray beard and bulging eyes. He smiled a toothy grin at them.

"If you wouldn't mind coming with us, the baron would like a word."

CHAPTER FOURTEEN

ANDY'S HEART WAS IN HER throat. They were cornered, with no weapons and nowhere to go. She silently cursed herself for letting her guard down. She glanced at Allen and saw that he was probably thinking the same. The four men entered the room and surrounded them. One of them stepped close to Andy and raised his hand to her full curls.

"Well, aren't you a pretty one."

"Don't touch her," Allen snarled.

Allen took a step forward, but before he could do more than that, the man behind him hit him over the head with the end of his gun, and he fell to his knees.

"Don't!" she cried.

One man handcuffed Allen while he was still dazed, before he could recuperate. The man that had touched her hair laughed. "If you don't want us to hurt your boyfriend, what'll you do for us?"

He stepped close to her and leaned his face in to smell her. Andy backhanded him with all the strength in her mechanical arm, and he went reeling backward. The other man to her left moved too quickly for her to react, punching the side of her face hard enough to send her to the floor. He lifted his gun to her head.

"Why shouldn't we blow you both away right here and be done with it? You'll receive no better from the baron."

Andy looked at Allen, and she knew what he was going to say. She shook her head, trying to stop him, but he spoke anyway.

"She's the lady of Lord Captain Bran."

This caused the men to pause. "What are you talking about?"

"Surely you've heard that Lord Captain Bran has taken a lady. That's big news around here."

"Yeah, we heard," one man said with a shrug.

"Well, that's her. I think the baron will want to at least meet the lady of Lord Captain Bran."

The man who held the gun to Andy's head narrowed his eyes. "If that's true, then I reckon you'll be in just as serious trouble with him after what we just saw."

Allen cast his eyes down to Andy. "Yeah, well, I'd rather be dealt with by my own captain."

"I don't know," said the man holding Allen still. "I've never seen the baron that mad before. I think he'll kill you both, regardless."

Allen looked desperate now. "Even so, you want that to be on the baron's hands. Because if you kill her and the lord captain finds out, it'll be you he comes after."

This seemed to frighten them, and they all looked at each other.

"Fine," one of them growled. "Let's handcuff them both and take them to see the baron."

They pulled Andy roughly to her feet and secured her hands behind her back with the cuffs. They walked with a man holding each of their arms, with Andy and two of the men in front. Once out in the street, they started walking, but not toward the busy city. They walked deeper into the abandoned ruins.

They led them into a massive old building. It looked like it was once a cathedral, with high reaching towers and pieces of colored glass still clinging to the frames of the windowsills. The smell of mold and dust seemed to fill her lungs and coat her mouth as they shuffled through the broken glass and paper that littered the ground. Andy couldn't turn to look at Allen, but she could hear him and the men who held him stomping heavily over the debris.

They walked all the way through the church and into a small back room with a confessional. The man on her left released her arm and slid a panel on the confessional up to reveal a keypad. He punched in several numbers, too quickly for her to see which, and the door slid open. Andy was pulled into what looked like the inside of an elevator. Allen was shoved in after her, and the door slid shut once more. It was a tight fit with all six of them in the small space. The man closest to the front pressed a button, and Andy felt them move upward. Everyone was silent as they rattled on. Allen turned to glance back at her once, but he was given a hard yank on his arm that made him turn back around. The elevator finally came to a stop, and the door opened once again.

Andy had thought they would go back to the palace, but that didn't appear to be the case. They were in a dimly lit hallway. Metal paneling covered the walls, and the floor was a dark gray. For the first time since being at the station, they looked like they were on a ship. They marched down the hall for a few minutes until stopping in front of a door. It opened, and they were escorted inside. Andy's stomach dropped.

"Mars!"

Mars was chained to the wall by her wrists, her head hanging between her shoulders and a trail of blood streaming from her nose. Her head snapped up at the sound of Andy's voice and a look of dismay crossed her face.

"No, shit, no. Andy, Allen, are you both OK?"

"Shut up!" one of the men ordered. "Your little friend here hasn't been so helpful. Maybe with you two here, it'll loosen her tongue."

They were dragged roughly across the room to where two cages

202 K. M. WATTS

sat, each about six feet long and four feet tall. Once Andy and Allen were securely inside, the cages were locked, and the men left the room.

"Mars, what happened?" Allen asked. "I thought you got away."

Mars shook her head. "We did, at first. But when we tried to escape to the loading docks, a trap had been set. Arlo got away with the bag of stolen goods, but they caught me. How did they find you?"

Andy shared a glance with Allen. "We let our guard down."

Just then the doors opened, and a woman and three men walked in. The woman smiled when she saw Andy and Allen in the cages. She had light auburn hair and full lips that had been painted with bright red lipstick. Her brown eyes moved from Andy to Allen. She motioned to the chains.

"Put them on the wall with their friend."

They pulled both Allen then Andy from their cages and moved them to the wall, where they cuffed their wrists to the chains and then backed away.

"You can leave," the woman said, without giving the men another glance. They did as they were told and closed the door behind them, leaving just her and one other man. He was a hulking thing, at least six and half feet tall.

The woman stood with her hands folded in front of her and her head tilted slightly to the side.

"Listen," Allen began. "You can turn back now. This is Lady Andy, she's—"

"I know who she is," the woman snapped.

"Then you know how bad of an idea it is to do what you're doing."

The woman laughed, a harsh, unpleasant sound that cut the air. "I don't think you quite understand the situation. My father doesn't care who you are. He isn't afraid of Lord Captain Bran. He can't touch me or my father."

"Your father?" Allen asked with a frown. "You're the baron's daughter?"

She nodded. "You may refer to me as Lady Vaila."

"Vaila—" Allen began, but she quickly cut him off again.

"*Lady* Vaila. I was born into royalty, not given the title by whomever I slept with." Her eyes shot daggers into Andy. "Given such, you will refer to me with my correct title."

She turned and walked to a chair that sat against the far wall. "Now, if you tell me what I want to know, this will be easy. If you don't, well, let's just say you shouldn't choose that option."

"What do you want to know?" Andy asked.

"We've already asked your pretty little friend here, and her answers have been less than forthcoming. Where are the items that were stolen from my father?"

Allen shook his head. "We don't know. We weren't even with them."

Vaila tapped her nails against the arm of the chair. "Maybe you're telling the truth. But unfortunately, I know *she* isn't. Perhaps the only way to get the information we want is with a bit of persuasion."

Vaila waved her hand. The hulking brute of a man walked toward Allen. Everyone was silent for a moment, then he lashed out. His fist connected with the side of Allen's face and Andy couldn't help but scream.

"No! Don't!"

Vaila's eyes moved to Andy now. "Do you have something to say?"

"We don't know anything! Beating us won't solve anything."

Vaila was quiet for a moment before looking at the man. "Continue."

He hit Allen again and again. Mars yanked against her restraints and kicked out, but she was too far to actually reach them. Andy tried to twist her wrists free, but even her mechanical arm was no use. The metal was too thick and too tight. Blood dripped from Allen's mouth and dotted the floor.

"Stop! Please, stop!" Andy screamed. The man alternated his hits between Allen's face and stomach.

"Please, I'll do whatever you want! Just stop hurting him!"

"Viktor, hold on," Vaila said.

The man stopped and took a step back. Allen hung from his chains, his head down and his breathing heavy. Vaila stood and walked to Andy.

"What, exactly, will you do?"

"Whatever you want. Just stop hurting him."

She tilted her head. "Interesting. They told me what they heard you saying to each other, but I didn't know if it was true." She looked at Allen and then back at Andy. "You are the lady of Lord Captain Bran, yet it's this handsome young man that you have feelings for."

A smile spread across her lips. "How scandalous. I've met plenty of gold diggers, but with Lord Captain Bran's reputation, I didn't think anyone would be stupid enough to try such a thing with him."

Andy didn't respond. What was she supposed to say? Certainly not the truth. Vaila reached out and ran a finger down Andy's cheek. "So pretty. I bet you've been the ruin of many men."

"Don't touch her!" Mars snarled.

Vaila's eyes darted to Mars and her smile grew even more. "And women, it would seem. I bet everyone just falls over themselves for these lovely golden eyes, don't they?"

The curve of her sharp nail scratched Andy's cheek, but she refused to wince. Up this close, Vaila's perfume was overpowering. It made Andy's head spin.

Vaila pulled her hand away and leaned back, a smug smile in place. "Viktor, come. I'll be back."

They left, and Andy let out a shuddering breath. "Allen, are you OK?"

He tilted his head toward her and gave a crooked smile. "Peachy. Don't worry about me, I've had worse."

"It's true," Mars said. "When he first joined the crew, he started a fight with a gang of dark market dealers. It was seven to one, and if Arlo and I hadn't stepped in I'm pretty sure they would've killed him."

Allen shrugged. "Nah, I was holding my own. Besides, if they didn't want to get into a fight, they should've left that poor tavern girl alone. I wasn't about to sit by and watch them harass her."

Mars rolled her eyes. "Always the gallant hero."

"If I remember correctly, you're the one who helped *comfort* her after the fact."

Mars's mouth curved into a devious smile. "What can I say? I have a nice shoulder to cry on."

"Hey, guys," Andy interrupted. "Not that this memory lane isn't great, but we need to find a way out of here. This situation is bad."

"Don't worry, you'll be fine. Regardless of what they say, they won't kill the lord captain's lady," Allen said.

Andy frowned. "You think that matters to me? Do you really think I could live with myself if I survived, and they killed you both? No. We need to find a way for all three of us to get out of here. Mars, do you really have no idea where Arlo went?"

She shook her head. "They'd closed off a lot of escape routes, but Arlo's resourceful. They know people everywhere. Maybe they were able to get a message out."

Andy chewed her lip. That was a big maybe, and it wasn't something they could rely on. But as it was, there was no way for them to get out of this situation on their own. There were likely hundreds of armed men outside those doors between them and the outside, and even then, any possible exit would be blocked off. They were trapped.

The doors slid open once more. Vaila was back, only this time she was with a tall, grim faced, balding man. His eyes were steely and cold, and his mouth formed a hard line. He looked between the three of them.

"This is the one?" he asked, motioning to Andy.

"That's her," Vaila confirmed.

Emotionless eyes roamed over her body. "She's not quite what I expected from the lord captain's lady."

Vaila smiled. "Not pretty enough for you, Daddy?"

So, this was the baron. Well, if she wasn't what he was expecting, then he surely wasn't, either. This thin, bald man hardly instilled fear into her. She felt a sudden surge of bravery.

"Listen, you need to let us go. My lord will come for me. If he finds me here and sees what you've done to his lady, he will kill you and everyone you hold dear."

The baron stared down at her for a moment before a cruel smile spread across his face.

"You are a foolish little girl. I'm not afraid of Lord Captain Bran. Of course, outside of my station, he is incredibly powerful. But he can't touch me here. I could kill you all and he could do nothing. Luckily for you, I don't plan on doing that. Not yet, at least. You stole some items from me. I want them back. If your lord captain wants you, he will return my possessions and pay a hefty price for all my trouble."

He stalked toward them, each step deliberate.

"If he will not pay the price, well. My daughter has plans for the three of you. Let me just say, you should truly hope that he feels strongly for you."

"The lord captain loves Lady Andy," Allen said, trying to sound confident.

Andy knew this was a lie. If the lord captain knew who she was, then it was likely she was just a payday for him. If the baron asked a price too close to what he would charge in ransom, would he just give her up as a lost cause? A part of her thought yes, he would.

The baron moved to stand beside Allen. "From what I've heard, you have feelings for her as well. Is that true?"

Allen didn't look at Andy. "I was tasked with caring for and protecting her."

"I see," the baron said and nodded. He turned to his daughter. "Call for Viktor."

Vaila nodded and left the room, returning a moment later with the massive brutish man.

"Put them both in the cage," he instructed, motioning to Allen and Mars. "Leave her on the wall."

Viktor lumbered toward Allen, his small eyes almost gleaming with malice. Allen tried to fight him off, but he was weak with exhaustion and no match for the enormous man. Viktor threw him on the floor of the cage and locked it before Allen could do anything. Mars put up a bit more of a fight, landing a hard kick to the man's chest, but ultimately she too was tossed into a cage.

"What are you doing?" Allen asked, panic clear in his tone.

"Leave her alone!" Mars cried. "She's innocent in all this. She didn't even know what we were doing!"

Nobody acknowledged them. Viktor came back to stand in front of Andy and looked to the baron for further instructions.

"Hit her."

Andy tried to brace herself, but the impact of his fist on her face had her seeing stars. The taste of iron flooded her mouth as blood pooled against her tongue. Allen and Mars shouted.

"No! Stop it! Please!"

"What are you gaining from this? She knows nothing!"

The baron ignored them. "Hit her again."

Again, the force of Viktor's fist slammed her head back into the wall. With the third hit, she felt blood drip from her mouth.

Allen was beating his fists on the wall of his cage, a cry of pure, desperate rage escaping him. Mars had shoved her fingers through the bars and was shaking them.

"Stop it! What do you want from me? I'll do what you want, just stop hurting her!" Mars screamed.

The baron walked in front of Andy. "Have you had enough?"

She looked up at him with an intense hatred. Who did he think he was? She was the crown princess of Celestine. He would not get the satisfaction of seeing her crumble. She spat the blood that had pooled in her mouth right at his face. Vaila let out an audible gasp. The baron reached up and slowly wiped the blood away. His fist shot out and hit her right in the stomach with more strength than she would have thought he possessed. Andy would have doubled over if she could, but given her restraints, she could only try to twist away.

"From what I've been told, you seem to inspire the dedication of all sorts of people. First, Lord Captain Bran makes you his lady after years of turning down offers from the most beautiful women in the galaxy. Then, my men overhear this young man confess his love for you." He turned to look at Mars. "Tell me, do you love her as well?"

Mars's lip curled into a snarl. "Go fuck yourself."

The baron smirked. "Just as I thought. It's impressive really, even if I don't see the appeal. A modern day Helen of Troy. It's too bad none of these people see what their love for you really is. Weakness. I suppose soon we will see if Lord Captain Bran truly has gone soft."

He reached up and ran the back of his fingers over her cheek. His small, cold eyes held hers for longer than she would have liked before he finally looked away.

"Viktor, put her back into her cage. We'll continue this later."

Andy didn't have any energy to do more than sag against the man once her shackles had been removed. He dragged her to the cage Mars was in and threw her to the floor before locking it again. Once the other three had left the room, Mars immediately crawled over to Andy and gripped her face in her hands.

"Andy, hey, are you all right?"

"Yeah, yeah, I'm fine. My head just hurts a little."

Truthfully, she didn't *sound* fine. Her words came out slurred and her eyes felt heavier with every second. And that pain on the back of her head was more of a pulsing throb, radiating down her neck.

Mars reached around to the back of Andy's head, and when she pulled her hand back, there was a small amount of blood on her fingers.

"Shit," Mars cursed. "That's not good."

"What?" Allen asked, panic clear in his voice. "Mars, what's not good?"

"I think she has a concussion. They hit her head pretty hard."

"Isn't there anything you can do?" he asked, his voice rising.

"Allen, I don't exactly have my medical kit here! Until we can get out, the things I can do are limited."

"Mars, she's bleeding! You have to do something. What good are all those years of medical training if you can't even use them!"

"Hey, don't you raise your voice at me! You're the one who was supposed to protect her. How could you have let your guard down?"

"Hey, hey, guys," Andy murmured, raising her hand. "Please, stop arguing. You're making my head hurt worse."

Allen gripped the bars of his cage and rested his forehead against them. "Andy, I'm sorry for getting you into this."

"You didn't get me into anything."

Mars shook her head. "You're right. I did. I never should have convinced you to come here."

Andy wrapped her hand around Mars's and pushed her fingers through the bars to touch Allen's. "Listen to me. You both need to stop viewing me as some damsel that needs to be saved and protected. I wanted to come here. It was my choice, and I wouldn't have let either of you convince me out of it. So, stop blaming yourselves, or I swear I'll throw myself out an airlock."

They both chuckled.

Allen wrapped his fingers around hers. "You know we would just get ourselves killed trying to save you."

She smiled. "Idiot."

"We're going to get you out of here, OK?" Allen said, conviction heavy in his voice.

Andy closed her eyes. She knew there was nothing they could do, that he wanted to believe his own words, but if they wanted to kill her, there was nothing he could do to stop them. She wouldn't tell him that, of course. She wouldn't take his hope. But at the moment, she was too tired to care. It felt as though she hadn't slept in years, and now sleep was pressing in on her with the weight of an ocean.

"Andy? Andy, wake up," Mars said, her soft hands patting at Andy's cheeks.

"Andy!" Allen cried. "No, don't fall asleep!"

Their voices seemed distant, like she was hearing them from the bottom of a pool. But they sounded panicked, and that frightened her. She struggled against the pull of sleep and opened her eyes. Mars was directly over her, and Allen had shifted so he was within her line of sight. They wore matching expressions of fear and concern.

"Andy, what's wrong? Sit up, open your eyes wider!" Allen said.

But she couldn't. The pull was just too strong. Everything seemed to spin around her, and then nothing. A complete blackness surrounded everything, like a blanket with the density of Earth had covered her. She couldn't move. She tried to listen for a sound, but there was nothing. It felt as if she had just been thrown into the vast emptiness of space, but even that wasn't right. There were stars in space.

Finally, after what seemed like an eternity, she heard something. A hollow *bang, bang, bang* echoed around her. It sounded like something hitting against metal. Andy tried to turn her head to the sound and was surprised to feel that she could move again. Also, the blackness wasn't so dark anymore. She opened her eyes, and the harsh lights overhead made her squint. Her head was no longer on the cold ground, but rather cushioned by something soft and firm. She turned to the sound and saw Allen still beside her in his cell. He was banging his fist against the bars, slowly and methodically. His forehead was still pressed to the bars, but his eyes were closed. Andy frowned.

"Allen?"

His eyes snapped open in an instant. "Andy? Oh, thank God!"

There was a gentle press of fingers to her cheek turning her head until she was looking up at Mars. Ah, it was Mars's lap she was resting on.

"Hey beautiful. You really had us worried there. How are you feeling?"

She groaned and stretched her neck. "My head's still throbbing, but it doesn't hurt as bad."

Andy rolled onto her side and pushed herself up so that she was sitting. "How long was I out for?"

Allen shrugged. "It's hard to say. A couple hours, maybe."

Andy pressed both of her hands to her face. "I think you were right about that concussion, Mars. That, or the chip in my head has been dislodged, which would be far worse."

"Why?" Allen asked, "What will happen if the chip gets dislodged?"

"Well, it keeps all of my organic parts in sync with my robotic parts. So, my guess is that my heart and left lung would stop working, along with my limbs and other synthetic parts. Basically, I would die."

"God, Andy, you should have told me about that! I didn't even consider the problem could be biomechanical," Mars scolded.

She snorted. "I'm sorry I didn't think to give you my entire previous medical history."

Allen shifted on the other side of the bars. "But do you think that's what happened?"

Andy shook her head. "I seem to be breathing fine. It's likely just a concussion."

"That still isn't good," Mars insisted. "We need to find a way out of here."

"Yeah, you don't say?" Andy deadpanned. "Did either of you come up with a plan while I was taking my little nap?"

Mars rolled her eyes. "We were sort of preoccupied with making sure you were still alive. It would affect the plan a bit if we were going to have to carry you out."

Before Andy could respond, the door opened once more and the baron and Vaila walked in. Vaila wore a smug, sadistic smile that twisted her pretty face unattractively. The baron stood in the middle of the room, his eyes moving between the three of them.

"We have attempted to contact Lord Captain Bran but have received no response."

The three stared at him, none sure of what to say. The baron continued. "We have relayed our terms and have told your captain that he has one hour to respond. If he does not, you will die."

Andy glanced at Allen and Mars. They wore the same worried expression as her own. Would the captain even care enough to respond? She looked back to the baron.

"What have you asked in ransom?"

Vaila answered, her twisted smile still on her face. "One hundred million pics, and ten of his best ships."

Andy's heart sank. That was a ridiculously large sum. Andy had come to understand the captain a bit, and it only made sense for him to cut his losses. The baron seemed to be of the same mind.

"I also told him that every minute he takes considering my offer will be a minute you are worse off. Viktor."

Viktor entered once more. She was really beginning to hate the sight of him.

"Take the lady from her cage and put her on the wall."

"No!" Allen shouted. "You already gave her a concussion. Any more could kill her!"

The baron nodded. "Fine. Avoid her head. Anywhere else is fine."

Allen flew into a rage of curses she had never heard before. He kicked at the door to his cage furiously, but this only made the baron laugh. When Viktor opened the cage door Mars launched herself at him, digging her nails into the flesh of his arm. But in this position her range of motion was limited and she was unable to do more than crouch. Viktor leveled a hard kick to her chest while simultaneously dragging Andy from the cage. Mars fell back, only to scramble up once more, but it was too late. The cage door locked into place. Andy was secured to the wall once more, and Viktor squared up. She could sense that when he hit her this time, it would be worse than before. As he lifted his fist, she tensed up, but a loud sound from the hall made them all stop. The baron scowled.

"What the hell are they doing out there?"

Another loud bang and yelling made him stand up. Vaila frowned, looking at her father. "Father, what's going on?"

Before he could answer, the door slid open. Andy let out a laugh that sounded more like a sob. Lord Captain Bran strode in, flanked by several of his men with guns. The baron took several steps back. "How the hell did you get past my defenses?"

The captain didn't answer. Instead, his eyes moved around the room. He wore the same deadly calm expression as when he had killed those five men. Until his eyes found Andy, and then a look of pure fury crossed his face. He turned back to the baron.

"I believe you have something of mine, and I've come to get her back."

CHAPTER FIFTEEN

THE BARON SEEMED TO REGAIN his senses and straightened up. "I gave you my terms. If you want her back, you can pay my price."

The captain shook his head slowly. "I don't think you understand. I wasn't asking."

The baron sneered. "Do you know who I am?"

The captain took three quick steps toward him, so that he was directly in his personal space. Viktor tried to step between them, but two of the captain's men stopped him. The captain raised an eyebrow.

"Yes, I know who you are. You're a little worm with perceived power, just because you lock yourself in here and think that makes you safe. It does not."

The baron puffed out his chest. "I'm not afraid of you. If you even touch me, you'll never leave this station alive. Neither will your whore."

The captain's jaw tightened, and his eyes narrowed. "You will never refer to her in that way again. I'll be leaving with her now."

Captain Bran walked toward Andy, but the baron side-stepped in front of him. "I'm afraid I cannot allow that. Guards!"

There were several seconds of silence in which the baron looked to the door expectantly. His face quickly fell, however, when he realized that nobody was coming. The captain smiled and walked around him. As he did, he snatched the set of keys that hung on Viktor's belt. He didn't look at Andy's face as he unlocked the shackles. When her wrists were free, she slumped forward, but he was able to catch her easily. He made to lift her in his arms, but she pushed him away.

"I can walk fine on my own."

He frowned but didn't argue. One of the captain's men took the keys and freed Allen and Mars, who both immediately came to stand beside Andy. The baron stood silently in the middle of the room the whole time, quietly seething but unable to do anything to stop what was happening. He was outnumbered. Without speaking another word, the captain led them out of the room.

The baron shouted out behind them, though, desperate to get the last word. "You have made a serious enemy today, Captain Bran! I truly hope your whore is worth your future destruction!"

The captain stopped, his face still expressionless. He turned back, walked the few steps to the baron, and struck him in the face. The baron fell to the ground, and Vaila shrieked. The captain pulled the baron to his feet and hit him again and again. Blood pooled in his mouth and splattered the floor, some landing on the captain's boots. There was no rage or passion behind what he did, only a cold and calculating man who sought retribution how he saw fit. Viktor stood stiffly, with his hands balled into fists, but the multiple guns trained on him forced him to not intervene. Vaila was pressed to the corner, no longer wearing her smug smile.

Finally, the captain stopped, throwing the baron to the floor. He pulled a cloth from his pocket and wiped his bloody knuckles.

"Never presume to threaten me again." He tucked the cloth back into his pocket and strode out of the room, everyone else following behind.

The halls were mostly empty, except for some of their own people stationed at the end of each corridor. Andy quickened her pace, so that she was beside the captain.

"We can't leave yet. Arlo is still somewhere in the lower levels."

He didn't look at her as he spoke, and his voice was hard as steel. "Arlo already made their way back to the ship earlier today. They're the one who first alerted us to your situation."

"But how did you get in? Where are all the baron's soldiers?"

The captain didn't answer for a moment, and when he did, he still didn't look at her. "The baron's soldiers aren't as loyal as he would like to believe. It wasn't difficult to pay off the right people."

Andy wanted to ask more questions, but his tone suggested she shouldn't press further. They reached a massive elevator and climbed in. Andy stood with the captain in front of her and Allen and Mars behind her. At one point, as they raced upward, Andy felt Allen momentarily press his hand into hers. The sensation gave her both a sense of relief and fear. They had been saved from the baron, but what would the captain do? They had disobeyed a direct order. Andy was already a prisoner, so she doubted he would do much to her, but what about Allen? He had been in charge of her, and he allowed her to leave the ship. And Mars, who had been the one to encourage them to disobey. Andy had been selfish. Would the captain kill Allen because of her stupid mistake? Would he punish Mars? No, she wouldn't let him.

They left the elevator and walked out onto the loading docks, though they were in a different section that she hadn't seen before. The elevator let out just a few meters from the entrance to their ship. Armed pirates were everywhere. As soon as they saw the captain they jumped into action, flanking their group and ushering them into the ship. Andy glanced back once they were on board and saw the airlock door sliding shut. Everyone was silent as they walked. Nothing but the sound of boots echoed through the halls. The captain stopped and turned.

"I will see Allen and Lady Andy privately in my study. Now." His voice was low and dangerous, and it made Andy afraid. Not necessarily for herself, but for Allen.

Mars stepped forward. "If you're going to be angry with anyone, it should be me. Don't punish them."

The captain's eyes flicked to her. "You and I will talk later. But you were not the one in charge of guarding Lady Andy. Now, go back to your quarters."

Mars looked like she wanted to argue, but Andy rested her hand on her arm and shook her head. She didn't need anyone else suffering from her mistake. Reluctantly, Mars backed away down the hall with the rest of the crew.

Everyone else filtered off as they made their way to the study. Andy felt the ship sway as they took off. When they reached the study, the captain stood aside and motioned for them to enter first.

The room was colder than Andy remembered it, and a bit darker. She took one chair across from the desk and Allen took the other. The captain entered, then closed and locked the door behind him. The sound of the lock made Andy's heart sink. For several unnerving seconds, the captain stood silently behind them. The only things Andy could hear were her own breathing and the sound of her heart hammering away inside her ribs.

She spoke, needing to break the tense silence. "It's my fault, what happened. Please don't blame anyone else."

"No," Allen cried, "that isn't true! If you have to blame someone, blame me!"

The captain walked around so that he was behind his desk and sat down, still not saying a word. He pressed his fingertips together and leaned back in his chair.

Andy shook her head at Allen. "You know that isn't true. I made you take me into the station, even though you didn't want to!" She turned to the captain. "I manipulated him into taking me.

Please don't punish him. I'll take whatever punishment you deem fit."

"Andy!" Allen snapped, standing up. "Stop lying. You aren't to blame!"

"Enough!" the captain snapped, finally. "Sit down."

Allen did as he was told. The captain leaned forward on his desk. "It would appear that you are both at fault. You both made poor decisions that nearly got you killed. You disobeyed a direct order."

Andy's mouth was dry. She tried to moisten it with saliva, but none would come. The captain continued. "What you did was idiotic and dangerous, though I'm sure you both already know that. Lady Andy doesn't seem to know better, but I expected better from you, Allen."

Andy's face burned red. She didn't appreciate him speaking to her like a child, but she knew now wasn't the time to talk back.

Allen's mouth curled down at the corners. "I'm sorry, Captain. What I did was wrong and foolish. I put Lady Andy in danger. Please, punish me and not her."

The captain rested his elbows on his desk and sighed. "I will think about what your punishment will be. You may leave now."

Andy raised her eyebrows, surprised by how easy that had been. They both made to stand, but the captain spoke. "No, not you, Lady Andy. Allen, leave us."

Allen stood, looking from Andy to the captain. Then he shook his head. "No."

The captain's eyes flashed up to him. "Excuse me?"

Allen straightened his back. "I'm sorry, Captain, but I won't leave her alone with you. I told you, she doesn't deserve punishment."

The captain raised an eyebrow, and after a moment Andy thought she saw a hint of a smile cross his lips. "Allen, I promise I will not harm her. She will be safe here with me, I give you my word."

Allen looked at Andy, and she nodded. She didn't want him getting into more trouble for her. Allen sighed and, after a pause, turned and walked to the door. He opened it but stopped before walking out. "I'll wait for you outside your room."

The door slid shut behind him. She hadn't realized it but having him there with her had been giving her a sense of comfort. That was gone now. She turned back to the captain and saw that he was still staring at the door. After a moment he stood and walked to the window, looking out with his hands folded behind his back. Andy wasn't sure if she should say something, but she didn't have to wonder long.

"I think he's in love with you."

Andy stared at his back. He didn't sound angry, only matter-of-fact, but she didn't like it. To admit that to him could be dangerous. "No, that's not—" she began, but he cut her off.

"It's all right, I don't mind. It's better, even, that he does."

Andy didn't know what to say. She licked her lips. "Why do you say that?"

The captain shrugged. "Love inspires devotion. Protection."

Andy stared down at her hands. What could she possibly say to that?

"Do you love him back?"

Andy's eyes snapped back up to him. She hadn't been expecting the question, though she supposed she should have.

"I don't know."

The captain nodded again. "Do you want to be with him?"

"I don't owe you an answer to that."

"No, you don't. But you can trust me, Andromeda."

She scoffed and shook her head. "I highly doubt—" She stopped mid-sentence. "What did you call me?"

Captain Bran looked over his shoulder at her, one eyebrow raised. Andy felt something like heat rising in her chest. She stood abruptly.

"What did you call me?" It was a dangerous question, but she had to know. She couldn't live with the thought hanging over her head anymore.

"I called you by your name. Your name is Andromeda."

Andy felt as though he had shoved her hard in the chest and was finding it difficult to breathe. So, it was all coming out. He knew who she was. She nodded.

"Yes, that is my name." She straightened up and lifted her chin. There was no point in pretending anymore. "I am Princess Andromeda of Celestine, and I am not afraid of you."

He turned fully and smiled. "That's good. I don't want you to be afraid of me."

"You want everyone to be afraid of you."

"Not everyone." He walked back around to his chair and sat down.

She still stood with her arms crossed over her chest. "Why don't you want me to be afraid?"

He chuckled. "I would have better luck trying to frighten a lion."

She frowned. "What are you talking about?"

"From what I've seen, you're pretty fearless."

"Then you don't know me well at all. I'm afraid all the time." She didn't know why she had told him this. She didn't want him knowing she was afraid. His eyes roamed her face, as though hoping to find something there that he currently couldn't see.

"Andy, I don't want you to be afraid of me."

She scoffed. "Well, perhaps you shouldn't have kidnapped me and locked me on a ship for ransom!"

His brow creased. "I'm not holding you for ransom."

She blinked. "What? Then why do you still have me? Let me go!"

He was silent as he looked down at his hands. She felt both fear and rage boiling up inside her. "What is wrong with you? If you don't want money, then what do you want from me? What other gain could you possibly have for keeping me here? I'm not going to sleep with you, if that's what you're into!"

He held his hands up, defensively. "I already told you, I want nothing like that."

Andy couldn't help her fury, as her voice rose to a shout. "Then, why? Tell me why you won't let me go! I deserve to know that, at least!"

"Please, lower your voice."

"Do not tell me what to do," she snapped. "You are not my father."

As she watched his face, she noticed his eyes tighten slightly. Before he replied, he took a deep breath. "Yes, I am."

CHAPTER SIXTEEN

ANDY STARED AT HIM, SURE she had heard wrong. "Excuse me?"

"This will all be bit difficult for me to explain to you, so I thought instead I would show you." He removed a cloth from an object on his desk. It was round and flat, with several golden buttons on top and two cords that protruded from both sides.

Andy stared at it. She had seen one of these before. "That's a mind connector." She had read about them and seen them on television. They allowed someone to look directly into the mind and memories of another. "Those were outlawed. How did you—" She stopped midsentence. Of course he could get one, he was a pirate.

"Wait, are you seriously going to try to convince me that *you* are my father?"

"Andy, I am."

She began to giggle, then full on laughed. He had lost his mind. "How stupid do you think I am?"

"I don't think you're stupid at all. I'm counting on that, actually. Please, let me show you. If, when I'm finished, you still don't believe me, I'll let you say your piece."

Andy still wore a smirk, but sat. There was no way he would make her believe such a ridiculous claim. He smiled, looking relieved that she would cooperate. He passed one wire to her, which had a flat pad on the end.

"Now if you could just place that on your left temple."

Andy stared at it with apprehension while the captain placed his own onto his temple. "It's all right, see? It won't hurt."

Andy hesitated for only a moment longer before she pressed it to her head. Captain Bran turned some dials on the main machine and pressed a few buttons.

"Now, what happens next may be disorienting, so prepare yourself."

Andy opened her mouth to ask what he meant, but before she could, something odd happened. It was as if someone had slid a filter over her eyes. The images before her changed, like someone had switched the channel in her brain to a different network. As the image cleared, she turned her head to look around. She was in the room of a ship, though it was nothing like the one she had just been in. It was mostly empty but for a single desk and two men that stood beside it. They leaned over several papers and maps. At first, Andy thought she didn't recognize either of them, but as she looked at the taller of the two, she realized with surprise that it was the captain. He looked much younger, by at least twenty years, with a clean-shaven face and blond curls that hung past his chin.

Andy wanted to move closer, and as soon as the thought entered her head, she slid across the room to be beside him. The sensation made her dizzy.

"If you want to move around in here, all you need to do is think it."

Andy gave a bit of a jolt and turned her head to see the older captain standing beside her.

"What the hell is going on?"

He raised an eyebrow at her. "I thought you said you knew what a mind connector was."

Andy narrowed her eyes. "So, what? We're in your mind?"

He tilted his head from side to side. "Yes, sort of. My memories, or at least an approximation of them. The mind is a funny thing. This was me, twenty years ago."

Andy glanced back at the young Captain Bran. As she watched him, he straightened up and spoke. "I think we've done enough planning. It begins in a week, and I want to be there by the first day."

The other man beside him tapped his fingers on the table. He was older and shorter than the captain.

The older Captain Bran shifted across the room. "He was my first mate. Jonas Belton was his name. He taught me everything I know about being a pirate. I wouldn't have made it a year without him. He passed away three years ago." The captain looked down at his old first mate with a hint of sadness in his eyes. "But anyway, this story isn't about him."

Jonas looked at the young captain. "This is dangerous, Bran. I'm still not sure about it."

The young captain dropped himself into a chair. "Are you serious? We aren't backing out now. This will be the biggest score of our career. Celestine will be ripe for the picking. Can you tell me another time when this will be at all possible? The first anniversary of the king and queen will be a month-long celebration, and every duke, lord, and lady will be in attendance. We have my forged credentials. I'll pass easy enough for a lord. Besides, nobody will pay any attention to me."

Jonas screwed up his mouth. "I suppose. It's just—"

The young captain leapt up. "It'll be all right, Jonas. Trust me, OK?"

The scene changed again in a blur of color. Andy blinked several times. When she looked around and saw where she was, she almost cried. She stood on the top balcony of the palace overlooking the Celestine gardens. In that moment, she was home. It took her a moment to realize that the young captain stood to her left, in conversation with a man she didn't know.

"I can't believe you've never been here before," the man said to the captain. "I thought every lord and lady had vacationed on Celestine at least once."

The captain laughed and shrugged. "Well, I guess I am now. There was never much of a reason to come before."

Laughter carried up to them from the garden below. The captain turned to find the source of the voices, and Andy saw a look of wonderment cross his face. She looked down, and this time let out an audible gasp. It was her mother. She walked through the garden accompanied by two of her ladies. A golden gown of silk was draped elegantly over her body, and a crown of gold leaves and pearls sat atop her raven hair. Andy had never seen her mother so young or carefree. The sight of her took her breath away. Apparently, she wasn't the only one.

"Who is that?" the captain asked.

The other man looked at him like he was insane. "You're joking, right? She's the reason we're all here. That's Queen Adella."

The young captain looked back down at the queen, his face a mixture of mischief and awe. "I think I'd like to meet her."

"But you can't just walk up to the queen!" the man said, but the captain wasn't listening. He had already made his way across the balcony to the staircase. Andy floated along behind him. She noted the older captain was still beside her.

"She was the most beautiful person I had ever seen. I'd done research on the king before making my move, but I hadn't thought to look into the queen as well. I had foolishly thought it was unimportant. Nobody's beauty had ever moved me like hers did."

They descended the stairs as the young captain approached the queen. Before he could get within fifteen feet, however, several armed guards stepped between them, blocking his view.

The young captain flashed a charming smile, but the guards only glowered. "You are not permitted to approach the queen without a formal invitation."

A lilting voice spoke from behind the guards. "Charlie, Beck, it's fine. Please, allow him through."

The guards' frowns tightened, but they did as she said. They stepped aside so that Adella was in full view. The young captain straightened his shoulders and approached. He dipped into a bow, though his eyes never left her face. Andy watched as her mother broke into a smile, her eyes curious at this bold young man.

"Your Majesty. It is an honor to meet you."

She extended a hand, which he took, and pressed his forehead to her ring. She raised a delicate eyebrow. "I apologize, sir, but I don't believe that I know you."

He laughed and shook his head. "No, unfortunately we have never been acquainted. I am Lord Brandigan of Carwhell."

"Ah, well Lord Brandigan, my ladies and I were just about to make another round about the garden. Would you care to walk with us?"

A hint of mischief flashed through his eyes again. "It would be my honor."

The scene shifted again. Andy blinked hard. "I hate that."

"I apologize, but it is necessary," the captain said beside her.

They were still in the gardens, but it was dark now. She turned at the sound of voices. Her mother and the captain were walking toward them. Andy wasn't sure how she knew it was two weeks later, perhaps because the captain knew. Her mother and the captain walked close together, closer than was socially acceptable. The sight of them like that made Andy's stomach twist. She leaned in to hear what her mother was saying.

"I've tried as much as I can, I just don't think there's anything for it. He doesn't love me. And as much as I wanted to in the beginning, I don't think I can love him either."

Andy wanted to recoil at these words. Was she talking about her father? That couldn't be true, surely.

"These sorts of things take time," the young captain said.

Andy could tell by the way he said it he didn't mean it. Her mother shook her head. "I've given it a year. I don't want this. I don't want to wake up in twenty years and wonder where my life went. I want an adventure, and I want freedom, and I want love. True love."

They had stopped beside a fountain now. The captain frowned. "Do you think you could ever have that?"

Her mother looked up at him, and as she did, the light of the stars reflected off her eyes. "I think I could, with the right man."

Before Andy could prepare herself, her mother leaned forward and pressed her lips to the captain's. He didn't hesitate as he pulled her closer. Andy wanted to run away, to drive the image from her mind, but she couldn't move. The sight of her mother kissing another man made her nauseated. She spoke through gritted teeth. "Get me out of here."

"I'm sorry, Andy, I can't do that," the captain said. "I need you to see. To understand."

"My mother would never do this! She is the most respectable person I have ever known, and she would not have an affair, regardless of how she felt about her husband."

The captain gave her a sad sort of smile. "She was nineteen and terribly lonely. It's quite easy to fall in love when you're young, when the world seems full of hope and possibilities."

Andy clenched her teeth. This wasn't fair. These memories were a bastardization of what her mother was. Before she could voice this, however, the scene shifted again.

They were inside the castle, in one of the smaller guest rooms. Another two weeks had passed. The captain sat in a chair near the door with his fingertips pressed together and his eyes not moving from the handle. As soon as it turned, he leapt from the chair. Her mother rushed into the room and closed the door behind her. She locked it and then turned to him. Her cheeks were flushed a bright pink beneath her tanned skin, and her eyes were wide and joyful. She laughed as she ran into his arms and spoke through the kisses she planted on him.

"I've missed you so much. It's been impossible to get away for these past two days."

The captain nestled his face into her hair and breathed in deeply. "I know. I haven't been able to stop thinking of you."

She pushed him backward onto the bed and climbed onto him. "I'm tired of restraining myself. I want you, all of you."

The captain pushed her back by her shoulders. "Are you sure?"

Her mother brushed her hair out of her face. "Of course I'm sure. My husband can have his whores, I only want you."

The captain laughed. "Am I your whore now?"

Adella ran a hand across his cheek. "Of course not. I love you."

This seemed to take the captain by surprise. His eyes widened, and he sat up. A look of worry crossed her mother's face.

"I'm sorry, I shouldn't have said that."

"No, no, it's all right. It's more than all right. It's just, I never thought a woman like you would ever love a man like me. I love you too."

Her mother smiled. "You do?"

"I do. I've never been so sure of anything in my life."

He flipped her onto her back and kissed her. Andy knew what was going to happen next.

"Stop!" she shrieked.

To her relief, the scene shifted again.

"I'm sorry about that," the captain said, embarrassment thick in his voice. "I got caught up in my own memory."

The sound of footsteps made Andy turn. Her mother was half running down the hall, her heels echoing against the tiles. She wore a look of dismay and fear. Three months had passed now, Andy knew. The captain stood nearby, hidden behind a column. As she approached, he reached out and pulled her into him.

He ran a hand through her hair. "There you are. It took you long enough."

Adella bit her lip and stepped away from him. "Something has happened, Bran."

The smile fell from his face. "What is it? Have we been discovered?"

Adella shook her head. "No, not that. But something else. Bran, I'm pregnant."

The captain stood still as what looked like shock rolled over him. "Pregnant? Are you sure?"

"Yes, I'm sure!" her mother cried.

He was frozen for a moment longer before he broke into an enormous smile. "You're going to have a baby? And is it—"

"Yours? Yes, of course, it's yours!"

The captain laughed. "That's wonderful, Ella! Why are you so upset?"

She bowed her head. "I didn't recognize the symptoms, so I went to the doctor. That's how I found out. They called my husband down and told us together. We are to announce it tonight."

The smile slid from the captain's face. "You will announce it as his child? He will raise it as his own?"

Adella threw her hands in the air. "Of course he will! You knew this was a possibility. What else could I do? If anybody ever found out, you would be executed, and I would be divorced and sent back to my family in shame." Tears flooded her eyes. "This has to end, Bran. For our own safety."

The captain shook his head. "Just give me some time, Ella. Give me a chance, I will find a way for us to be together."

Andy was ready this time when the scene shifted. Adella sat in front of the captain as he held her hand in his. "Ella, I think I've figured out a way for us to be together. But for it to work, I need to tell you something. The truth, about me."

Adella frowned. "What are you talking about?"

Captain Bran took a deep breath. "I'm not exactly who you think I am. I'm not a lord, I have no title. My name really is Bran. I'm a captain of a ship though, and I think I've found a way for us to run away together, so we can be a family."

Adella blinked a few times. "Wait, slow down. If you aren't a lord, how did you get invited here?"

"I forged documents."

"But why? All so that you could attend a party?"

The captain looked down. "No, not exactly. Ella, as I said, I'm the captain of a ship. A pirate ship."

Adella drew her hands away from him. "That's not funny, Bran, don't joke about that."

"I wish I were, but I'm not. I originally came here to loot."

Adella stared at him in silence. When she said nothing, he continued.

"But then I met you! You changed everything. I told my first mate that we couldn't do this. He wasn't pleased, but I talked him out of it. All I want now is you."

Adella shook her head back and forth. "You lied to me?"

"What else could I do? I'm telling you now, because I have a plan. I can get you and our baby out of here. We can go where nobody will find us and be free and happy. Isn't that what you've always wanted?"

"But how can I trust you? You've been lying to me this whole time!"

"No! Not this whole time. I love you more than anything. I am still the same person you've gotten to know these past months."

She paced back and forth, her fingers twisted together. The captain watched her in silence for a few moments before speaking again. "Do you want to come away with me?"

She pressed her hands over her eyes. "No. Well, yes, but I don't know. I need to think."

Another shift. They were now back in the garden, and the captain watched as Adella walked toward him. She stopped a few feet away.

"Please, let me talk first. I don't fully understand everything you told me yesterday. I'm worried that I don't know you as well as I thought I did, and I'm afraid. How can I not be? But I know I love you. And I know I don't want to be locked inside this cage any longer. So I'm willing to take the risk, whatever the outcome may be. So, tell me, what is your plan?"

The captain made to embrace her, but before he could, the scene changed. The captain was now on the bridge of a ship. A crewman stood beside him and was speaking.

"Everything went according to plan. They were able to knock out her guards and left enough scraps of her dress to make it look like a kidnapping. They'll be arriving soon, and we'll need to leave as soon as they are on board. It may be at least an hour before anyone discovers she's gone, but once they do, we have to be far from here."

The captain nodded. "Good. Prepare for takeoff."

The scene shifted again, and this time they were on an Earth beach. It was deserted but for four people. Her mother and the captain were there, as well as the first mate and a man Andy didn't know. Her mother wore a flowing white dress, and her stomach was quite round now, at least seven months along. She held hands with the captain as the other man spoke.

"Do you take this woman to be your wife in all matters of both heaven and earth? Will you protect her, love her, and devote yourself to her in every way deemed fit?"

The captain smiled. "I do."

"And do you take this man to be your husband in all matters of both heaven and earth? Will you protect him, love him, and devote yourself to him in every way deemed fit?"

Adella laughed. "I do."

"Well then, I pronounce you husband and wife!"

The captain pulled Adella into a kiss just as the scene changed. The first thing Andy processed were the screams. Her mother lay on a bed with her feet in the air. The captain paced near the door, a fist pressed to his mouth. He tried to get closer.

"Doctor, is everything all right?"

"It's fine. This is completely normal for a natural birth. Now please, Captain, step back. She's about to crown."

A moment later the shrill sound of a newborn echoed throughout the room. The doctor chuckled as he held the baby up. "Your healthy baby girl is here, Captain. Would you like to hold her?"

The captain rushed forward as the doctor turned and handed him the sticky white baby. Andy couldn't help but notice the thick mass of curls she had. She squalled loudly, her little fists curled to her shoulders and her legs kicked feebly. As soon as the captain took her into his arms and held her to his chest, the baby calmed. She curled into him, her screams now soft mewls. The captain laughed and tried to blink the tears from his eyes.

"Adella, she's so beautiful. Our girl is amazing."

Though Adella looked exhausted, gave a radiant smile. "Let me see her."

The captain took a step forward, but as he did, the baby opened her eyes. If Andy had any reservations about who the baby was, they were gone the moment she saw them. Bright gold shone from beneath the partially hooded lids. The captain gasped and recoiled, his expression of joy transformed into a mask of horror. He shook his head. "No."

Adella sat up, her tone now sharp and urgent. "Bran? What's the matter? What's wrong?"

The captain could do nothing but shake his head and stare down at the baby.

"That was the most horrifying moment of my life."

Andy looked at the captain beside her. His eyes were heavy and distant, sorrow etched into the lines of his face as he relived the memory. "The happiest moment of my life became the most heart-breaking in an instant. I loved you the moment I saw you, but I knew what happened to babies born with moon sickness. The thought of losing you destroyed me."

As he spoke, she watched her mother take the baby. She looked into her eyes and broke into tears, her face pressed against her new-born. The next scenes shifted quickly, each showing her a glimpse as the captain spoke. "The doctors told us there was nothing we could do. There was no cure, nobody knew why babies with moon sickness died. So we cherished every moment we could with you, knowing any moment could be our last.

A scene of the captain rocking and singing to her shifted into her mother giving her a bath. The next showed both lying beside her while they stroked her cheeks and talked to her. Her mother read her books, then the captain kissed her forehead before laying her in her crib.

"But then something incredible happened. Two weeks came and went. No baby had ever lived more that fourteen days. Your mother found hope, and though I wanted to be a realist, it was infectious. We decided you would live, and you did. You thrived, even. You gained weight and developed at a fantastic rate. The first time I heard you laugh, I cried. You were ours, and we weren't going to give you up. But then everything changed."

Andy was pulled into what looked like a battle scene. Men fought all around her, and the screams of combat echoed in the air. Her eyes found the captain. He shot a man down and ran another through with a blade.

"Another ship attacked us, one larger and better equipped than mine. Somehow, we beat them back and survived, but your mother had finally seen the other side of this life."

Andy watched as the captain raced down the halls. He stopped at a storage hatch and yanked it open. Her mother was huddled inside, her baby bundled up and held tightly to her chest. The scene shifted, and the captain and her mother now stood closely together in a dimly lit room. Baby Andromeda slept soundly in her crib nearby, oblivious to the pair's whispers.

"Bran, they could have found us. They almost did. They would have killed us both."

The captain held her mother's shoulders. "I can protect you! You know that."

Her mother pulled away. "Today, sure. But what about next time?"

"I will always protect you both."

"Are you so sure about that?"

"Yes!"

"Sure enough to bet my life on it? To bet hers?" her mother asked, motioning to the sleeping baby.

The captain faltered. "Adella… "

Her mother shook her head. "Bran, I love you, and I love this life. But I love her more. We can't be selfish anymore, we don't have that luxury. We thought we were going to lose her, but we were given a miracle. I won't squander that. Her life is more important than my happiness, and I hope you feel the same."

The captain took a step back and closed his eyes. "So, what? You'll go back? Back to a miserable life with a husband who doesn't love you and keeps you in a gilded cage?"

"If a cage is what will keep her safe, then yes. If it were just me in danger, I would choose this life every time. But it isn't. Please, try to understand."

He ran a hand over her cheek. "I do. Of course I do. I'll give up this life for her."

The scene shifted once more. The captain and Andy's mother stood near the loading door. Baby Andy was wrapped in blankets and bundled in her mother's arms. The captain kissed her mother firmly on the lips, their faces lingering a moment longer once the kiss had ended. Her mother pulled an envelope from the inside of her coat and slid it into his hands, then removed the ring from her finger and handed that to him as well.

"I love you, Ella. I always will."

She smiled, though there was no joy in it. "I know. I doubt I will ever love another."

They kissed again, then he took the baby from her arms. He ran a thumb over her tiny cheek. "Good-bye, my sweet Andromeda. You take my heart with you when you leave, and you will always hold it for as long as you live, even if you don't know it."

The baby showed a gummy smile and reached a small fist up to him. He kissed it gently, before handing her back to her mother. The act of letting her go seemed to cause him physical pain, as his face crumbled into sadness and tears formed in the corners of his eyes.

"Letting you two go was the hardest thing I ever had to do. But it needed to be done. A pirate ship was no place for a baby."

When the scene changed again, Andy noticed a distinct difference in the captain. He was older now, with his curls cut shorter as they were now, and thin lines had formed around his eyes. He was in the dining room with his crew.

"Hey, Captain, did you hear the news?" one man asked.

The captain barely looked up from his screen. "What news?"

"About the crown princess of Celestine."

The captain froze with his cup halfway to his mouth. "What about her?"

"There was an accident. Apparently, her pod ship crashed, and she was ripped out. The news said she was dead."

"No, that ain't what I heard!" another man shouted. "She's not dead, just horribly disfigured. In my opinion, this is just karma on the king. Serves him right, always trying to take our ships down."

But the captain wasn't listening. He had already leapt from his chair and was out the door.

The captain was now crouched inside a dark space, which Andy realized was a closet. She heard a door open and close, and the captain pushed the closet door open. Adella was in the room with her back to them. The captain cleared his throat, and she spun around, her eyes wide. When they fell on the captain, she looked as if she were staring at a ghost.

"Bran?" She spoke his name as if it were a word she had never heard before. "What—what are you doing here?"

He continued to stare at her as though he had found all the answers to the universe. "My God, Adella. You're still as beautiful as the first day I saw you."

But Adella only shook her head. "You cannot be here. Why have you come?"

"I heard what happened. Please, Ella, tell me it isn't true. Our Andromeda, is she still alive?"

Her expression softened. "Yes, she's alive. She was badly injured, but they were able to save her."

He let out a breath. "Good. And is she disfigured?"

Adella smiled gently. "No. They used robotics. She'll look just as she did before. Here."

She went to her vanity and opened the first drawer. She pulled out a picture and brought it to him. Thirteen-year-old Andromeda stared up at him with bright gold eyes, her black curls loose around her shoulders.

He let out an incredulous laugh. "She's stunning. Just as beautiful as you."

"More so," her mother corrected.

"Can I see her?"

Adella looked at him like he had lost his mind. "See her? Of course you cannot! Bran, you need to leave."

"Adella." He reached out to her face, but she pulled sharply away.

"Don't. I'm not the same girl I was thirteen years ago. I'm not nineteen anymore. I'm a mother to more than just Andromeda now. And I'm a queen."

He pressed his lips together. "Do you love him?"

Adella sighed. "I can't do this now. You have to go."

"You took my daughter from me, the least you can do is give me an answer."

Adella bared her teeth. "How dare you? We both made that decision, because it was the right one. I owe you nothing!"

They stared each other down for several seconds before her face calmed, and she let out a sigh. "Yes, of course I love him."

"So, it wasn't true. What you told me? That you would never love another man."

She threw up her hands. "Bran, I was young. We both were. I moved on, didn't you?"

He shook his head. "No, never. How could I? Who could possibly compare to you? You are the only woman I have ever loved."

Adella seemed to deflate. "Bran, what do you want from me? I'm not the same person you knew all those years ago."

He looked down at the picture. "No, I suppose not."

The scene faded from view, and Andy realized she was back in the captain's office. He had removed his scanner. She blinked and felt tears on her cheeks. Andy shook her head slowly.

"No, th-that can't be true. It doesn't make any sense. People would have known if my mother disappeared for ten months. I would know!"

The captain shook his head. "They covered it up. They told the public she had gone away to have a relaxing pregnancy and to give birth. Whether it was to avoid scandal or protect her, I'm not sure. From what I gathered, they really believed she was kidnapped. The king was just happy to have his pet wife back, and he believed you were his. Everything went back to normal."

Andy stared through him. How could this be? She simply couldn't believe it, and yet she had watched it unfold right before her eyes. Was it possible to fake such detailed memories? "I-I don't believe you."

He sighed. "I knew it would take some convincing. It sounds insane. I mean, what are the chances? But it is true."

Andy twisted a curl anxiously around her finger. "No, I'm the daughter of the king. I'm the crown princess of Celestine."

"No, Andromeda, you aren't. Where did you think you got your curls from?"

Andy looked at the curl around her fingers. "It's a recessive trait."

"No, it isn't. It's a common trait in my family. Have you never wondered what the name of this ship is?"

Andy frowned. "I didn't even know it had a name."

The captain reached into his desk and pulled out a paper. He slid it across the desk to her, and she reluctantly leaned forward to read it. It was some sort of ship ledger, and at the top was the full name of the ship. The *Andromeda*. Andy swallowed hard.

"Andromeda is also a constellation. That's just a coincidence."

The captain reached below his desk and lifted out a large chest. It was the same one she had found in her room. He opened the lid and pulled out the baby clothes.

"These were yours. I'm sure you can't remember, but I bought them for you at one of the outer stations."

"You told me your family was dead."

"No, I told you my child had been taken from me. You were." He continued looking through the chest and pulled out the ring. "This was the ring I gave your mother when we married." He set that on the desk as well, then pulled out the letter. "I worried when you found this that you had read it. It was far too soon for you to find out. But I think you're ready."

He slid the letter to her, and she reached out to take it. She didn't want to read it, but it was like something else had taken over. She looked at the initials on the front. "Who is A.C.C.?"

"Your mother."

Andy shook her head. "No, my mother's initials are A.C.F., Adella Cornelia Farrington."

He smiled softly. "Not at that time. She took my last name while she was with me. Adella Cornelia Crane. It's the last name you were born with as well. I think Andromeda Crane sounds better than Andromeda Farrington."

She pulled a sheet of paper out of the envelope, and her heart began to pound quickly in her chest. It was her mother's handwriting. With a feeling of dread, she read.

To my sweet Bran.

Even though I must leave you now. I need you to know that my love for you will never fade. You are the first and last man I will ever love. I must do this, though, for the light of our lives.

our dear Andromeda. I know that you already know this, and I know that this breaks your heart. Even though we will not be able to spend our years together, know that you will never leave my mind. You are the father of my child and keeper of my heart. When I married you, I took my vows seriously, and I still do. My hope is that someday we will find our way back to each other, and you will get to see our baby again. You know she loves you as well. This is my last gift to you.

Your love,
Adella

Andy finished reading and continued to stare at the letter. Tears hung in her eyes as she slowly shook her head back and forth. "No. No, it's not possible. You—you can't be my... "

"Andy, I know this is a lot to throw on you. I want to give you time to come to terms with this. You can take as much time as you need, and when you are ready, you can come to me."

Andy leapt up and threw the letter onto the table. "No! No, this is bullshit! I don't believe you." Her voice quavered with every word.

The captain stared at her. "Yes, you do."

Andy closed her eyes. How could this be happening? Her entire life was built around the fact that she was the crown princess of Celestine, daughter of King Alder. How could this man come in and change that in a matter of minutes? It was too much. She spun around and left the room. She raced down the hall and turned her face away from anyone she passed to keep her tears from being seen. When she reached her room, she was relieved to see that Allen wasn't there. She didn't need him to see her fall apart. She rushed inside and closed the door before throwing herself onto the bed. Everything she'd kept bottled up seemed to flow over in that moment. She sobbed into the pillow.

How could the captain be her father? Her mother would never do that. Was she truly capable of doing something so traitorous? Andy had seen the letter with her own eyes, and it was surely her mother's handwriting. And those memories. How else would he have known with such detail what her castle looked like? How could he remember her mother's voice with such detail? Could it be possible that this was just an elaborate plot the captain had constructed?

There was a knock at the door, and before she could answer, it slid open. Allen walked in and froze when he saw her in tears. He closed the door and rushed to her side.

"What did he do, Andy? Did he hurt you?"

Andy pressed her face into her hands and tried to control her sobbing. How could she tell him what he had told her? If he knew the truth, would he even still care to help her? She shook her head.

Allen tried to pull her hands from her face. "Then what, Andy? Please talk to me. What happened?"

She slid her hands down from her eyes so that she could look at him. His eyes were wide, and his brows were lowered. He searched her face, as though hoping to find the answers there. She needed to talk to someone about this, and she supposed he was the best option. She wiped her face and took several deep breaths.

"He told me something, something I wish he hadn't."

Allen sat beside her on the bed. "What did he tell you?"

Andy chewed her lip and stared at her hands. "The truth, I think."

She told him everything the captain had shown her. She told him about the letter and the ring, and about the mind connector and the memories she'd seen.

When she finished, he remained silent for several seconds. He stared into the distance, his eyes unfocused. "Do you really believe him then?"

Andy shrugged. "I don't want to. If it is true, then that makes my whole life a lie."

Allen frowned and tilted his head. "How?"

"What do you mean how?" she asked as she stood up. "If he is my father, then what does that make me? I was raised to be the queen of Celestine. The only one who can be a ruler of Celestine is the firstborn of the current ruler. If the king isn't my father, then who am I?"

Allen watched her quietly. "I don't think who made you changes who you are at all. Just because the king didn't make you, that doesn't make you any less his daughter."

"I feel like he would disagree."

Allen raised his brows. "Do you? Do you think if your father found out you weren't biologically his, he would throw out eighteen years of loving and raising you? Your parents aren't who make you, your parents are the people who love and take care of you."

Andy wrapped her arms around herself. The truth was, she didn't know. She didn't know if this would change how her father saw her. Would he strip her of her title and home? Would he really throw her into disgrace? She loved her father, and she knew he loved her, but would this be big enough to destroy everything?

"You know," Allen said slowly, "there is a way for you to find out for sure."

She looked up. "What?"

"You could have Mars do a blood test. She'd have the answer within minutes."

Andy shook her head quickly. "No. No, I don't want to know."

She turned away and walked to the window. She heard Allen get off the bed and walk to her. "Andy, not knowing the truth won't protect you. It'll break you. If you know for sure, you can be in control of what happens."

Andy squeezed her eyes shut as the tears forced their way out. She didn't want to tell him that she didn't need a blood test. In her heart, she already knew the truth. But he was right. Not knowing for sure would pick away at her forever. She nodded.

"Ok, fine. Let's go to Mars."

CHAPTER SEVENTEEN

THE MOMENT ANDY STEPPED FOOT through the door to the medical wing, she was accosted by a blur of white hair. Mars's arms wrapped tight around Andy's shoulders; her face pressed to the curve of her neck. Andy hugged her back, taking a few calming breaths and inhaling her floral perfume. When Mars pulled back, she brought her hands up to cradle Andy's face.

"Are you OK? What happened? Why does it look like you've been crying? If the captain did anything to you, I swear I'll undertake a mutiny."

Andy chuckled, pressing her cheek into Mars's palm. "I'm OK physically."

Her face creased with concern. "But emotionally?"

She let out a breath. "There's actually a reason we came to see you."

A few minutes later Andy sat silently as Mars drew her blood. Allen had told her the situation quickly and quietly, making her understand that discretion was incredibly important. Mars still seemed shocked and confused, but she was doing what they asked with no further questions. Once she had the blood, she went to her lab. She pulled a small vial of blood labeled "Captain" from the freezer, then inserted both vials into the machine on her desk and clicked away on her keypad. When she was done, she turned back to them.

"OK, so let me just get a few things straight. You think you are the daughter of the captain, and it's just a coincidence that our crew boarded your ship and took you captive?"

Andy nodded, still feeling numb. Mars blinked several times before continuing. "All right. So how did the captain know it was you if he hadn't seen you since you were an infant?"

Andy wasn't sure how to answer that without revealing her full identity, so instead she shrugged. Mars shook her head and leaned back against her desk.

"This is insane. Well, I guess this explains why the captain has been so protective of you. It also explains why he was so angry at us for raiding the baron."

Andy didn't know what to say. Her stomach was in knots as she stared at the machine. If it told her what she thought it would, what would she do? Would she tell her father? Would she confront her mother? Would she keep it a secret for the rest of her life? Every option made her nauseated. The machine beeped and Mars sat up. She glanced back at Andy before turning the screen so she could see. Andy didn't want to look, but she did. She read the words slowly before nodding.

It was what she had expected. She was not the true crown princess. Everything was a lie. Part of her wanted to cry, or scream, or throw things around the room. But she didn't. She took a deep, shuddering breath. A breakdown wasn't an option. She had to deal with this. She stood and walked to the door, and Allen was quick to follow.

"Where are you going?"

"To talk to him."

He frowned. "What are you going to say?"

"I don't know. But I need to figure this out. What else can I do? Should I lock myself in my room and refuse food or water? What good would that do?"

"Don't get me wrong," Allen said, keeping up with her quick pace, "I'm glad you're going to talk with him. I just want to know if you're ready. You just found out; maybe you should take some time to process."

Andy rolled her eyes. "Why? All that would do is make me angrier." She stopped outside his office. "Do you want to come in with me?"

Allen looked taken aback. She knew there was no reason for him to come in, but she also knew that him being there would make her feel better. But he shook his head.

"I don't think this is my place. You and the captain need to figure this out."

He was right, of course. She took a deep breath and knocked on the door. There was a moment of silence before he answered.

"Come in."

She glanced at Allen one last time before sliding the door open and walking in. The captain still sat behind his desk, and his eyes widened when he saw it was her.

"Andromeda. I wasn't expecting you to come back so soon."

She closed the door and moved to the chair across from him. She stared at him for several moments before speaking.

"Why?"

He furrowed his brow. "Why what?"

"Why did you choose to tell me?"

"I thought you deserved to know."

Andy shook her head and bared her teeth. "No. Don't you dare say you did this for me. I would have been better off never knowing. You did this for you. What did you think would happen when I found out? Did you think I would jump up into your arms and cry with joy? Did you think I wanted to have to question my whole life?"

The captain sat forward. "Andy, you deserved to know where you come from."

"No!" she shouted. She took another deep breath, forcing herself to be calm. "No. You did this for you."

He shrugged. "Maybe I did. Maybe I wanted, for once in my life, to be able to talk to my daughter. I have done nothing but think about you since the day you were born. All I have ever wanted was a relationship with you."

She scoffed. "And the way you did that was by kidnapping me?"

"I didn't do that intentionally. If coincidence hadn't brought you into my path, I would have let you be for the rest of your life. But once I had you, what other choice did I have?"

"Do not try to justify this! You said you gave me up so that I could be happy—well, I was! I was happy just living my life the way it was."

He raised his eyebrows. "Really? You think you were happy living that perfect little life that had been meticulously planned out for you? You were happy marrying someone you didn't choose and only going where others told you to go?" He shook his head. "No. I've seen it since you've been here. You're like your mother. You want love and adventure and *choice*. That was something they would never give you. You'll go back and live out a numb life next to a man who you'll grow disgusted with over time, who will never love you the way you want."

Andy squeezed her fists so tight she felt her nails dig into her skin. "Yeah, well, my mother seemed to end up pretty happy with my father."

"No, she was content. There is a difference. Do you honestly think you can go back to whichever prince you are promised to after this and be happy?"

She opened her mouth to respond but stopped. She hadn't allowed herself to think about that. An image of Eden ran through her head, and she found nothing but indifference. Once, perhaps, she could have seen something growing between them. But now?

"Perhaps it would be difficult at first, but in time it would grow easier."

The captain gave her a sad, almost pitying smile. "No, it wouldn't. Take it from someone who has had true love. No one else is ever the same. It's like going from having your favorite, flavorful dish every day to eating nothing but plain oats. It'll leave your mouth dry, and you'll constantly be thinking, 'God, if I could only just have one more bite of what I had, I would give up eating ever again.' Unfortunately, you won't know that until it's too late."

She looked away. She wouldn't admit to him that she thought he was right. The idea of going back and marrying someone she barely knew made her feel sick. After a moment, she looked back at him.

"You're right. I want the choice. That's all I've ever wanted. But how is being here with you any better? You keep me a prisoner against my will. You keep me away from my family. So, don't make yourself out to be some great champion of choice when you have taken mine away."

He leaned back in his chair. "OK, fine. I'll take you back if that's your choice. If that is truly what you want, I'll let you choose."

She blinked several times. She hadn't expected that. "Really? You'll take me back?"

He nodded. "If that's what you want."

She lowered her eyes. "I have to go back. My kingdom needs me."

The captain slammed his hand down on his desk, making her jump. "You see, there it is again! You do everything for everyone else. The truth is, your kingdom doesn't need you. They will go on just fine without you. You have sisters who could take up that duty, if you wanted. The truth is that you are afraid. You've had people telling you what to do your whole life, and you're terrified that if given the choice, you will choose wrong."

Andy stood, her chair scraping against the floor. "Don't try acting like you know me! You've never been there!"

"I told you, you're just like your mother. She was afraid too. She wasn't truly free until she let that go and decided for herself what she wanted. Once she did that, she never looked back. That is the true measure of a ruler. Their decisiveness in themselves, and their ability to know what is right."

Andy breathed heavily, her mouth full of saliva that had quickly collected as she stood there motionless. After a moment, she spoke quietly. "But what if I don't know what the right thing to do is?"

He walked around his desk and stood in front of her. "Close your eyes."

She frowned. "No."

"Trust me." He spoke gently.

Reluctantly, she did as he said. He continued, soft and calm. "Forget, for a moment, that you have anybody relying on you. Forget all the expectations of others. Pretend that it's just you, and only your opinion matters. Now, picture what you want. Picture your ideal life."

As she followed his instructions, an image formed in her head. She was running. Through corridors, through stations, on Earth. Her hair whipped around, and she felt weightless. She felt free. Allen was beside her, laughing along with her, and Mars was on her other side. She could picture it so clearly. She could do what she wanted. There would be no doors closed to her just because of who she had been born. Her love could belong to whomever she wished.

She opened her eyes and found the captain smiling. "Now, did any of what you just pictured involve being queen?"

She let out a shaky breath and shook her head. "But I have to go back to my family."

He nodded and placed a hand on her shoulder. "They aren't going anywhere. If you want to do something for yourself for once, even for just a little while, you can always go back when you're ready."

250 K. M. WATTS

She pulled away from his reach. "But I can't remain a prisoner here anymore! I'm not a child, and I don't want you telling me what to do."

He folded both of his hands in front of himself. "You're right. From now on, as long as you choose to be here, you have free rein. You can do what you like and go where you want."

Andy inhaled and exhaled slowly. It felt as if a chain had been broken away.

"Wait, what about the crew?"

He frowned. "What about them?"

"They think I'm your lady." Before, it had only been a little creepy, but now, knowing who he was...

"Ah, right. I had forgotten about that."

"Yes, and can I ask, if you knew who I was, why on Earth would you tell everybody I'm your lady?"

He shrugged. "I couldn't very well tell everybody you're my daughter. It was the safest route to follow."

She wrinkled her nose, but let the matter drop. "OK, but still, what are we going to tell everyone?"

He leaned back against his desk. "It would be too dangerous to change the story now. The safest course of action may be to just go along with what they already believe."

"No, absolutely not. How am I supposed to be free around here if I'm still living that ridiculous charade? Surely we can come up with a better excuse that doesn't leave me in such a precarious situation."

"Andy, we can't tell anybody the truth. It would put you in danger. Even telling Allen and Mars is a risk, but I understand why you did. I trust my crew with doing their jobs and staying loyal, but they are still pirates. They live outside the law, and if someone offered them the right price, who knows what they would do."

She crossed her arms. "I understand that. I'm not saying we should march through the halls announcing that the crown princess of Celestine is on board. All I'm asking is for a position that allows me to actually be one of them. Not some kept pet."

The captain sighed and pinched the bridge of his nose. "Very well. We'll tell them I have granted you freedom from me and have made you an official member of the crew. This could still put you in danger. Allen and I can't be around to protect you twenty-four seven."

She placed her hands on her hips. "So give me a gun and I'll protect myself."

He raised an eyebrow. "Andy, you couldn't kill that man before."

"Yeah, well, there's a bit of a difference in killing someone in cold blood and stopping them from hurting me."

He tapped his finger on the desk before he smiled and reached into his desk drawer. He pulled out a gun and handed it to her.

"Just make sure that before you pull the trigger, you're ready for what follows."

"I have a feeling that's not something I could ever prepare for."

A haunted sort of smile crossed his face. "No, I don't imagine it is."

CHAPTER EIGHTEEN

OVER THE NEXT WEEK, ANDY did her best to blend into the new role. The crew had seemed surprised when the captain told them she was no longer his lady but a full member of the crew. She spent nearly all her time with Mars and Allen, given they were the only ones who knew most of her secrets.

The sound of gentle tapping awoke her from sleep. She opened her eyes slowly, blinking hard against the light of the room. Just as always, she couldn't tell what time it was supposed to be. She rolled over, and then immediately let out a shriek. Mars was sitting on the bed beside her, watching her with a small smile and tapping her nails against her com screen.

"Morning, sleepyhead."

"Mars," Andy groaned as she sat up. "What the hell are you doing?"

Mars brushed a strand of hair from her face. It was shoulder length and in tight curls now. Andy liked this look best.

"I was waiting for you to wake up. You're a deep sleeper, you know."

Andy rolled her eyes but smiled. "Yes, I've been told. But why are you watching me sleep?"

"Captain wants everyone to meet up in the observation chamber in an hour. I volunteered to come get you."

Andy sat up and scooted back so that she was sitting beside Mars against the headboard. "Why does he want us all there?"

"Don't know. Nothing bad, probably."

"That's *very* reassuring."

Mars snorted. "Hey, I never claimed to have a great bedside manner."

Andy laughed and tugged on one of Mars's curls. "On the contrary, I think you have excellent bedside manner."

Mars stilled and raised her eyebrows, a slow smile creeping onto her face. "Is that so?"

Andy felt her cheeks warm. "Um, well, yes."

Mars rolled onto her side so that she was looking up at her. "And tell me, what else do you like about me?"

For a moment, Andy considered making a joke about it, but Mars was looking at her with what seemed like a challenge in her eyes. So instead, she rolled onto her side so that they were facing each other.

"I like that you're brave. I like that you're bold. You don't care what people think about you, and you make sure they know it. You're completely unapologetic about what you want. You're completely unafraid."

As she spoke, Mars's smile had slid from her lips. The look she gave her now was full of questions and something else Andy wasn't sure she could pinpoint. When Mars spoke, her voice was quiet.

"I don't know about all that. I'm afraid plenty of the time. And I definitely don't always go after what I want."

Andy raised an eyebrow. "Like when?"

Rather than answer, Mars reached out and ran her thumb across Andy's jaw. Andy inhaled sharply, her eyes going slightly wide. The feeling of Mars's thumb on her skin was like a live wire, connecting every nerve in her body to that single point. But then it was gone. Mars tucked her hand beneath her head and gave her a smile.

"So, how are you enjoying all this freedom?"

Andy blinked, her mind still filled with the sensation of Mars's touch. "Um, what?"

"Your freedom. Now that you can come and go as you like, do whatever you want. How is it?"

"Oh, it's good, I suppose. I don't really know what to do with it." Andy bit her lip, focusing on a small spot on her pillow.

"What is it?"

"Does not wanting to go back to Celestine make me a bad person? I mean, I miss my family, but when I was with them, I always felt so suffocated. Like I was living out a perfectly scripted life that I had no say in and nobody had asked if I wanted. And I just did it, whatever they wanted, without question. Now, at least I can choose what happens to me."

Mars smiled and shook her head. "That doesn't make you a bad person, that makes you human. I think I would go insane if people were always telling me what to do and how to do it. We have to find our own way in this universe."

Andy sighed. "I feel like whatever I do, I'll be losing and gaining something."

Mars stared at her, and for a moment she thought she was going to touch her again. She wanted her to.

"Then I guess you just need to decide what you can live without, and what's worth fighting for."

"What if I do the wrong thing?"

Mars slid her hand into Andy's, intertwining their fingers. "I can't answer that for you. But I think you should do whatever will make you most happy."

Andy chewed her lip and stared into Mars's dark eyes. She wasn't sure how long they lay there, but the sound of someone clearing their throat made them both jump. Allen stood in the doorway, his hands braced on either side of the door and a mischievous smile on his face.

"Hey, you two, we're supposed to be at the observation chamber in twenty minutes."

Mars pulled her hand away from Andy and sat up. "Yeah, I know. That's what I came here to tell Andy."

"Well, your cuddling session looked lovely, but Captain doesn't like to wait."

Andy climbed out of bed and grabbed some clothes from her trunk. Before she closed the bathroom door, she stuck her tongue out at him and heard him chuckle.

Fifteen minutes later, the three of them made their way into the observation chamber. Andy wasn't sure why she expected there to still be blood on the floor, but she was relieved to find it sparkling clean. The rest of the crew had already assembled and were gathered around the room. Andy spotted the captain standing on the raised dais. When he made eye contact with her, he smiled and gave a small nod. Ever since he had told her who he was, he had been giving her space. He didn't sleep in his own room anymore, leaving it entirely for her. She had suggested taking one of the smaller crew rooms, but he had refused. She knew he was still worried for her safety and keeping her in his more private quarters made him feel better.

She still hadn't fully come to terms with who he was to her. It was doubtful that they could ever have the relationship he wanted. She had a father, one who had raised her. Just because he had helped to make her didn't make him her dad. But whenever she would think that, the memory of him holding her and weeping would flash through her mind. Or the memory of him singing to her, or kissing her, or giving her up. He loved her. She knew that, and she couldn't help but feel guilty that she didn't feel the same. But she was doing the best she could.

When it looked like the crew was all there, the captain spoke.

"Just a few hours ago, I received a transmission informing me of a rogue ship in my district. It is believed that they are smuggling illegal cargo and have broken article three of our code."

Andy leaned over to Allen. "Isn't all cargo you take out here illegal?"

He snorted. "Yeah, but this is doubly bad. Article three of the code states that any ship operating out here must give thirty percent of its bounty to the ruling lord captain it's under. This one seems to have decided it wants to branch out on its own, possibly in a bid to become a new lord captain. That rarely works out for them."

Andy raised an eyebrow and focused back on the captain.

"Now, I could send one of my other squadrons out to deal with them. But I thought, since it's been so long since you've all had some fun, we would go after the bastards ourselves."

The room erupted into cheers. Andy looked around, startled at the enthusiasm for destroying another crew. Allen seemed to notice her surprise and smirked.

"As the main crew of the lord captain's, we don't get to raid as often as other ships. It's always good to let everyone release some steam."

Andy scrunched up her nose. "By killing a bunch of people?"

He shrugged. "We don't kill all of them. Their captain and leaders of the ship, yeah, but the rest of the crew get the option of joining one of our other ships or being exiled."

"Exiled from being a pirate? That sounds a bit counterintuitive, don't you think?"

"Hey, despite what you think, we have rules out here. They know the consequences of breaking them."

Andy looked back to the captain, who was laughing with the men standing near the front. He straightened up and spoke to the room once again.

"They seem to have disabled their tracking system, but they don't appear to be the brightest bunch. Because it's one of my ships, our crew was able to hack in and get their location. They've stopped in midspace and haven't moved in a while. We should be on them in the next eight hours.

"I expect all of you to prepare yourselves and be ready when the time comes. The crew is smaller, and the ship is less well equipped, but we still can't risk any screwups. We have our own precious cargo aboard, after all."

At this, he looked to Andy. She could only hold his gaze for a few moments before looking away. It was too much. She had heard of unrequited love between romantic partners, but between family? It wasn't that she disliked him. In fact, ever since finding out the truth, she liked him quite a bit. But love was something else. Love had to be earned.

People began to stream out of the room and the captain approached the three of them.

"Allen, I hoped you would help with the initial attack on the ship. You're one of my best in a fight, and I would like for this to go smoothly."

Allen nodded. "Of course. I'll meet with the other men and make a plan of attack."

"Excellent. And Mars, I'll have you stationed with a team at the entrance of the ship, to make sure none of them can get on board."

Mars did a little salute. "Aye, aye, Captain."

He smirked and turned away, but Andy stopped him. "Wait, what about me?"

A frown creased his forehead. "Absolutely not. You aren't battle trained. I don't need you getting hurt, or one of these two getting hurt trying to protect you."

Andy folded her arms. Honestly, she couldn't argue with that. She had never been in a proper battle before, especially not with rogue pirates. But she also didn't want to just sit around doing nothing. She was a part of the crew now, after all.

"Fine, but let me do something else. I can work on the deck."

"Andy, the deck will be filled with skilled professionals. I know you want to help, but this isn't something that will be beneficial. You're with mechanical."

"Yes, but the rest of the mechanics will be fighting as well!"

"And if you were thoroughly trained in combat, then I would have no problem with you joining them, but you're not."

Andy ground her teeth together. She highly doubted that, but it would do no good to argue this point.

"Fine. I'll just sit in my room and do nothing."

He smiled. "Thank you."

She had the overwhelming urge to do something unladylike but reined it in. She watched him walk away. Allen nudged her.

"Trust me, it's better this way. You wouldn't enjoy being there for the initial attack. I'll come get you when it's over so you can watch the pardoning of the crew members who swear fealty."

"Yeah," Mars agreed. "Plus, when this is over, I'll show you the loot I was able to keep from the baron. Captain took a bunch of the good stuff, but I still have plenty of interesting items. They're in a box in my room."

Andy shrugged. She hated feeling useless, but they were right. She didn't want to get anyone hurt by being reckless. One thing she knew was that as soon as this was over, she was going to force Mars and Allen to train her until she was good enough to fight alongside them. Doing nothing had never been her strong suit.

Eight hours later found Andy pacing back and forth across her room. She had been told they were coming up on the ship nearly an hour ago and had been sent away while the others prepared. It would be a lie to say she wasn't nervous. People that she now deeply cared for were about to be thrown into an extremely dangerous situation, and she could do nothing to help. She didn't even know if they had boarded the other ship yet. She assumed she would hear some sort of commotion when it happened, but really, she had no idea.

She stopped pacing and walked to the door. Even with her ear pressed to it, she could hear nothing but silence.

"Damn it!" she cried, kicking the desk with the toe of her boot.

If she had to stay here and do nothing, it was going to drive her to madness. She chewed her lip for a moment, considering her options. Going down to the loading doors was out of the question. She couldn't risk distracting the crew. But if she went to the main deck, surely she wouldn't be in the way. At least she would know what was happening. With her mind made up, she slid open the door and walked into the hall.

Again, nothing but silence. Her booted footsteps echoed in the empty halls, giving off an eerie feeling, like she was walking through a ghost ship. There were normally crew members making their way up and down these halls, but right now they all had specific jobs. As she turned down a hall to her left, she stopped. There was a faint sound coming from back the way she had come. It was almost a grating sound, like metal being scraped against metal. The ship should not be making that sound. Her curiosity getting the better of her, Andy turned back. The further down she walked, the louder it became. Picking up her pace, she rounded the corner and stopped.

A side panel was open in the ship's wall. She was fairly sure it led down into the cargo hold. None of that mattered at the moment, however, because six men she didn't recognize were standing outside of it and helping a seventh man out. Andy's breath caught in her chest. These men were most certainly not from her crew, which meant they were from the other crew. They caught sight of her only a moment after she did them.

"Hey!" one cried, pointing at her. "Get her! Don't let her alert the others!"

Without another thought, Andy turned and ran. She was horribly aware that she was without a weapon and incredibly outnumbered. The men stood between her and her room where her gun was. She could try to make her way to the main deck, but it was pretty far, and if she made one wrong turn, she would be dead. The sound of them chasing her was loud, their boots slamming against the metal floor and their breathing rough. Her own pounding heart didn't help. She racked her brain for any inkling of where to go. An idea came to her.

Mars's room was close, just down the next hall. There was no guarantee there would be any weapons there, but it was the best plan she had.

Her boots skidded against the floor as she turned left. Her momentum almost made her slam into the wall, but she was able to regain control and righted herself. The men were closer now. She made the last turn and ran into Mars's door.

Oh God, please don't let it be locked.

She hit the panel button, and it slid open. But there was no time to relax. Running in, she tried to close it behind her, but a thick boot slid in the way. With a startled shriek, she backed up and looked around wildly. There had to be something here she could use. There was a box on the desk, and it looked like it was filled with all sorts of objects. The items Mars had stolen from the baron!

Andy ran for it, but as soon as her hand closed around the top, she felt a hand grab the ends of her curls and yank. She fell back with a cry of pain, the box of objects falling and its contents scattering across the floor. A thick hand wrapped around her neck and slammed her down, and a man loomed over her, his face scarred and ugly.

"Where did you think you were going, little girl?" His voice was like shoes on gravel.

The hand tightened, cutting off oxygen, and Andy panicked. He was at an angle that made it difficult to kick, but that didn't negate the fact that her legs were extraordinarily strong. Bringing them up, she clamped them around his waist and squeezed. His eyes widened and after a moment she heard one of his ribs crack. His grip on her throat loosened, and she gasped for air. She rolled and shoved him to the side, scrambling around for something to use as a weapon.

She hadn't noticed the other man who had been waiting by the door until he grabbed her by the back of her shirt. Her eyes fell on a wooden box that had fallen open when it was thrown with the rest of the items. Her heart surged. A long, curved blade lay half outside the box, glistening in the florescent lights. She tried to reach for it, but the hand holding her pulled her back. A kick to the shin forced him to the floor. The moment he let go of her, she surged forward and wrapped her hand around the handle of the blade.

The moment her skin came into contact with it, a surge of energy unlike anything she had ever felt before shot through her. A gasp forced its way out of her. Her eyes were transfixed on the blade, which, if she wasn't mistaken, had begun to let off a glow. That, mixed with the sensation that it was pulsing against her palm, gave the terrible impression that it was alive.

Andy had become so transfixed by the blade that she momentarily forgot the reason she had come here in the first place. A swift kick to her side brought her back to reality. She rolled over with a groan. The man whom she had kicked was now on top of her and had pulled a gun.

"Didn't want to waste my bullets on you, but I think this will be worth it."

At the same time as he lifted the gun to her head, Andy brought the blade up and slashed at his shoulder. Due to the angle, the cut was shallow. But that didn't seem to matter. The moment it cut into his skin, his eyes went wide, and he fell back off her. She could do little more than watch in horror as he stumbled across the room, something white and opaque seeping from his wound and connecting to the blade. The blade began to vibrate with purpose now, and Andy had a bizarre feeling that it was happy. Andy inexplicably knew what was happening to the man. His soul, or life essence, was being sucked from him. She had no idea how she knew this; it was as if the blade was communicating with her. The man fell to the floor, his body going still and his eyes staring blankly at the ceiling.

Andy dropped the blade with a cry and crawled backward away from it. The man whose ribs she had cracked had recovered somewhat and had watched what had happened.

"What the hell did you do to him?" he shouted, reaching for the fallen blade.

"No, don't!" she tried to warn him. Somehow, she knew that if he touched the blade, it would not end well for him.

Sure enough, as soon as the blade was in his hand, he let out a terrible scream. He fell to his knees as his hand turned to ash and crumbled, followed by the rest of him. Andy stared in open-mouthed horror as he disintegrated before her eyes. The blade clattered back onto the floor, and a silence filled the room. Andy felt as though she were glued to the spot, her eyes not moving from the blade. She was aware of a commotion outside the room but couldn't seem to make her body react.

The door slid open, and a man walked in, weapon drawn and looking furious. His eyes traveled from the soulless man to the pile of dust, to Andy. He moved toward her, but a flash of dark curls behind him and a blade to his throat drew him to a stop.

"I suggest you drop your weapon and surrender, if you aren't a complete idiot," Mars said.

The man was still for a moment, but then turned and raised his gun. Mars was quicker, yanking his head back by his hair and slicing his throat. He fell to the ground, blood pooling around him.

Mars remained standing where she was, looking around the room. When her eyes fell on Andy, she approached slowly.

"Andy, hey, are you all right?"

Andy still couldn't draw her eyes away from the dead man. Her mind felt cloudy and slow. Mars drew closer, moving slowly, as though she were comforting a frightened animal.

"Andy, what happened? How did you end up here?"

It took her a moment, but finally Andy was able to look at Mars. She knew how she must look. Her hair was likely a mess, her face pale and eyes haunted.

"I-I don't know. I didn't mean to. I was just trying to defend myself. I didn't know it would do that."

Mars knelt down beside her. "Didn't know what would do what?"

Andy pointed a shaking finger at the blade. Mars reached for it, but Andy grabbed ahold of her and screamed.

"No! Don't touch it! It turned him to ash."

Mars's brows knitted together, looking at the pile beside the blade. "Wait, are you telling me that was a person?"

Andy nodded. "Yes. I grabbed it to protect myself. I cut that other man, and it-it—" How could she explain what had happened without sounding crazy? "It was like it sucked the life out of him. It was vibrating and glowing. And then I dropped it and the other man took it. But as soon as he touched it, that happened."

Mars's eyes were wide. "Jesus. When I first saw it, I knew there was something wrong with it. That's why I left it in its box. But why didn't you turn to dust?"

All Andy could do was shake her head. She didn't know. The memory of what that man had said, the one who had tried to kidnap and mutilate her, flashed through her mind.

You don't know what you are?

She forced that thought back. If she thought about that right now, she was sure she would have a breakdown. Mars pulled her into a hug, cradling her head and pressing her face into her shoulder. Her warm pressure was grounding, the sharp scent of sanitizing soap and jasmine forcing her into the present. She brought her arms up and wrapped them tightly around Mars.

"Hey, it's OK. It's fine. You're fine."

Andy wanted to agree, to assure Mars that she would be all right. But in that moment, she really wasn't sure.

CHAPTER NINETEEN

ANDY SAT ACROSS FROM THE captain, a three-course dinner set out before her. It had been a week since the raid of the other ship. Andy was doing her best to get past what had happened, but the nightmares that came every night refused to let her forget. The captain was trying to distract her the best he could, and she appreciated him for trying. The blade had been carefully handled and put back in its box, then placed it in the trunk where the captain kept all of his other important items. She couldn't lie, she didn't like having it so close, but it was better than leaving it where anybody else could get to it. She twisted the gem on the necklace she wore, glancing up at the captain. It was the necklace Eden had given her. It had initially been taken when she came here, but the captain had given it back. Part of her felt guilty wearing it, but really it meant nothing to her. It was just a pretty bit of jewelry.

"So, are there any medical conditions on your side of the family that I should know about?"

He looked up at her as he put a piece of chicken in his mouth. "You mean besides homicide and kleptomania? Considering you survived moon sickness, I'd say you're safe."

She put her fork down slowly. "Yes, I've been thinking about that. About how I'm the only one to have ever survived it. What does it mean?"

He seemed to consider it before he looked down at his plate. "So little is known about the disease. When you were born with it, your mother and I did tireless research for weeks. There were a few odd cases where babies were born with it but no bodies were ever documented. As far as we could see, there was no proof those babies lived. It's likely they were just born to poor families who abandoned them and didn't report the death."

Andy nodded. "But it must mean something, right? I was able to hold that blade, but when the other man touched it, it destroyed him."

The captain sighed. "I don't know what that means. I admit, it's odd. I honestly haven't put more thought into it beyond being immensely grateful you survived. Even when I couldn't see you, when it had been years since I looked into your eyes, I would think of you and worry that you weren't happy. I would dream of you... all the time." He closed his eyes as he said the last bit, as though it caused him pain.

She frowned. "What were the dreams?"

"There were different ones. For about a year after you left, I would dream that I could hear you crying, somewhere on the ship. I would race around, desperate to find you. But I never did."

Andy swallowed hard. "And the others?"

"After a few years, the dream changed. I would see a golden-eyed little girl running through the gardens of Celestine. You would see me, and I would reach out to you, but you were afraid. You didn't know me. You would run away in terror.

"There were a few others after that. One where you were on a sinking ship, an Earth one. You would call out for me, beg me to save you, but I couldn't. I could never get to you. After your accident, I would dream that I was watching your ship take off, with a feeling of dread. I could never remember why until it was too late. Then your ship would explode, with me helpless on the ground."

"Jeez," Andy whispered. "It seems like you only had nightmares about me."

He smiled. "No, there was one happy dream I would have. I dreamed I walked on a beach with your mother's hand in mine. She had never left me. You would run ahead, your black curls flying behind you. You would shriek with laughter as the cold waves jumped at you, each time trying to dodge them. Waking from that dream was the worst."

Andy lowered her eyes. "I'm sorry you didn't get to have the life you wanted."

He nodded. "So am I."

Silence stretched between them. She picked at her food as she tried to think of something to say. She had always been uncomfortable with silence. It always felt as though with every second that someone didn't speak, an invisible balloon was filling and would eventually pop. It filled her whole body with tension. The captain chuckled softly. She looked at him.

"What?"

He shook his head. "You're just like your mother. I can see you sitting there, racking your brain for something to say. She didn't like silence either."

Andy narrowed her eyes. "That's not true. I've been alone with my mother enough times to know that she can let a silence stretch on forever."

"Then I suppose she got better at pretending."

Andy leaned back in her chair. "The more I think about it, the more I realize we were all pretending. Some less than others. My sister Rosetta always said what was on her mind. My father would get so mad at her. One time, during a royal banquet, she asked my mother's aunt, the Duchess of Brazine, why her face was so hairy."

Andy giggled. "Rosetta's bold. She never cared what anybody thought and made sure people knew it." She let out a sigh. "I was never like that. I've always cared too much. Even when I try to pretend I don't, I'm no good at acting. I used to want to be just like Rosetta."

The captain folded his hands over his chest. "It helps that she didn't have the weight of an entire kingdom on her shoulders."

Andy inhaled deeply. "Yes, I suppose it does. Perhaps she *would* make a better queen."

"Saying whatever is on your mind doesn't make you a great leader. Sure, sometimes you have to demand attention and be heard, but you must also know when to be silent and let things remain as they are."

She pursed her lips. "Do you think that's why my father has allowed the outer stations to become overrun with crime and poverty? Why he lets people remain enslaved within his domain?"

The captain stood and walked to a cabinet that contained several vials of alcohol. He poured a glass for himself, then walked back to his chair and sat before he took a sip. "Andy, I don't hide the fact that I don't like King Alder. Part of it is indeed because of my anger and jealousy. He has the life I always dreamed of having. But another part of my dislike stems from the way he rules. He sits in an ivory tower and watches the little people toil away for his benefit, all while allowing the millions under his rule to live in poverty. And I'm not even talking about the outer stations. Stations Seven through Ten are shitholes, run by cruel lords that were put into power by the circumstances of their birth."

Andy wanted to defend her father, but she couldn't bring herself to say the words. Even the thought of saying it was for the greater good left a nasty taste in her mouth. The captain went on.

"But, in a way, I also understand him. He and I share some of the same traits. They're traits I don't like, but I have them all the same. I have significant power out here. If I wanted, I could throw all my resources into changing the way things are. I could make a difference. But I don't. Do you know why?"

Andy raised an eyebrow. "Because you're selfish?"

He held up his glass to her. "Exactly. Both the king and I are selfish. We put the needs of ourselves and our family before the needs of the others. That is the way of most people, even if they won't admit it."

Andy looked down. "I'm selfish too."

He shrugged. "Perhaps. Everyone must be sometimes. It's nothing to be ashamed of."

"But you just said it's a trait you don't like."

"That's because selfishness becomes a problem when it is your driving factor. Nearly every decision I have ever made has been selfish. Now look at my life."

Andy laughed. "Yes, look at your poor miserable life. You have an untold amount of money, a loyal crew, and the respect and power to live as you wish."

He leaned back and balanced his glass between his fingers. "True. And yet what do I have that I have not bought? I have no wife to love me, no children to remember me." He took a small sip of alcohol. "What good is a legacy if there is no one to honor it?"

Andy watched him in silence for several moments. "I'll remember you."

His eyes flashed up to her, and a faint smile crossed his face. "Thank you." He looked back down at his glass. "One of the only selfless decisions I've ever made was killing my brother. And that selflessness destroyed my family."

"No." Andy shook her head. "Your brother destroyed your family. He was a monster. What would have happened if you hadn't stopped him? He would have continued to beat your mother and abuse your sister. He deserved to die."

"But was that my decision? I could have stopped him and called the police. He would have gone to prison."

"Would he? You've told me your family was influential. Would your father not have gotten him off lightly?"

The captain's eyes remained on his glass, as though searching the depths within. "I've asked myself that question a million times. That's what I told myself after I fled. It's the only thing that stopped me from putting a bullet in my head for a long time. The truth is, I don't know. I never will. I do know that I'll never be able to unsee him, dead on the floor at my feet. I'll never forget the screams of my sister, only thirteen, as she looked from his dead body to me. She was afraid of me, just like you were when you first saw me."

Andy didn't know what to say. Should she comfort him? How? He looked back at her then and straightened up.

"I'm sorry, I didn't mean to pull you into my twisted little world."

She shook her head. "It's fine. Really. I-I enjoy having someone to talk about these sorts of things with. Insecurities. God knows I have enough of them to last a lifetime." She smiled, almost playfully. "It's nice to have an adult figure in my life who I don't think is perfect."

A snicker broke through his serious expression. "Well, I am happy to provide you with an attainable moral figure. Now, it's getting late. You should get back to your room so that you can rest."

Andy nodded. "All right. I'll see you in the morning?"

He lifted his glass to her. "Of course. Sleep well, Andromeda."

"Good night, Bran."

His eyes widened slightly, seemingly taken off-guard by her causal use of his name. It was a step up from Captain. He smiled as she closed the door behind her. She leaned back against it and closed her eyes. They were making progress. With a push-off from the door, she made her way down the hall when a low whistle caught her attention. She came to a stop and turned. Allen was standing at the end of the hall, his tall frame leaning up against the wall of the ship.

"Hey there, Princess. Could I ask you to spare a minute?"

Andy rolled her eyes but smiled. She hadn't had as much one-on-one time with him as she would have liked since she found out the captain was her father. Allen had been bogged down with crew duties, and Andy had been fairly distracted. But as she let her eyes roam over his broad shoulders and devious smirk, the memory of his mouth on hers and his hands in her hair raced back. A warm heat rose in her cheeks.

"Oh, I don't know. It'll truly be a tremendous burden on me. But, if you must."

He scoffed as he approached her. "I just got a good look at what it would be like to be your subject. Horrible."

She swung to smack his arm, but he caught her wrist in his hand. Andy sucked in a breath at the sudden contact, his strong fingers wrapped easily around her wrist and his face so close she could feel his breath ghosting across her cheeks. The lids of his eyes drooped and his mouth fell open slightly as he took in her flushed skin. Allen swallowed, looking from her hand to her face.

"Will you come with me?"

Any quip that she would normally have thrown at him died on her lips at the rasp in his voice. Her mouth had gone dry, so all she could do was nod mutely.

Allen shifted his hold on her so that he was gripping her hand instead of her wrist and led her down the hall. After a minute of walking, she knew where he was leading her. They came to a stop beneath the hatch to the sky dome, and he gave her a sly smile.

"What do you say? For old times' sake?"

Andy rolled her eyes. "It's only been a couple months."

He seemed to take this as a yes and climbed the ladder. The door opened, and he climbed through. Andy followed him up. It was every bit as beautiful as she remembered. Space stretched around them in every direction. The last time she had been here, she was a captive on a hostile pirate ship. Now, she was part of the crew. She was a free woman with a sea of possibilities stretched out before her. She laid down on her back, and Allen joined her.

"Life is weird."

Allen turned his head slightly to look at her. "How so?"

"I mean with everything I've gone through in these past few months. I've done things I never could have imagined doing before. Hell, even the panic attacks have lessened. I didn't even notice their absence at first. I think… I think the mask I wore my whole life was slowly suffocating me."

Allen remained silent but reached out to rest his hand over hers.

"And in the meantime, I've met pirates, I've run from the law, I've… " She looked over and met his eye. "I've met people that I care deeply for."

He raised an eyebrow. "Oh? Someone good, I hope?"

Andy huffed a quiet laugh. "Yes, I think he's very good."

The cheeky smile Allen wore slid off his face as he looked into her eyes. Once again, that charge of energy crackled in the air between them. Allen licked his lips.

"I know we haven't really talked about what happened on Station Twelve. About what I said and did."

Andy sat up and pressed her cheek to her knees, keeping her eyes still on him. "Did you not mean it?"

Allen sat up as well, his eyes distant. "No, I did. I do. The way I feel about you, Andy, I've never felt this way for anyone before. You're all I think about. I worry about you constantly." He snorted. "It's exhausting, honestly. And trust me, it's all right if you don't feel the same. I don't expect anything from you. You don't owe me anything; I just want you to be happy."

Andy chewed her lip. "What if I don't know how to love properly?"

A slow smile spread across his face, like the first rays of light on a horizon that had been dark for too long. "Then I'll have to love you enough for the both of us."

Andy's breath came out in a rush. She reached out slowly, as though not to scare him, and cupped his jaw in her palm. He stilled, his breath coming in short shudders. Slowly, she dragged her thumb over his lips, the soft fullness of them a contrast to the roughness of his jaw. He hadn't shaved in a couple of days, and the barest hint of red stubble shadowed his skin. When she slid her thumb off his lip, a small amount of moisture came with it.

"You're the kindest man I've ever met."

As soon as the words left her mouth, it was as if all the fight went out of him. He leaned forward into her palm and closed his eyes tightly, as though that would help fight off the onslaught of emotion he was feeling. Andy continued. She needed him to know.

"You are so damn kind. You always think about everyone else."

"That's not—"

"Hush. None of that right now."

He moaned and pressed harder against her palm. Confident, self-assured Allen was coming apart in her hands all because of a few kind words. She felt as though a door that she had never seen before was being opened into his soul. As though it had been an awfully long time since he had experienced genuine affection and love. It made her heart ache for him.

"You are constantly willing to risk your life for others. And while I wish you wouldn't, because I need you to be safe, I love that quality in you. Despite the front you put up, you love other people and care about them. And you're so smart. Even if it drives me insane sometimes, I love your wit."

She moved her hand up and rubbed against the velvety softness of his eyelids. Pale eyelashes fluttered against the warm tone of his cheeks.

"I love that you're brave. I love that you're independent. I love that you're funny."

At this, he finally opened his eyes, and his expression was filled with mirth.

"Oh, you think I'm funny, do you? I thought you found me to be insufferable."

She nodded in mock seriousness. "Oh yes, I do. Completely unbearable to be around."

Allen broke into laughter. "Well, I'll try to be a bit more bearable."

Andy shook her head. "Don't you dare."

And then she was leaning forward, bringing her lips to his in a gentle press. His hands wound their way into her hair, tugging gently at the roots and making her feel lightheaded. She gasped and leaned further against him, both of her hands gripping the sides of his face. With the barest of pressure, she bit down on his bottom lip and pulled. This rewarded her with the desired response, as he groaned loudly and pulled back, his eyes wide and his lips already pink and swollen.

"Jesus, Andromeda. What are you trying to do, kill me?"

She laughed. "If you can be killed with a kiss, I'd worry for your health."

She flopped back down, and Allen followed suit, though they were now much closer than before. His knuckles brushed against hers, and the contact made the hair on her arms stand on end. Without thinking too hard about it, she intertwined their fingers. When she glanced at Allen, he was smiling.

"So, Andy, I let you in on a little bit about me. What about you? Have you ever been in love before?"

Andy considered the question for a moment, then nodded. "I thought I was, when I was sixteen."

"What was their name?"

"Catalina. She was the daughter of a lord. We only knew each other for two months, as she went back home after that, but those two months were some of my best. I think I might have fallen in love with her if she had stayed longer, but she was the closest I came. She was fascinating and beautiful, and she didn't live by the rules that had been set out for her. She made me feel like I could do anything."

Allen looked up at the stars. "She sounds great."

"She was. Then her father married her off to some lord, and I never saw her again." Andy knew how bitter she sounded, and it was because she was. How had it taken her this long to fully understand the horrible nature of the way they were treated? Catalina had been so full of life, and though she hadn't seen her in years, she couldn't bear the thought of her flame being extinguished for the sake of an alliance. The same way hers would be if she let her parents marry her off.

Andy realized it had been a minute since either of them had spoken and glanced back at Allen. Only then did she realize that she probably shouldn't rave about how wonderful an ex was. "Oh, but you don't have to worry. That was over two years ago."

Allen gave her a gentle smile. "Andy, I'm not jealous. You don't owe me your past, or even your future, for that matter. I'll gladly take whatever you'll give me. I don't want to own you."

Andy rolled toward him. "If you keep talking like that, I'm going to begin to think that I'm the one who doesn't deserve you."

"Hmm." He stroked the back of her hand with his thumb. "I don't think anyone deserves anyone. Even if the circumstances weren't great, I'm glad I met you. Not sure what I'd be doing right now if I hadn't."

She smirked. "Oh, you would have been fine. You probably would have met some daring, beautiful pirate girl, likely named Gilda, who though jaded by this world would have been inexplicably drawn to you. You two would gallivant across the stars together in lustful bliss."

He raised an eyebrow. "Well then, what am I doing here with you? Get out of here!" He gave her shoulder a playful push.

Andy gasped in mock outrage. "Well, if that's how you feel. I won't stand in yours and Gilda's way."

She rolled away from him, but he caught her arm and pulled her back. He lifted her and rolled her so that she sat atop him, her legs straddling his sides. He held both her hands in his own. "I don't want Gilda."

She leaned forward so that their faces were closer together. "Then what do you want?"

He lifted his face to hers and kissed her slowly. Andy leaned into him. Her breath caught in her chest as he ran his hands over her thighs and onto her hips. She ran her fingers from the crook in his collarbone down to his chest. He pulled out of their kiss and stared up at her.

"Andy, when I say I want you, I don't just mean this." He motioned with his eyes to where their pelvises met. "I mean, I want all of you. I want your smile and your laughter, your anger and your sorrow. Your morning breath and those wild curls. I want every part of you you're willing to give me."

Andy ran her hands through his hair. "Allen, I know. I know you."

She leaned into him, her cheek pressed to his chest. They lay there for several minutes, the gentle thump of his heart against her face. The warmth of his body felt like home, a home that she never wanted to leave.

She sat back up and began to speak, but before she could utter a word, she was thrown roughly to the side. The back of her head slammed against the glass of the dome before she crumpled to the floor. She could hear Allen shouting something, but he sounded extremely far away. She opened her eyes and saw that he was over her, with his hands on her face.

"Andy! Andy, are you all right?" he shouted.

She pushed herself up onto her elbow, her head still pounding. "I think so. What happened?"

"We must be under attack. Come on, we need to get to the main bridge."

He pulled her up, and they made their way back down the ladder. They ran down the halls hand in hand until they reached the main bridge. The room was in chaos. Crew members ran from screen to screen, shouting over each other to be heard. The captain appeared in the doorway and pushed past Andy and Allen.

"What happened?" he demanded.

One pilot spoke up. "We were hit. They struck us on the southern side below the engine bay. It wasn't a critical hit, and we suffered little damage, but if they hit us again a little higher up, it could be catastrophic."

The captain stared at the screen that showed the analytics. "Who? Who is attacking us?"

Before the pilot could answer, another crew member spoke up. "Captain, there is an incoming screen call from the other ship. What would you like me to do?"

He turned and sat in his chair. "Accept it."

The screen was blank for a moment before it lit up, and a face appeared. Andy couldn't help the gasp that escaped her. Eden stared out of the screen, his eyes directed at the captain. Even though she knew she wasn't in the shot, she took a step back behind Allen. How had Eden found her?

"Lord Captain Bran, I am Prince Eden of Someron. I have detected that my fiancé, Princess Andromeda of Celestine, is currently aboard your ship. Am I correct in this assumption?"

The crew looked around at each other, confused frowns on all their faces. All except Mars. Andy noticed her turn to look sharply at her, and she tentatively glanced back. Mars's eyes were wide for a moment, before understanding crept over her face.

"Would you believe me even if I said she was not on this ship?"

Eden raised an eyebrow. "No, I would not. I know you have her. Has she been harmed?"

"I can assure you she is in perfectly good health. Would you like to see her?"

Eden straightened up, as though surprised the captain was making this so easy. "Yes, I would."

The captain turned and motioned for her to step forward. Every eye on the bridge was on her now. Andy felt as though her stomach were twisted into knots. She should be happy. This was her fiancé, her dashing prince, and he had come to rescue her. But she was not happy. She wanted to take Allen's hand and run. Run from this ship, run from her responsibilities, run from her future that had finally caught up with her and had come to claim her. But she couldn't. It was too late for that now.

She wasn't sure why, but she had assumed that when the time came, it would be her decision to go back. That she would just decide that now was the time to leave, that she had finished with Allen and Mars and was ready to go back to her real life. But she realized, now in this moment, that would never have happened. She never wanted to go back to being a princess locked away in her castle or to a perfect prince who said all the right things. She wanted to explore the galaxy and be free to make her own choices and mistakes. But that was no longer an option. She took a deep breath and stepped forward, releasing Allen's hand. As soon as she lost the warmth of his touch, it felt as though something vital had been ripped from her. But she continued forward, nonetheless.

She stepped into view of Eden, and his face immediately broke into a relieved smile. "Thank God, Andromeda. I thought you were dead. Are you all right?"

Andy nodded and forced a smile onto her face to match his. "Yes, I'm fine."

"Good." He turned his attention back to the captain. "You will hand her over to me now, or we will fire again. This time we will not miss your main engine bay."

The captain shook his head. "If you fire on us, you risk killing your beloved princess. You wouldn't risk that."

"If we take out your primary engine, you will still have forty minutes left until you reach critical oxygen levels. The nearest ship that could assist you is at least two hours away. You would be dead before they reached you. However, that would be plenty of time for my crew to swarm your ship and take her back by force. I am giving you the option. Give her to me freely and live or keep her from me and die."

The captain chuckled. "Boy, if you think your ship is truly superior to mine, you are mistaken. We can handle anything you throw at us."

Eden set his jaw. "Very well, if that is your choice."

"No!" Andy cried. Both the captain and Eden looked to her. She turned to the captain and shook her head. "No. Please, don't fight him. It's time for me to go home."

He frowned. "Andy… "

"I know. But it's time that you let me go."

He stared at her, his face mostly expressionless, except for his eyes, which burned with unsaid emotion. But then he composed his face and nodded before looking back at Eden.

"Very well. We will prepare the princess for transport."

CHAPTER TWENTY

ANDY STOOD IN THE ROOM that she had occupied for the last five months. She'd never come to think of this as home, but it held comfort that she hadn't realized before. She'd packed a bag with the few belongings she had, and it now sat on the bed in front of her. The sound of the door made her turn. Allen stood in the doorway, his hands in his pockets and his eyes on her packed bag.

"Are you ready to go?"

Andy ran her fingers over the smooth surface of the bed sheets. "No. But I have no choice."

Allen moved to stand in front of her. "Yes, you do. We can fight. I know we can take them on, if we just—"

"Allen," Andy interrupted. "I can't. I must go back. It's time. We both knew this couldn't last forever, we've talked about this."

"Yeah, I know. I just thought we'd have more time."

Andy picked absently at the collar of his shirt. "So did I."

He reached into his pocket and pulled something out. He placed it in her hand, and she saw it was a com. "I've programmed it to send a direct message to me. Once you're in Celestine, it won't work, but I thought if you ever needed me while outside of your kingdom, you might want to send me a message. Just push the middle button twice, and it'll send me a direct call."

Andy smiled and slid it into her pocket. "Thank you."

"I wouldn't change a thing, you know."

Something fragile inside Andy cracked, a delicate hope she hadn't even realized she'd been safeguarding until this very moment. "No, neither would I."

Allen's smile became sad as he ran his thumb across her cheekbone. "I'm really going to miss you. The only good-byes I've ever known were on the other side of death."

She swallowed hard, trying her best to not let him see how her heart was breaking. "Well. I'll live happy knowing this isn't quite so permanent. Perhaps we'll see each other again someday."

She wouldn't let the last time he saw her be filled with sadness. This would be the last memory she had with him, and she wanted to keep it for a lifetime.

Allen nodded. "I'm counting on it."

Andy turned and lifted her bag. As she turned back to Allen, she placed her hand on his chest.

"Good-bye."

She made to walk past him and out the door, but before she could, Allen took ahold of her elbow and spun her back toward him. Andy dropped her bag and threw her arms around his shoulders, kissing him as she'd kissed no one before. She had read so many books that described kissing someone you loved as feeling like electricity and fire. This felt nothing like that. This felt like home. Like she was safe and wanted and loved. She didn't want to lose this. She wanted him to ask her to stay again. To tell her they could run away from her responsibilities and her duty. To be free with him. But she knew he wouldn't. He understood what had to be done just as well as she did. Allen held his hands to her face for a moment before letting go. He took a deep breath and straightened up.

"Good-bye, Andromeda."

Andy smiled through the emotion that threatened to choke her. "Good-bye, Allen."

She turned and picked up her bag and walked to the door. But before she left, she turned back one last time. "I just want you to know that even though he is my duty, you are my choice."

With that, she walked out, letting the door slide shut behind her. She had to leave now, otherwise she knew she wouldn't be able to do it. Even now, as she walked down the hall, she imagined him rushing out of the room and running after her. He would call to her, and she would turn and run back to him. But that didn't happen, and she was glad. If he did that, he wouldn't be the Allen that she loved. He knew she had to do this, and he wouldn't make it any more difficult than it needed to be.

She rounded the corner and stopped. Mars was standing just ahead, leaning against the wall with her arms crossed over her chest.

"So, a princess, huh? I should have guessed, really. All that talk of duty makes a lot more sense now."

Andy dropped her chin, averting her eyes. "Are you mad? That I didn't tell you?"

"No, I'm not mad." Mars pushed off the wall and took a few steps toward her. "I get it. Did Allen know?"

Tentatively, Andy nodded. "He knew from the beginning. He met me on Celestine."

Mars stared at her for a moment and then burst into laughter. "Of course he did. And he told no one. Classic Allen. He was just protecting you."

Again, Andy nodded.

Mars gave her a contemplative look. "You know, if you had told me, I would have protected you as well. Allen isn't the only one who cares about you."

An ache seized at her heart. "Yeah, I know, Mars. I care about you too, more than you can know. I wish… I wish I had more time."

"Yeah, me too."

In two long strides Mars was in front of her and her arms were pulling her in for a tight hug. Andy buried her face in her soft curls. Mars was smaller than Allen, but she hugged her with the same ferocity and desperation.

"I'm going to miss you, Princess."

"I know. I'll miss you too."

Mars pulled back but kept both of her hands on either side of Andy's face, cradling it. Then, with a gentleness that broke Andy's heart all over again, she pressed the softest of kisses to the corner of Andy's mouth. It was hesitant, as if afraid of Andy's response. And that just wouldn't do. Andy shifted her mouth until she could capture Mars's fully, her hand coming up to rest against the one already holding her cheek. Mars inhaled sharply, a frantic little sound escaping her as she leaned into the kiss. It was warm, and soft, and it ripped open the wound in Andy's heart all over again. When she finally broke the kiss, Mars let their foreheads rest against each other.

"Don't go."

Andy's face crumpled. "I have to."

"No, you don't," Mars breathed against her mouth. "We'll take care of you. Let Allen be the self-sacrificing one. I don't mind being selfish if it means we get to keep you. Look at me, you're making me beg. I never beg, ask anyone."

A small laugh from Andy made their noses brush. "I don't doubt that. I still have to go."

Mars's thumb stroked across her cheekbone. "It was worth a shot, huh?"

Andy nodded, leaning into the hand on her face. "Yeah, it was."

Mars swooped in to press one final kiss to her mouth. Andy barely had any time to savor it before Mars was stepping away and breaking the contact. She missed it immediately.

"Right, well. You'd better get going then."

Without another word, she stepped around her, hurrying away down the hall. Andy remained where she was for several minutes. She worried that if she tried to walk, her legs would give out. But eventually, she knew she had to go.

She reached the loading bay, where they would dock onto the other ship, and she would cross over. She wasn't sure who she had expected to be there, but it was only the captain. He stood facing away from her with his hands behind his back. She cleared her throat, and he turned to face her. He smiled and took a few steps toward her.

"This is the second time I've had to give you up."

She chewed her lip nervously. "Bran—"

He held up his hand. "No, it's OK. I'm not expecting you to make a profound change and realize that you love me and think of me as your dad. I understand that, for you, he will always be your dad. I just need to know that you understand I love you, and even if I never see you again, having the privilege of knowing you for these past few months has been the greatest gift I ever could have received."

Andy smiled. "I know." She set her bag down and stepped forward to wrap her arms around him. He seemed surprised but recovered quickly and embraced her back. She had never been this close to him before, never realized what he smelled like. She pulled back.

He frowned. "What's wrong?"

She shook her head. "Nothing, it's just, you smell like cinnamon and oak."

"So?"

"My mother's favorite perfume smells of cinnamon and oak."

A smile spread across his face. He ran his hand over her hair. "I'm going to miss you."

She nodded. "I wish I could have gotten to know you better."

"As do I."

The sound of bolts connecting made them step apart quickly. They were docking. It was time for her to leave. She looked back up at him. "For what it's worth, I'm proud to have a father like you."

A look of surprise crossed his face, but before he could respond, the hatch door opened, and several armed men ran through. They spotted her immediately.

The man nearest to her shouted. "Princess Andromeda! Quickly, come with us!"

She barely had time to look back at the captain before the man took her by the arm and pulled her roughly away. She and the armed man ran back through first, with the others following behind, their guns still pointed at the captain. It happened so quickly, she barely had time to register what was going on. She stared back through the door at the captain for a moment more before it slid shut and he was gone.

She couldn't stand there for too long, however, because the men were already trying to pull her away.

"Come, Your Majesty. We're to bring you directly to Prince Eden."

She let them pull her away and down the hall. She barely noticed where they were taking her. Her mind hung back, clinging to the ship and family she was leaving behind. She didn't come back to herself until she heard her name.

"Andromeda!" Eden raced toward her down the hall. He wrapped his arms around her and pulled her into a tight embrace. She slowly lifted her arms to hug him back. She needed to keep up appearances. He pulled back and looked down at her. "Thank God. Everyone believed you were dead, but I never stopped trying to find you."

She gave him a small smile. "Thank you. I appreciate your dedication."

Eden frowned, as though finding something strange about her words. She probably sounded cold. He quickly replaced his frown with a smile and took her hand.

"Come, you must be exhausted. You'll have to tell me what those monsters did to you, and we can have the doctor look you over."

All she could bring herself to do was nod mutely. They wound their way down the hall and through a door to a lavishly designed room, not unlike the captain's. Eden took a seat behind a large desk, but Andromeda couldn't bring herself to sit. She moved to the window, looking out to see the outside of the *Andromeda*. They would be pulling away any minute now, and she would be alone once more.

After a few moments, Eden spoke. "Andromeda, what happened to you?"

She inhaled deeply and closed her eyes. What could she tell him? Certainly not the truth, at least not all of it.

"The pirates kidnapped me."

"Did they hurt you?"

"No."

"What did they want?"

She shrugged. "I suppose they wanted to ransom me."

She heard Eden shift in his chair. "They had you for nearly five months. We never once received any demands."

What did he want her to say? "They didn't exactly share their plans with me."

"Did they assault you?"

She spun around. "What? No!"

"Can you blame me for asking? They are pirates, they have a reputation for doing that."

"No, no. They didn't. They never made me do something I didn't want to do."

The taste of Allen's and Mars's lips still lingered on her mouth. In her mind she saw their smiles and the way they looked at her, the way that they saw her for herself, not just for her status. She closed her eyes and pushed back the tears. She knew Eden was watching her, and she knew she wouldn't be able to explain why she was crying.

It was only then a question came to her. "How did you find me?"

He wagged his finger at her. "Ah, that was a bit of luck. You know the necklace I got you? Before I gave it to you, I had a tracker put in for security. Until yesterday, it was completely offline. Then, I got a hit. It showed me right where you would be."

Andy blinked, trying to absorb this. He had given her a tracker? It had been inactive until she took it out of its box. She wanted to curse herself. This was all her fault.

"I see."

"Your family has missed you terribly. They've kept your kidnapping a secret, but they've been frantically searching everywhere for you. Not a simple task."

"I've missed them as well."

She turned back to the window. The other ship was still docked. A part of her wished they would just go. Seeing it there, a place that housed the people she'd come to think of as home, was nearly unbearable. They were still in reach, a dream on the edges of consciousness that called her back to their warm embrace. An image of Allen and Mars flashed through her mind, their soft touches a ghost on her skin. She'd never realized home didn't have to be a place. Sometimes home was the people you loved.

A shaky breath escaped her. Loved. She loved them. What was she doing? How could she give them up, just like that? She didn't belong in a palace. She belonged with them. A resolve unlike anything she'd ever felt formed in her mind, weighed down by the revelation.

"Eden, you have to let me go back."

His brow creased. "What?"

"Look, I know this is going to be hard to understand. But I want to go back. All my life I've been trapped. Stuck in a role I didn't want. But for these past few months, I've finally been free. Please, this is what I want. Just... just tell them you couldn't find me."

He continued to stare at her, his expression completely blank.

"I know this is difficult to understand. But we wouldn't be happy together. You deserve someone who loves you, and that's never going to be me. Just, come with me and talk to the captain."

She turned and walked for the door. But when she reached it and pushed the panel, it didn't open. She frowned and pushed it again.

"Eden, please, unlock the door."

Behind her, he let out a heavy sigh. "You just couldn't make this easy, could you?"

Andy turned around and froze. Eden had walked to the front of his desk, and in his hand was a gun, directed at her. "What the hell are you doing?"

He leaned back against the desk. "This wasn't how I wanted it to go. I would have wished for this to be painless, preferably in your sleep."

Andy's heart lurched in her chest. "Eden, what the *hell* are you talking about?"

"Yes, I do imagine this is difficult for you to understand."

She shook her head, her eyes moving from the gun to his face. "Eden, I don't know what's going on, but put the gun away."

"Yeah, I can't do that. Can't have loose threads wandering around."

"Loose threads to *what*?"

He lurched up from the desk. "To getting what I want!"

For the first time since Andromeda had met him, his mask of politeness slipped and revealed a hint of something beneath. Something wild and unhinged, and it sent a tremor of fear through her.

She held up her hands, tying to placate. "OK, calm down. Why don't you tell me what it is you want?"

He scoffed and turned his head away, shaking it slightly. It would be the perfect opportunity to strike back, to try to disarm him, but he was too far away. He'd pull the trigger before she got near enough. Instead, she slipped her hand into her pocket and pressed the button on the com Allen had given her.

"That's a complicated question that you don't need all the answers to. What I will tell you is that I want to be king. And for me to get what I want, unfortunately, you need to be out of the picture."

Her mind raced, trying to understand what he was saying. "That doesn't make sense. You'll be king someday, whether you marry me or not."

He began to approach her, slowly. "Yeah, but see, I'm done waiting for someday. And I don't just want Someron. If I want control of both Someron and Celestine, and eventually every other kingdom, then I need a child with the heir of Celestine. I've spoken to doctors, and I know the chances of me ever having a child with you."

His eyes ran down the length of her body. "Not with all the metal and wires that make up your body. I won't wait another fifteen years while you try in vain to give me an heir. Your sister will give me one quickly."

Andy gritted her teeth, fury seething through her body. "That still doesn't make any sense. If you kill me, my father will have you executed."

"Mmm," he nodded. "Yes, he would. But see, I didn't kill you. I tried to save you. But though I gave it my most valiant effort to save my beloved fiancé, the horrid pirates shot and killed you. I will be devastated, obviously, and there will be a mourning period. But when that's over, I will be free to marry your sister Rosetta."

"Eden you're sick in the head. This will never work. Your father's healthy, it'll be a long time before you're crowned king."

The corner of Eden's lip curled into a cruel smirk. "He was healthy. Unfortunately for him, he fell rather ill with an unknown virus. His condition has deteriorated rapidly over this last week, and he'll likely already be gone by the time I return."

Andy's sucked in a breath. "You poisoned your own father?"

He shrugged. "Why not?"

"Why not? Because he's your father! He loves you!"

He let out a sharp laugh, though there was no humor in it. "Loves me? He doesn't love me. The only person he ever loved was my older brother. Kasian could do no wrong. My entire childhood, I watched my father do everything with him. They went hunting together, they played chess together, my father brought him along to every council meeting and allowed him to stand beside his throne at court. I used to beg him to let me come along. All I wanted was for my father to see me as he saw Kasian. Every time, my father would laugh and tell me it wasn't my place. I would not be king, so I didn't need to do kingly things. Even my mother preferred my younger sister. I knew that as long as my brother was around, I would be nothing. So, I got rid of him."

The pieces clicked into place for Andy. "You killed him too."

He nodded. "It wasn't too difficult to hide the explosive charge on the ship. I set it so that it would go off once they were out in orbit. You should have heard the way my mother screamed when they told her the news. And my father, I had never seen him cry before. I had to pretend to be distraught, but I had never felt so much joy. Finally, my father was forced to accept me as his heir."

Andy bared her teeth. "You're psychotic. You'll kill your own family for power."

Eden tilted his head, the deadness of his eyes sending a shiver down her spine. "I would kill everyone for power."

"Why didn't you just attack the ship while I was on it? Why go through the trouble of bringing me here?"

He sucked his teeth. "While it would have been easier to simply blast you out of space, it wouldn't have been clean. Your family would only have my word that you're dead. But if I bring them your body, they'll have no doubt. Your sister will be named heir, she will give me a child, and then she and the rest of your family will die in a tragic accident. Even now, I have my people stationed close to them. If anything goes wrong, well, let's just say I have a backup plan."

Andy fought to keep her breathing even, to stop the panic from boiling up. "Don't you fucking touch my family."

"If it makes you feel any better, you won't actually have to see it happen. When you think about it like that, me killing you first is actually a kindness."

He lifted the gun and aimed. Andy tensed, prepared to feel the sting of a bullet, when a powerful force hit the ship. Both were thrown to the floor. Eden still held the gun, but Andy was the first to recover. She flung herself forward, grabbing for the gun. He moved it out of her reach, but she caught ahold of his arm. She dragged him toward her, but his fist caught her in the side of her head. The force of the hit made her dizzy, but she held on. She used her legs to push herself on top of him, though she was now at an awkward side angle.

"Get off me, you stupid bitch!" Eden snarled.

He grabbed a handful of her curls and pulled her head backward. She grunted in pain but managed to reach forward and wrap her bionic hand around his throat. A sound like a cannon went off, and for a moment Andy wasn't sure what had happened. But then she felt it. A searing hot pain cut through her stomach, making Andy to fall off him.

She rolled onto her back and looked down. The stain of blood had already begun to cover the front of her shirt, and it grew larger every second. Eden sat up, and even he looked shocked by what he had done. Andy pressed her hand to her stomach, as though it would keep the blood from pouring out of her. Eden stood.

"This is your fault. You did this!"

It sounded as though he was trying to convince himself more than her, but she wasn't paying attention. There was another hit to the ship that made Eden stumble, but Andy barely processed it. She gasped for breath, and she felt the floor beneath her was now slick with blood. A darkness crept in around the corners of her vision. She knew she was about to black out. Before she did, she registered the sound of people shouting and guns firing. Just before she slid into darkness, she saw a flash of red hair over her and a panic-stricken voice.

"Andromeda! No, no, no, no! Please, God, no. Andy, stay with me!"

And then there was nothing.

CHAPTER
TWENTY-ONE

THE FIRST THING ANDROMEDA WAS aware of was the sound of voices. At first, they were distant and indistinguishable, but as she focused on them, they became clear. There were three of them.

"Why hasn't she woken up?"

"She went through a traumatic experience and lost a lot of blood. The transfusion was successful, and I was able to fully close the wound, but the mind is a delicate thing. She'll wake up when she's ready."

"And you're sure there will be no permanent damage?"

"I can't be sure of anything with this sort of thing. But I don't think so. The bullet went straight through and missed most major organs. The ones it did hit, I was able to treat. You need to be patient."

"Patient? How can I be patient with her life?"

"Hey, don't yell at me, Allen. I know how much you care for her, and I care for her too. I've done the best I can. Do you want me to lie to you? You know I can't and won't do that."

"OK, calm down, you two. Mars, I know you've done everything that you can, and I appreciate it more than you know. All we can do now is be here for her and make her comfortable."

Andy drifted back into the darkness. As she drifted, she was plagued by dreams and nightmares. She was standing at the window of a ship. They flew high above the moon. The Kingdom of Celestine sat within its many domes, shiny and gleaming and perfect. As though looking through a telescope, she could see her castle perfectly. And there was her family, all standing on the lawn. They turned their faces up to look at her. They smiled and waved, and she realized they could see her as well. She smiled and waved back. What came next happened so fast, she barely had time to register it. It looked as though a bomb had gone off inside the castle, and within seconds, it engulfed the entire dome in flames. She watched in horror as the fire ripped through her family and destroyed her home. She screamed and slammed her hands against the window, but it was too late. They were gone.

Andy peeled her eyes open and closed them again. There was a dim light above her, but her eyes weren't used to it. She turned her head to the side and opened them again. She immediately saw Allen. He was reclined in an oversized chair, asleep. She shifted her body and groaned. Her whole torso felt sore. At the sound of her movement, Allen's eyes snapped open, and he sat up.

"Andy! Oh, thank God." He took her hand in his. "How do you feel?"

She grimaced as she pushed a button to raise her bed into a sitting position. "I'm having vivid flashbacks of my first accident. You didn't put more metal into me, did you?"

Allen smirked. "No, we were luckily able to avoid that."

Allen pressed a button on his com, and a moment later, Mars rushed in followed by the captain. They both made their way to the end of her bed.

"See," Mars said, waving her hand at Andy, "I told you it wouldn't take too long for her to wake up."

Andy shifted and gritted her teeth. "How long have I been out?"

"Four days," the captain answered.

Andy looked at him sharply, then at Allen. "Prince Eden. He shot me."

The captain frowned. "We know. We heard everything over the call to Allen."

"How did you get me off that ship?"

"The prince vastly underestimated us. We were still anchored when you alerted us, so it was relatively easy to launch a counterattack," the captain said.

"We have to alert someone. He was poisoning his father; we need to stop it!"

Mars shook her head sadly. "It's too late." She turned to the screen on the wall. "Screen on. Play Someron Communication Network." To Andy, she said, "This has been running since yesterday."

The screen turned on to show the outside of what she believed to be the royal palace of Someron. A woman's voice spoke over the image in a calm tone.

"With the death of King Beckett and the return of Prince Eden, sources close to the royal family say that a coronation will happen quickly. It will likely take place within the week. Upon his return to Earth, His Royal Majesty wept openly at the news of his father."

As she watched, the image changed to that of her own capitol. "Meanwhile, King Alder and Queen Adella have continued to refuse comment on why their daughter, Princess Andromeda, has yet to marry Prince Eden. Celestine remains in a media blackout, leaving many to speculate that the princess is ill or has refused the hand of our prince."

Mars commanded it off. Andy closed her eyes. "He actually did it. I half expected him to be bluffing."

Andy opened her eyes and looked down at herself for the first time. Her stomach was wrapped heavily in bandages. That monster had done this. And now, now he was going to kill her family. Her sisters, her father, her mother. He wanted to take them all from her. She felt something then, an emotion that until this moment she had never truly felt. Hatred. It burned in her chest, threatening to choke her if she allowed it. It infected her sorrow, like blood tainting water. Its red tendrils crept their way around her heart and, like a mist, filled her mind. She hated him. The image of his blue eyes made her want to scream.

"I-I think I need a minute to myself. To think."

"Of course," Captain said. "Just call for us when you're ready."

He walked out, and Allen and Mars reluctantly followed. Andy lay there in her bed, imagining his face, his voice, his laugh. Every memory was like a fiery poker, digging its way deeper into her soul. Did he really think that she would lie down and let him do this? He had intended for the shot to be fatal. Luckily, he hadn't accounted for her crew. And they truly were hers, she realized.

Eventually she slid her legs off the bed and stood. She dressed in the simple clothes that Mars had left her, only barely cringing at the pain. When she was dressed and her hair combed, she called for Allen, Mars, and the captain to rejoin her.

They all walked in cautiously. Allen was the first to speak.

"Andy, are you all right?"

She stared out the window. "I will be."

Mars took a careful step forward. "Is there anything we can get you?"

Andy shook her head. "I didn't call you here for comfort."

The captain's voice was low and restrained. "Andy, what are you thinking?"

She turned back to look at them. "Prince Eden wants to take something from me. He has hurt and killed countless people. He needs to be stopped."

"Are you going to go back to your family? To warn them about Eden?" Allen asked.

"I can't do that. He told me he has people near them, people who I assume will kill them if anything goes wrong. If I try to get near them, there's a strong possibility Eden will have them killed. I can't risk that. I'll have to do this without the help of my family."

Allen raised his eyebrows. "Then how?"

The captain answered for her. "With us."

Andy looked at him.

"That's why I called you here. I want to know if you'll help me in destroying him. I'll do it on my own if I must, but it will be easier if I have your support."

"So, what?" Mars asked. "You want to catch this prince and make him serve trial?"

"No." Andromeda's voice came out harsh, the bitterness in her heart seeping out. "He told me what he did, that's enough of a trial for me. I can't risk him escaping or hurting the people I love. He needs to die."

Mars and Allen glanced at each other, while the captain remained quiet and focused on her. She took a deep breath.

"Look. This is where I belong. I can't go back to my old life; I know that now. And there are things about me that even I don't understand. Maybe I never will. But I won't abandon my family. So, if I ever want to live any semblance of a normal life, this is something I need to do."

There was a long silence, and Andy noticed Allen looking at her with no small amount of concern.

Finally, the captain nodded. "I will help you in whatever you need."

"Yeah," Mars agreed. "So will I."

Andy looked at Allen. She refused to acknowledge the sadness written all over his face. She held his gaze. "Will you help me, Allen?"

It seemed like forever before he finally let out a sigh and nodded. "Always."

She let out a breath. She had worried that he would refuse her, though it made no sense for him to. He had shown he was capable of violence. Why would he not help her get her own justice?

"Thank you." She turned back to the window. "Then let us begin."

ABOUT THE AUTHOR

BORN IN ARIZONA, K.M. IS the oldest of four sisters. From a young age she felt a calling toward writing, spurred when she won her school's Young Author Award for best story. The desire to create stories only grew as she did and led her to attend college with a major in creative writing. K.M. strives to write rich and vibrant worlds, with a heavy focus on LGBTQ+ themes. As an advocate of LGBTQ+ rights, K.M. enjoys working within the community to build a sense of acceptance through stories. In her free time, she enjoys canyon hiking with her partner in her home state. *Born Andromeda* is her debut novel.

CONNECT WITH 🐦 kmwattsofficial
K.M. ONLINE 📷 k.m_watts